Everyman, I will go with thee,
and be thy guide

THE LESLIE PRICE
MEMORIAL LIBRARY

FIELD HOUSE

BRADFIELD COLLEGE

THE EVERYMAN
LIBRARY

*The Everyman Library was founded by J. M. Dent
in 1906. He chose the name Everyman because he wanted
to make available the best books ever written in every
field to the greatest number of people at the cheapest possible
price. He began with Boswell's 'Life of Johnson';
his one-thousandth title was Aristotle's 'Metaphysics',
by which time sales exceeded forty million.*

*Today Everyman paperbacks remain true to
J. M. Dent's aims and high standards, with a wide range
of titles at affordable prices in editions which address
the needs of today's readers. Each new text is reset to give
a clear, elegant page and to incorporate the latest thinking
and scholarship. Each book carries the pilgrim logo,
the character in 'Everyman', a medieval mystery play,
a proud link between Everyman
past and present.*

Tennessee Williams

THE NIGHT OF THE IGUANA

AND OTHER STORIES

Edited by
CHRISTOPHER BIGSBY
University of East Anglia

EVERYMAN
J. M. DENT · LONDON

Christopher Bigsby is consultant editor for the
Everyman American literature series.

Introduction and chronology © J. M. Dent 1995

J. M. Dent
Orion Publishing Group
Orion House
5 Upper St Martin's Lane
London WC2H 9EA

Typeset in Sabon by Deltatype Ltd, Ellesmere Port, Cheshire
Printed in Great Britain by
The Guernsey Press Co. Ltd, Guernsey, C.I.

British Library Cataloguing-in-Publication Data
is available upon request.

ISBN 0 460 87500 0

CONTENTS

NOTE ON THE AUTHOR AND EDITOR

TENNESSEE WILLIAMS was born in Columbus, Mississippi, in 1911. His playwriting career began in the 1930s but his first Broadway success came with *The Glass Menagerie* in 1945. He followed this with *A Streetcar Named Desire*, two years later, and then a series of plays which established his as a unique voice in the American theatre. These included: *Summer and Smoke, Cat on a Hot Tin Roof, Orpheus Descending, Suddenly Last Summer, Sweet Bird of Youth* and *The Night of the Iguana*.

Williams was also the author of three novels and several collections of short stories: *One Arm and Other Stories* (1948); *Hard Candy: A Book of Stories* (1954); *Three Players of a Summer Game and Other Stories* (1960); *The Knightly Quest: A Novella and Four Short Stories* (1966); *Eight Mortal Ladies Possessed: A Book of Stories* (1974); *It Happened the Day the Sun Rose, and Other Stories* (1982).

CHRISTOPHER BIGSBY has published more than twenty books on American and British culture. His works include the three volume *Critical Introduction to Twentieth Century American Drama*, and *Modern American Drama 1945–1990*. He is also the author of a novel, *Hester* (1994), and has written plays for radio and television. He is a regular broadcaster and is Professor of American studies at the University of East Anglia in Norwich, England.

CHRONOLOGY OF WILLIAMS'S LIFE

1911	Thomas Lanier Williams born in Columbus, Mississippi, the son of Cornelius Coffin Williams and Edwina Dakin Williams
1913	The family move to Tennessee
1918	The family move to St Louis, Missouri
1923	Williams begins school
1927	Publishes his first work, an essay in *Smart Set* magazine: 'Can a Good Wife be a Good Sport?'
1928	Publishes his first short story, 'The Vengeance of Nitocris', in *Weird Tales*
1929	Enters the University of Missouri at Columbia
1932	Father withdraws him from the University. He works for the International Shoe Company, an experience reflected in *The Glass Menagerie*
1933	Wins $10 for 'Stella for Star', in *Story* magazine
1935	Writes a one-act play, *Cairo! Shanghai! Bombay!* which is produced in Memphis, Tennessee. Attends Washington University, St Louis, Missouri
1936	Two short plays, *The Magic Tower* and *Headlines* produced. His story 'Twenty-Seven Wagons Full of Cotton' published in *Manuscript*
1937	*Candles in the Sun* and *The Fugitive Kind* staged in St Louis. Leaves for the University of Iowa, Iowa City. His sister Rose undergoes a lobotomy
1938	Graduates from the University of Iowa. Goes to Chicago and then New Orleans

1939   He is awarded $100 by the Group Theatre and his plays
        are sent to an agent, Audrey Wood. *Not About
        Nightingales* produced in St Louis. 'The Field of Blue
        Children' is published by *Story* magazine. He is awarded
        a $1000 Rockefeller grant

1940   His play *The Long Goodbye* is staged at the New School
        for Social Research in New York. *Battle of Angels* opens
        in Boston

1941   *Battle of Angels* closes after brief and unsuccessful run.
        Begins work on 'Portrait of a Girl in Glass'

1942   *This Property is Condemned* produced in New York

1943   Six month contract as MGM scriptwriter. Turns
        'Portrait of a Girl in Glass' into a screenplay called *The
        Gentleman Caller*. *You Touched Me*, written with
        Donald Windham, opens in Cleveland

1944   Awarded $1000 by the American Academy of Arts and
        Letters. *The Purification* produced in Pasadena. *The
        Glass Menagerie* opens in Chicago

1945   *Stairs to the Roof* produced in Pasadena. *The Glass
        Menagerie* opens in New York to much critical acclaim.
        You Touched Me opens in New York

1947   *A Streetcar Named Desire* opens on Broadway, winning
        the Pulitzer Prize. *Summer and Smoke* opens in Dallas

1948   *Summer and Smoke* opens in New York. 'One Arm' is
        published

1950   The film version of *The Glass Menagerie* is released and
        The Roman Spring of Mrs Stone is published

1951   *The Rose Tattoo* opens in New York and wins a Tony
        Award. The Film of *A Streetcar Named Desire* is released

1953   *Camino Real* opens in New York

1954   Short Story collection *Hard Candy* published

1955   *Cat on a Hot Tin Roof* opens in New York, winning the
        Pulitzer Prize and the Drama Critics' Circle Award. The
        film of the *Rose Tattoo* is released

1956   *Baby Doll*, a film based on *Twenty-Seven Wagons Full of Cotton*, is released and blacklisted by the Catholic Church

1957   *Orpheus Descending* opens in New York

1958   *Garden District* (*Suddenly Last Summer* and *Something Unspoken*) opens off-Broadway

1959   *Sweet Bird of Youth* opens in New York, as does *I Rise in Flame, Cried the Phoenix*. A one-act version of *The Night of the Iguana* is staged at the Spoleto Festival and the film version of *Suddenly Last Summer* is released

1960   *Period of Adjustment* opens in New York and *Fugitive Kind*, the film version of *Orpheus Descending*, is released

1961   *The Night of the Iguana* opens in New York. Film versions of *Summer and Smoke* and *The Roman Spring of Mrs Stone* released

1962   *The Night of the Iguana* wins the New York Drama Critics' Circle Award. *The Milk Train Doesn't Stop Here Anymore* opens at the Spoleto Festival. Film versions of *Sweet Bird of Youth* and *Period of Adjustment* released

1963   *The Milk Train Doesn't Stop Here Anymore* opens in New York

1964   Film version of *The Night of the Iguana* released

1966   *Slapstick Tragedy* opens in New York. Film version of *This Property is Condemned* released

1967   *The Two Character Play* receives its premiere at the Hampstead Theatre Club in London

1968   *Kingdom of Earth* opens in Philadelphia and then moves to New York. *BOOM*, film version of *The Milk Train Doesn't Stop Here Anymore* released

1969   Joins the Catholic Church. *In the Bar of a Tokyo Hotel* opens in New York. He is committed to a psychiatric hospital

1971   *Out Cry* (a version of *Two Character Play*) is produced in Chicago. *Confessional* is produced in Maine. Williams breaks with his long-term agent, Audrey Wood

INTRODUCTION

Thomas Lanier Williams was born in Columbus, Mississippi in 1911. He later gave several explanations for adopting the name Tennessee: it was a reference to family history, a schoolyard nickname given to him because of his southern accent, a reaction against his real name which made him sound like a romantic, and possibly effete, poet. Whatever the truth of this there is a sense in which he was his own construction, a self-conscious performer of his life who found in writing a protective world and in his public persona a necessary mask. For behind the confident, masculine-sounding 'Tennessee' was indeed the soul of a romantic poet exhibiting, like his characters, a profound mistrust of a reality which presented itself as the source of anxiety and menace.

A childhood illness left Tennessee Williams with a weak constitution and a preference for a less physical life than that led by his male contemporaries. He later described himself as a solitary child, more addicted to reading than to boisterous games. He began writing stories at the age of ten, finding companionship in a sister later to suffer from profound psychological problems. Together, as he later explained, they 'lived in [their] own imagination'. To his father, as to his school mates, he was a 'sissy', his writing providing primary evidence. His mother, however, encouraged him, reading aloud from Dickens. On the other hand she was deeply puritanical, affecting to be shocked by any direct sexual references, so that it is not difficult to see Williams's later career as a reaction against this upbringing. Indeed both the domineering father and fussily puritanical mother make appearances in his drama.

At the age of sixteen he won third prize in a *Smart Set* competition for an essay called 'Can a Good Wife be a Good Sport', and published a gothic story in *Weird Tales*. At eighteen he went to university where he became aware of his homosexuality but repressed it. In 1934 his father withdrew him from university and for three years he worked in a shoe factory, where his

namesake Tom works in 'Portrait of a Girl in Glass', which later
became his first successful stage play, *The Glass Menagerie*.
Thereafter he returned to university and began his stage career by
writing plays for a radical St Louis theatre company.

For Williams, writing became an escape, and the lies of fiction a
protection against the disturbing urgencies of the real. As he
himself confessed, he 'discovered in writing . . . an escape from a
world of reality in which I felt acutely uncomfortable. It
immediately became my place of retreat, my cave, my refuge.'[1]
Several of the characters in these stories adopt the same strategy.
They are artists of one kind or another: writers in 'The Important
Thing', 'Portrait of a Girl in Glass', 'Two for a Party', 'The Field of
Blue Children', 'The Angel in the Alcove', and 'The Night of the
Iguana'; a musician in 'The Resemblance Between a Violin Case
and a Coffin'. They are fantasists, reshaping the world to serve
their psychic needs. So, Laura, in 'Portrait of a Girl in Glass', turns
to her glass menagerie for consolation, in a story in which the
narrator, like that of 'The Resemblance Between a Violin Case
and a Coffin', bears Williams's own first name. In the words of the
narrator of the latter story, 'it was then . . . that I began to find life
unsatisfactory as an explanation of itself and was forced to adopt
the method of the artist of not explaining but putting the blocks
together in some other way that seemed more significant to him.
Which is a rather fancy way of saying I started writing.'[2]

It is, indeed, possible to read these stories as a kind of spiritual
autobiography written by a man still coming to terms with his
sexuality, the mental collapse of his sister, the difficulties which he
had with his parents and, following what appeared to be a form of
heart seizure, his sense of mortality. Certainly they are laced
through with personal references and frequently address his own
sense that the artist must always be at odds with and oppressed by
a society instinctively hostile towards the free spirit. The young
girl in 'Three Players of a Summer Game' was based on a
childhood friend, Hazel Kramer, whom Williams had met when
she was nine and he was eleven. The incident in which she
removed a fig leaf from a male statue occurred in the St Louis Art
Gallery. The *New Yorker* magazine showed that it was scarcely
less puritanical than Williams's mother when it cut the incident
from their published version. 'The Resemblance Between a Violin
Case and a Coffin' is even more directly personal not only, like

'Portrait of a Girl in Glass', reflecting his relationship with his sister, Rose, but also identifying his own first homosexual feelings.

In 1938, having graduated from the State University of Iowa, Tennessee Williams went in search of work with the WPA (the government relief agency) in Chicago. He was unsuccessful and drifted south, to New Orleans, where he lived in a series of boarding houses. In the registers kept by a succession of landladies he listed his occupation as 'writer', then a piece of fantasy. He lived a bohemian life and revelled in the eccentrics, the romantics, the down at heel people he met. It was a period on which he later drew for many of his plays and stories. Several of the stories in this volume were sketched out at this time or within a few years: 'The Field of Blue Children' in 1937, 'The Night of the Iguana' in 1940, 'Portrait of a Girl in Glass' in 1941, 'The Angel in the Alcove' and 'One Arm' in 1943. The surprise, perhaps, is that they already define many of the themes which were to become the identifying marks of his drama, not least his concern to place sexuality at the centre of his work.

It is tempting to see Williams's homosexuality as providing one reason for his interest in those marginalised and oppressed by society. Most of the characters in these stories, as in his plays, live in the interstices of life, existing in the half light, moving through a world at a tangent to the American dream of confident individualism. In several stories homosexuality is confronted directly as in his plays, dependent on Broadway producers and audiences, it is not. He describes those whose only currency, fast losing value, is sexual and whose survival depends on passing contacts with strangers. Indeed in stories and plays alike Williams explored, as few others did, the power of sexuality to liberate and enthral. Few of the sexual pairings in this volume, however, are truly liberating or redemptive. Such meaning as they generate is momentary, except, perhaps, in the case of 'One Arm', where, ironically, brief and furtive couplings are, the reader is asked to believe, treasured memories for those forced to live in shadows only momentarily lit by the fire of passion. It is hard, though, to see this as anything more than sentimentality.

Williams was a homosexual at a time and in a place where to be such was a criminal offence attracting draconian punishment. His work was, at least in part, a response to his sense of ambivalence and harassment. He was at odds with the values of a culture which

seemed to lean confidently into the future, but he was also aware
that he represented a challenge to its fundamental myths which
turned on notions of a fierce male individualism or a companionship drained of sexual content. Change the gender signs which
attach themselves to the young girl in 'The Important Thing' and
you have Williams himself:

> She was not like a girl. He wondered that he had never noticed
> before how anonymous was her gender, for this was the very
> central fact of her nature. She belonged nowhere, she fitted in no
> place at all, she had no home, no shell, no place of comfort or
> refuge, she was a fugitive with no place to run to.[3]

Gender, indeed, is none too secure in these stories. In
'Three Players of a Summer Game' a woman, with hair cut short,
reveals 'strong cords of muscle' and a 'strong arm' with 'fingers
clenched into a fist'. She has a 'male assurance'. In 'Two on a
Party' the woman prostitute recalls occasions when her lovers
were seemingly unaware of her gender. Androgyny seems to offer
its own kind of grace, transcending or denying boundaries whose
authority seems of a piece with those other divisions which serve
only to separate and define.

Yet his characters never quite bridge the gap between them.
They never communicate fully, clinging to one another out of a
sense of need which they can neither fully articulate nor define.
They bear the scars of their encounter with a harsh reality. Laura,
in 'Portrait of a Girl in Glass', recoils in horror from a public
world which requires her to adapt to its rhythms. A male
prostitute loses his arm in the navy and lives on to find that his
personal wound establishes a link with those who seek him out
because they feel some incompletion in their own lives. Even the
cat in 'The Malediction', which craves only warmth and companionship, has a crushed leg. For others the wounds are less
obvious, less physical, but real enough for all that.

Williams's characters are aware of some insufficiency, some
trauma, then, but often cannot quite recall the origin of the
wounds they bear. We are never told what makes Brick's world
collapse, in 'Three Players of a Summer Game', though in *Cat on a
Hot Tin Roof* we do learn that it was possibly a homosexual
relationship and his denial of it. We do not know why Laura, in
'Portrait of a Girl in Glass', is so pathologically shy, though in *The
Glass Menagerie* Williams chooses to give her a club foot, an

image for the mental instability which afflicted his sister on whom Laura was modelled. The fact is that the wound is a given. Their vocation is to find ways of surviving. That is, for the most part, the only meaning they can find in a life which is otherwise baffling.

In 'The Coming of Something to the Widow Holly', the protagonist visits a metaphysician because, as she explains, 'I'm terribly troubled. There seems to be something important left out of the picture.' 'What picture?' he asks her. 'My life,' she replies. 'And what is the element which appears to be missing?' he asks. 'An explanation,' she replies.[4] That same missing element haunts many of Williams's characters. Aware of a sense of loss and insufficiency they cannot find the words to explain their sense of incompletion. So they turn to drink, to a desperate sexuality, to art, to strangers, in order to obliterate the pain and fill the gap. But, like the two characters in 'The Important Thing', they can do no more than 'look with sorrowful understanding, unable to help each other except through knowing, each completely separate and alone. . . .' The writer thus becomes no more than a specific example of a general principle. As Williams was later to ask, rhetorically, 'What choice has the artist, now, but withdrawal into the caverns of his isolated being?'[5]

This collection of stories is a little like its most frequently recurring setting – the rooming house. Each story visits a separate room in which a desperate soul burns. Virtually all suffer from what the protagonist of 'The Angel in the Alcove' identifies as a 'profound psychic wound, a loss or a failure'.[6] Even the young seem doomed, dying of tuberculosis or pneumonia, afflicted by nameless fears and anxieties. More often his characters have passed some invisible point of no return. The bloom of youth is fading. An edgy defensiveness characterises their relationships with others.

The woman protagonist of 'The Night of the Iguana' is 'a spinster of thirty', with a 'frantic need to find comfort in people'. Her family, meanwhile, is described in a way which could effectively describe most of his characters. They display 'nervous talents and sickness', consisting, as they do, of 'drunkards and poets, gifted artists and sexual degenerates'.[7] The two homosexual men who fascinate and torment her are, for all their cruelty towards her, themselves driven to this spot by their own desperation and locked in a relationship which itself seems in a state of near collapse. One of them, like his companion, a writer,

is 'still not more than thirty', obviously a major divide for
Williams, and one which he had passed by the time he wrote this
story. The other is much older and, also like Williams himself,
aware that writing in fashion in the 1930s is no longer in vogue.
He has, we are told, 'a look that often goes with incurable
illness'.[8] Alma, in 'The Yellow Bird', is 'pushing thirty', while in
'Three Players of a Summer Game' Brick is described as 'not so
young any more'. And so it continues. One of the two prostitutes
in 'Two on a Party', once again a writer, is hard of hearing and
balding; his companion is heavy in the hips. Like most of
Williams's characters, then, these are in flight from what, in that
same story, is described as the 'one great terrible, worst of all
enemies, which is the fork-tailed, cloven-hoofed, pitchfork-
bearing devil of Time!'[9] They are 'birds flying together against the
wind';[10] lonely people. Like the priest in 'One Arm' his characters
virtually all have 'a little functional trouble of the heart'. As the
narrator was to say in the planned film version of the story, these
are 'the queer, the mutilated, the not-so-young-anymore with
their loneliness a terrible cry in their throats, muted, or stifled to
dumbness'.[11]

Williams celebrates those damaged by their encounter with
reality, those forced to inhabit the margins of a society which has
no room for people who choose not to be players in the American
game of acquiring and achieving. For the most part his characters
move in a world closed to those in tune with history and American
pieties having to do with progress and consumption. They stand
on street corners trading momentary companionship for survival.
They flit in and out of transients' hotels, hide in seedy apartments
or rooming houses, move on from city to city one step ahead of the
law and in flight from the growing evidence of their own
mortality. They are no longer in control of their lives, if they ever
were. They are deeply vulnerable and bear the marks of that
vulnerability.

There is undeniably a sentimental strain in Williams's work.
His protagonists somehow sustain their spiritual integrity in the
midst of corruption. Even his comic grotesques are granted a
certain absolution as their cruelty and paranoia are recast as mock
heroic battles against circumstance. His achievement, however,
was never that of the realist, either in his drama or fiction. Settings
are always metaphors, language an expression of the impulse to
remake the world with words, character the focus for

fundamental needs and aspirations made flesh and blood and then translated, often imperfectly, into symbol. In Williams's work all settings have symbolic significance, whether it be the dried up fountain of *Summer and Smoke*, which reflects the sterility of its female protagonist, or the threatening domestic jungle of *Suddenly Last Summer*. So it proves in 'Portrait of a Girl in Glass'. Outside the window is a hard and unforgiving world where a predatory dog tears the life out of cats cornered in a dead-end alley. Laura is such a creature. She, too, is trapped.

Williams had none of the realist's desire to document, explain, list, elaborate. The real, indeed, was his enemy. It was too sharp-edged, too ineluctable, too firmly linked to the demeaning facts of experience. Art was a protection against the real for him as it was the protection sought by his protagonists, and it is in that sense that these stories can be read autobiographically as he details the lives of those, like himself, too shy, vulnerable, paranoid, fearful, panic-stricken to function until a transfiguring imagination can recast a threatening world into a place charged with a kind of desperate hope.

Williams's world is characterised by decay, dissolution, madness, a nervous intensity bordering on insanity. In other words it exhibits all the elements of romanticism and in particular the southern gothic world of Poe and William Faulkner. And it is worth remembering that Williams was a southern writer whose regret at the loss of grace and style, whose alarm at the intrusion of crude materialism, have an historical as well as a personal foundation. His characters may feel by-passed by history but so, too, is the South which they inhabit.

These stories share nothing with the boiled down prose of Ernest Hemingway, the minimalist realism of Raymond Carver or the detached ironies of John Cheever. They operate at a higher temperature and humidity. The language is more ornate, lyrical, self-regarding. In that sense, too, Williams is very much a southern writer, kin to Faulkner and to Eudora Welty, though less concerned with the pressure of history than Faulkner and more direct than Welty in his treatment of sexuality. The bruised lyricism which characterises Williams's prose style – bruised in the sense that you can smell the decay which it masks – is a feature not only of his writing but of the language which he gives to his characters for whom words are a means to transform a prosaic and threatening reality into something more acceptable. So, a field of blue flowers becomes an inner resource when it is translated into sustaining metaphor. Blue flowers become 'blue children', a curious consolation to a woman who has otherwise surrendered her dreams to habit and banality.

Williams's language, though, is frequently, and sometimes absurdly, baroque, as though he were uneasy with the prosaic until it could be touched with lyricism. As Blanche Dubois, in *A Streetcar Named Desire*, throws a coloured shawl over a table lamp to soften its revealing white glare so he uses language to transform the crude facts of life and mortality. When the protagonist of 'One Arm' is killed in the electric chair Williams uses a transfiguring prose to elevate a tawdry death and charge it with significance:

> Bolts from across the frontiers of the unknown, the practically named and employed but illimitably mysterious power that first invested a static infinitude of space with heat and brilliance and motion, were channelled through Oliver's nerve cells for an instant and then shot back across those immense frontiers, having claimed and withdrawn whatever was theirs.[12]

The effect, as here, can be merely bathetic and mannered. It can also, however, charge Williams's work with precisely that sense of the poetic which he sees as evacuated from American life.

Tennessee Williams's reputation plainly turns on his drama. Author of *The Glass Menagerie*, *A Streetcar Named Desire*, *Suddenly Last Summer*, *Cat on a Hot Tin Roof* and half a dozen other classics of the theatre, he was perhaps the most purely original playwright America has produced. For all his admiration for Anton Chekhov and D. H. Lawrence, whose imprint is detectable, his strength lay in a vision which was in part deeply personal and in part a product of his Southern upbringing.

Williams wrote comparatively little fiction but what he did shared certain qualities and concerns with his drama. Indeed in several cases he tried out ideas, characters and situations in his stories which would later be transferred into plays. It is true in this collection of 'Portrait of a Girl in Glass', which became *The Glass Menagerie*, of 'Three Players of a Summer Game' which, radically transformed, became *Cat on a Hot Tin Roof* and of 'The Night of the Iguana' and 'One Arm'.

Williams was also a poet, and a poetic sensibility informs much of his work. It stains his language and, indeed, that of his characters who often have the souls, and sometimes the avocation, of poets. But though he wrote and published poetry it is his prose work which remains his real achievement – a prose work which is, in effect, so many notes from underground as he celebrates the lives of those who struggle to find some meaning in the seemingly arbitrary nature of experience.

His characters are caught in decline. The energy generated by youthful hope has dissipated. Above all they are isolated, lonely, desperate for human contact yet terrified of its implications and consequences. There is another world, dominated by the powerful, the rich, those oblivious to the sufferings of the dispossessed, but it is not their world. They huddle in their boarding houses, hotel rooms, dishevelled apartments and even prison cells, waiting for the end, sentenced, as a character in his play *Orpheus Descending* observes, to 'solitary confinement inside our own skins, for life!'[13] But that is not quite the whole story.

There is no doubt that Williams saw defeat as the primary fact of human life. Virtually none of his characters could be said to win their battles with experience but, as he once said of his sister Rose, mentally ill and irreparably harmed by a hasty lobotomy, 'high station in life is earned by the gallantry with which appalling experiences are survived with grace.'[14] It may sound odd for him to use such a phrase as 'high station' when neither his sister nor his characters could ever aspire to such while mere survival is not the grail they sought. He is not, however, referring to social role, material achievement or public distinction. What he values is a certain unconscious dignity, a desperate courage in the face of defeat, and though this often involves a profound self-deception, as one of his characters in 'The Lady of Larkspur Lotion', remarks, a character significantly called The Writer, 'There are no lies but the lies that are stuffed in the mouth by the hard-knuckled hand of need.'[15] Redemption, or whatever must pass as such, rests, in part, in the impulse to reach out to those similarly imprisoned in their isolated cells and in part in the power of the imagination to transform, transfigure and transcend the painful truths of human life.

CHRISTOPHER BIGSBY

References

1   Tennessee Williams, *Where I Live* (New York, 1978), p. 1.

2   Tennessee Williams, *The Night of the Iguana and Other Stories*, p. 158.

3   *Ibid.*, p. 56.

4   *Ibid.*, p. 85.

5   C. W. E. Bigsby, *A Critical Introduction to Twentieth Century American Drama*, Vol. 2 (Cambridge, 1984), p. 51.

6   *The Night of the Iguana and Other Stories*, p. 149.

7   *Ibid.*, p. 3.

8   *Ibid.*, p. 17.

9   *Ibid.*, p. 102.

10 *Ibid.*, p. 112.

11 Tennessee Williams, *Stopped Rocking and Other Screenplays* (New York, 1984), p. 253.

12 *The Night of the Iguana and Other Stories*, p. 72.

13 Tennessee Williams, *Five Plays by Tennessee Williams* (London, 1962), p. 324.

14 Tennessee Williams, *Memoirs* (New York, 1975), p. 252.

15 Tennessee Williams, *Twenty-Seven Wagon Loads of Cotton* (New York, 1966), p. 71.

THE NIGHT OF THE IGUANA

AND OTHER STORIES

THE NIGHT OF THE IGUANA

Opening onto the long south verandah of the Costa Verde hotel near Acapulco were ten sleeping-rooms, each with a hammock slung outside its screen door. Only three of these rooms were occupied at the present time, for it was between the seasons at Acapulco. The winter season when the resort was more popular with the cosmopolitan type of foreign tourists had been over for a couple of months and the summer season when ordinary Mexican and American vacationists thronged there had not yet started. The three remaining guests of the Costa Verde were from the States, and they included two men who were writers and a Miss Edith Jelkes who had been an instructor in art at an Episcopalian girls' school in Mississippi until she had suffered a sort of nervous breakdown and had given up her teaching position for a life of refined vagrancy, made possible by an inherited income of about two hundred dollars a month.

Miss Jelkes was a spinster of thirty with a wistful blonde prettiness and a somewhat archaic quality of refinement. She belonged to an historical Southern family of great but now moribund vitality whose latter generations had tended to split into two antithetical types, one in which the libido was pathologically distended and another in which it would seem to be all but dried up. The households were turbulently split and so, fairly often, were the personalities of their inmates. There had been an efflorescence among them of nervous talents and sickness, of drunkards and poets, gifted artists and sexual degenerates, together with fanatically proper and squeamish old ladies of both sexes who were condemned to live beneath the same roof with relatives whom they could only regard as monsters. Edith Jelkes was not strictly one or the other of the two basic types, which made it all the more difficult for her to cultivate any interior poise. She had been lucky enough to channel her somewhat morbid energy into a gift for painting. She painted canvases of an originality that might some day be noted, and in the meantime, since her retirement from teaching, she was combining her painting with travel and trying to evade her neurasthenia through the distraction of making new friends in new places. Perhaps some day she would come out on a kind of triumphant plateau as an artist or as a person or even perhaps as both. There might be a period of five or ten years in her life when she would serenely climb over the lightning-shot clouds of her immaturity and the waiting murk of decline. But perhaps is the right word to use. It would all depend on the next two years or so. For this reason she was particularly needful of sympathetic companionship, and the growing lack of it at the Costa Verde was really dangerous for her.

Miss Jelkes was outwardly such a dainty tea-pot that no one would guess that she could actually boil. She was so delicately made that rings and bracelets were never quite small enough originally to fit her but sections would have to be removed and the bands welded smaller. With her great translucent grey eyes and cloudy blonde hair and perpetual look of slightly hurt confusion, she could not pass unnoticed through any group of strangers, and she knew how to dress in accord with her unearthly type. The cloudy blonde hair was never without its flower and the throat of her cool white dresses would be set off by some vivid brooch of esoteric design. She loved the dramatic contrast of hot and cold colour, the splash of scarlet on snow, which was like a flag of her own unsettled components. Whenever she came into a restaurant or theatre or exhibition gallery, she could hear or imagine that she could hear a little murmurous wave of appreciation. This was important to her, it had come to be one of her necessary comforts. But now that the guests of the Costa Verde had dwindled to herself and the two young writers – no matter how cool and yet vivid her appearance, there was little comfort to her in the way of murmured appreciation. The two young writers were bafflingly indifferent to Miss Jelkes. They barely turned their heads when she strolled on to the front or back verandah where they were lying in hammocks or seated at a table always carrying on a curiously intimate-sounding conversation in tones never loud enough to be satisfactorily overheard by Miss Jelkes, and their responses to her friendly nods and Spanish phrases of greeting were barely distinct enough to pass for politeness.

Miss Jelkes was not at all inured to such off-hand treatment. What had made travel so agreeable to her was the remarkable facility with which she had struck up acquaintances wherever she had gone. She was a good talker, she had a fresh and witty way of observing things. The many places she had been in the last six years had supplied her with a reservoir of descriptive comment and humorous anecdote, and of course there was always the endless and epic chronicle of the Jelkes to regale people with. Since she had just about the right amount of income to take her to the sort of hotels and *pensions* that are frequented by professional people such as painters and writers or professors on Sabbatical leave, she had never before felt the lack of an appreciative audience. Things being as they were, she realized that the sensible action would be to simply withdraw to the Mexican capital where she had formed so many casual but nice connections among the American colony. Why she did not do this but remained on at the Costa Verde was not altogether clear to herself. Besides the lack of society there were other drawbacks to a continued stay. The food had begun to disagree with her, the Patrona of the hotel was becoming insolent and the service slovenly and her painting was showing signs of nervous distraction. There was every reason to leave, and yet she stayed on.

Miss Jelkes could not help knowing that she was actually conducting a siege of the two young writers, even though the reason for it was still entirely obscure.

She had set up her painting studio on the South verandah of the hotel where the writers worked in the mornings at their portable typewriters with their portable radio going off and on during pauses in their labour, but the comradeship of creation which she had hoped to establish was not forthcoming. Her eyes formed the habit of darting toward the two men as frequently as they did toward what she was painting, but her glances were not returned and her painting went into an irritating decline. She took to using her fingers more than her brushes, smearing and slapping on pigment with an impatient energy that defeated itself. Once in a while she would get up and wander as if absentmindedly down toward the writers' end of the long verandah, but when she did so, they would stop writing and stare blankly at their papers or into space until she had removed herself from their proximity, and once the younger writer had been so rude as to snatch his paper from the typewriter and turn it face down on the table as if he suspected her of trying to read it over his shoulder.

She had retaliated that evening by complaining to the Patrona that their portable radio was being played too loudly and too long, that it was keeping her awake at night, which she partially believed to be true, but the transmission of this complaint was not evidenced by any reduction in the volume or duration of the annoyance but by the writers' choice of a table at breakfast, the next morning, at the furthest possible distance from her own.

That day Miss Jelkes packed her luggage, thinking that she would surely withdraw the next morning, but her curiosity about the two writers, especially the older of the two, had now become so obsessive that not only her good sense but her strong natural dignity was being discarded.

Directly below the cliff on which the Costa Verde was planted there was a small private beach for the hotel guests. Because of her extremely fair skin it had been Miss Jelkes' practice to bathe only in the early morning or late afternoon when the glare was diminished. These hours did not coincide with those of the writers who usually swam and sun-bathed between two and six in the afternoon. Miss Jelkes now began to go down to the beach much earlier without admitting to herself that it was for the purpose of espionage. She would now go down to the beach about four o'clock in the afternoon and she would situate herself as close to the two young men as she could manage without being downright brazen. Bits of their background and history had begun to filter through this unsatisfactory contact. It became apparent that the younger of the men, who was about twenty-five, had been married and recently separated from a wife he called Kitty. More from the inflection of voices than the fragmentary sentences that she caught, Miss Jelkes received the impression that he was terribly concerned over some problem which the older man was trying to iron out for him. The younger one's voice would sometimes rise in agitation loudly enough to be overheard quite plainly. He would cry out phrases such as *For God's sake* or *What the Hell are you talking about!* Sometimes his language was so strong that Miss Jelkes winced with embarrassment and he would sometimes pound the wet sand with his palm and hammer it with his heels like a child in a tantrum. The older man's voice would also be lifted briefly. Don't be a fool, he would shout. Then his voice would drop to a low and placating tone. The conversation would fall below the level of audibility once more. It seemed that some argument was going on almost interminably between them. Once Miss Jelkes was astonished to see the younger one jump to his feet with an incoherent outcry and start kicking sand directly into the face of his older companion. He did it quite violently and hatefully, but the older man only laughed and grabbed the younger one's feet and restrained them until the youth dropped back beside him, and then they had surprised Miss Jelkes even further by locking their hands together and lying in silence until the incoming tide was lapping over their bodies. Then they had both jumped up, apparently in good humour, and made racing dives in the water.

Because of this troubled youth and wise counsellor air of their conversations it had at first struck Miss Jelkes, in the beginning of her preoccupation with them, that the younger man might be a war-veteran suffering from shock and that the older one might be a doctor who had brought him down to the Pacific resort while conducting a psychiatric treatment. This was before she discovered the name of the older man, on mail addressed to him. She had instantly recognized the name as one that she had seen time and again on the covers of literary magazines and as the author of a novel that had caused a good deal of controversy a few years ago. It was a novel that dealt with some sensational subject. She had not read it and could not remember what the subject was but the name was associated in her mind with a strongly social kind of writing which had been more in vogue about five years past than it was since the beginning of the war. However the writer was still not more than thirty. He was not good-looking but his face had distinction. There was something a little monkey-like in his face as there frequently is in the faces of serious young writers, a look that reminded Miss Jelkes of a small chimpanzee she had once seen in the corner of his cage at a zoo, just sitting there staring between the bars, while all his fellows were hopping and spinning about on their noisy iron trapeze. She remembered how she had been touched by his solitary position and lack-lustre eyes. She had wanted to give him some peanuts but the elephants had devoured all she had. She had returned to the vendor to buy some more but when she brought them to the chimpanzee's cage, he had evidently succumbed to the general impulse, for now every man Jack of them was hopping and spinning about on the clanking trapeze and not a one of them seemed a bit different from the others. Looking at this writer she felt almost an identical urge to share something with him, but the wish was thwarted again, in this instance by a studious will to ignore her. It was not accidental, the way that he kept his eyes off her. It was the same on the beach as it was on the hotel verandahs.

On the beach he wore next to nothing, a sort of brilliant diaper of printed cotton, twisted about his loins in a fashion that sometimes failed to even approximate decency, but he had a slight and graceful physique and an unconscious ease of movement which made the immodesty less offensive to Miss Jelkes than it was in the case of his friend. The younger man had been an athlete at college and he was massively constructed. His torso was burned the colour of an old penny and its emphatic gender still further exclaimed by luxuriant patterns of hair, sunbleached till it shone like masses of crisped and frizzed golden wire. Moreover his regard for propriety was so slight that he would get in and out of his colourful napkin as if he were standing in a private cabana. Miss Jelkes had to acknowledge that he owned a certain sculptural grandeur but the spinsterish side of her nature was still too strong to permit her to feel anything but a squeamish distaste. This reaction of Miss Jelkes was so strong on one occasion that when she had returned to the hotel she went directly to the Patrona to enquire if the younger gentleman could not be persuaded to change clothes in his room or, if this was too much to ask of him, that he might at least keep the dorsal side of his nudity toward the beach. The Patrona was very much interested in the complaint but not in a way that Miss Jelkes had hoped she would be. She laughed immoderately, translating phrases of Miss Jelkes' complaint into idiomatic Spanish, shouted to the waiters and the cook. All of them joined in the laughter and the noise was still going on when Miss Jelkes standing confused and indignant saw the two young men climbing up the hill. She retired quickly to her room on the hammock-verandah but she knew by the reverberating merriment on the other side that the writers were being told, and that all of the Costa Verde was holding her up to undisguised ridicule. She started packing at once, this time not even bothering to fold things neatly into her steamer trunk, and she was badly frightened, so much disturbed that it affected her stomach and the following day she was not well enough to undertake a journey.

It was this following day that the Iguana was caught.

The Iguana is a lizard, two or three feet in length, which the Mexicans regard as suitable for the table. They are not always eaten right after they are caught but being creatures that can survive for quite a while without food or drink, they are often held in captivity for some time before execution. Miss Jelkes had been told that they tasted rather like chicken, which opinion she ascribed to a typically Mexican way of glossing over an un-appetizing fact. What bothered her about the Iguana was the inhumanity of its treatment during its interval of captivity. She had seen them outside the huts of villagers, usually hitched to a short pole near the doorway and continually and hopelessly clawing at the dry earth within the orbit of the rope-length, while naked children squatted around it, poking it with sticks in the eyes and mouth.

Now the Patrona's adolescent son had captured one of these Iguanas and had fastened it to the base of a column under the hammock-verandah. Miss Jelkes was not aware of its presence until late the night of the capture. Then she had been disturbed by the scuffling sound it made and had slipped on her dressing-gown and had gone out in the bright moonlight to discover what the sound was caused by. She looked over the rail of the verandah and she saw the Iguana hitched to the base of the column nearest her doorway and making the most pitiful effort to scramble into the bushes just beyond the taut length of its rope. She uttered a little cry of horror as she made this discovery.

The two young writers were lying in hammocks at the other end of the verandah and as usual were carrying on a desultory conversation in tones not loud enough to carry to her bedroom.

Without stopping to think, and with a curious thrill of exultation, Miss Jelkes rushed down to their end of the verandah. As she drew near them she discovered that the two writers were engaged in drinking rum-coco, which is a drink prepared in the shell of a coconut by knocking a cap off it with a machete and pouring into the nut a mixture of rum, lemon, sugar and cracked ice. The drinking had been going on since supper and the floor beneath their two hammocks was littered with bits of white pulp and hairy brown fibre and was so slippery that Miss Jelkes barely kept her footing. The liquid had spilt over their faces, bare throats and chests, giving them an oily lustre, and about their hammocks was hanging a cloud of moist and heavy sweetness. Each had a leg thrown over the edge of the hammock with which he pushed himself lazily back and forth. If Miss Jelkes had been seeing them for the first time, the gross details of the spectacle would have been more than association with a few dissolute members of the Jelkes family had prepared her to stomach, and she would have scrupulously avoided a second glance at them. But Miss Jelkes had been changing more than she was aware of during this period of preoccupation with the two writers, her scruples were more undermined than she suspected, so that if the word *pigs* flashed through her mind for a moment, it failed to distract her even momentarily from what she was bent on doing. It was a form of hysteria that had taken hold of her, her action and her speech were without volition.

'Do you know what has happened!' she gasped as she came toward them. She came nearer than she would have consciously dared, so that she was standing directly over the young writer's prone figure. 'That horrible boy, the son of the Patrona, has tied up an Iguana beneath my bedroom. I heard him tying it up but I didn't know what it was. I've been listening to it for hours, ever since supper, and didn't know what it was. Just now I got up to investigate, I looked over the edge of the verandah and there it was, scuffling around at the end of its little rope!'

Neither of the writers said anything for a moment, but the older one had propped himself up a little to stare at Miss Jelkes.

'There *what* was?' he enquired.

'She is talking about the Iguana,' said the younger.

'Oh! Well, what about it?'

'How can I sleep?' cried Miss Jelkes. 'How could anyone sleep with that example of Indian savagery right underneath my door!'

'You have an aversion to lizards?' suggested the older writer.

'I have an aversion to brutality!' corrected Miss Jelkes.

'But the lizard is a very low grade of animal life. Isn't it a very low grade of animal life?' he asked his companion.

'Not as low as some,' said the younger writer. He was grinning maliciously at Miss Jelkes, but she did not notice him at all, her attention was fixed upon the older writer.

'At any rate,' said the writer, 'I don't believe it is capable of feeling half as badly over its misfortune as you seem to be feeling for it.'

'I don't agree with you,' said Miss Jelkes. 'I don't agree with you at all! We like to think that we are the only ones that are capable of suffering but that is just human conceit. We are not the only ones that are capable of suffering. Why, even plants have sensory impressions. I have seen some that closed their leaves when you touched them!'

She held out her hand and drew her slender fingers into a chalice that closed. As she did this she drew a deep, tortured breath with

her lips pursed and nostrils flaring and her eyes rolled heaven-
wards so that she looked like a female Saint on the rack.

The younger man chuckled but the older one continued to stare
at her gravely.

'I am sure,' she went on, 'that the Iguana has very definite
feelings, and you would be, too, if you had been listening to it,
scuffling around out there in that awful dry dust, trying to reach
the bushes with that rope twisted about its neck, making it almost
impossible for it to breathe!'

She clutched her throat as she spoke and with the other hand
made a clawing gesture in the air. The younger writer broke into a
laugh, the older one smiled at Miss Jelkes.

'You have a real gift,' he said, 'for vicarious experience.'

'Well, I just can't stand to witness suffering,' said Miss Jelkes. 'I
can endure it myself but I just can't stand to witness it in others, no
matter whether it's human suffering or animal suffering. And
there is so much suffering in the world, so much that is necessary
suffering, such as illnesses and accidents which cannot be
avoided. But there is so much unnecessary suffering, too, so much
that is inflicted simply because some people have a callous
disregard for the feelings of others. Sometimes it almost seems as
if the universe was designed by the Marquis de Sade!'

She threw back her head with an hysterical laugh.

'And I do not believe in the principle of atonement,' she went
on. 'Isn't it awful, isn't it really preposterous that practically all
our religions should be based on the principle of atonement when
there is really and truly no such thing as guilt?'

'I am sorry,' said the older writer. He rubbed his forehead. 'I am
not in any condition to talk about God.'

'Oh, I'm not talking about God,' said Miss Jelkes. 'I'm talking
about the Iguana!'

'She's trying to say that the Iguana is one of God's creatures,'
said the younger writer.

'But that one of God's creatures,' said the older, 'is now in the
possession of the Patrona's son!'

'That one of God's creatures,' Miss Jelkes exclaimed, 'is now
hitched to a post right underneath my door, and late as it is I have
a very good notion to go and wake up the Patrona and tell her that
they have got to turn it loose or at least to remove it some place
where I can't hear it!'

The younger writer was now laughing with drunken

vehemence. 'What are you bellowing over?' the older one asked him.

'If she goes and wakes up the Patrona, anything can happen!'

'What?' asked Miss Jelkes. She glanced uncertainly at both of them.

'That's quite true,' said the older. 'One thing these Mexicans will not tolerate is the interruption of sleep!'

'But what can she do but apologize and remove it!' demanded Miss Jelkes. 'Because, after all, it's a pretty outrageous thing to hitch a lizard beneath a woman's door and expect her to sleep with that noise going on all night!'

'It might not go on all night,' said the older writer.

'What's going to stop it?' asked Miss Jelkes.

'The Iguana might go to sleep.'

'Never!' said Miss Jelkes. 'The creature is frantic and what it is going through must be a nightmare!'

'You're bothered a good deal by noises?' asked the older writer. This was, of course, a dig at Miss Jelkes for her complaint about the radio. She recognized it as such and welcomed the chance it gave to defend and explain. In fact this struck her as being the golden moment for breaking all barriers down.

'That's true, I am!' she admitted breathlessly. 'You see, I had a nervous breakdown a few years ago, and while I'm ever so much better than I was, sleep is more necessary to me than it is to people who haven't gone through a terrible thing like that. Why, for months and months I wasn't able to sleep without a sedative tablet, sometimes two of them a night! Now I hate like anything to be a nuisance to people, to make unreasonable demands, because I am always so anxious to get along well with people, not only peaceably, but really *cordially* with them – even with strangers that I barely *speak* to – However it sometimes happens . . .'

She paused for a moment. A wonderful thought struck her.

'I know what I'll do!' she cried out. She gave the older writer a radiant smile.

'What's that?' asked the younger. His tone was full of suspicion but Miss Jelkes smiled at him, too.

'Why, I'll just move!' she said.

'Out of the Costa Verde?' suggested the younger.

'Oh, no, no, no! No, indeed! It's the nicest resort hotel I've ever stopped at! I mean that I'll change my room.'

'Where will you change it to?'

'Down here,' said Miss Jelkes, 'to this end of the verandah! I won't even wait till morning. I'll move right now. All these vacant rooms, there couldn't be any objection, and if there is, why, I'll just explain how totally impossible it was for me to sleep with that lizard's commotion all night!'

She turned quickly about on her heels, so quickly that she nearly toppled over on the slippery floor, caught her breath laughingly and rushed back to her bedroom. Blindly she swept up a few of her belongings in her arms and rushed back to the writers' end of the verandah where they were holding a whispered consultation.

'Which is your room?' she asked.

'We have two rooms,' said the younger writer coldly.

'Yes, one each,' said the older.

'Oh, of course!' said Miss Jelkes. 'But I don't want to make the embarrassing error of confiscating one of you gentlemen's beds!'

She laughed gaily at this. It was the sort of remark she would make to show new acquaintances how far from being formal and prudish she was. But the writers were not inclined to laugh with her, so she cleared her throat and started blindly toward the nearest door, dropping a comb and a mirror as she did so.

'Seven years bad luck!' said the younger man.

'It isn't broken!' she gasped.

'Will you help me?' she asked the older writer.

He got up unsteadily and put the dropped articles back on the disorderly pile in her arms.

'I'm sorry to be so much trouble!' she gasped pathetically. Then she turned to the nearest doorway.

'Is this one vacant?'

'No, that's mine,' said the younger.

'Then how about *this* one?'

'That one is mine,' said the older.

'Sounds like the Three Bears and Goldilocks!' laughed Miss Jelkes. 'Well, oh, dear – I guess I'll just have to take *this* one!'

She rushed to the screen door on the other side of the younger writer's room, excitingly aware as she did so that this would put her within close range of their nightly conversations, the mystery of which had tantalized her for weeks. Now she would be able to hear every word that passed between them unless they actually whispered in each other's ear!

She rushed into the bedroom and let the screen door slam.

She switched on the suspended light bulb and hastily plunged the articles borne with her about a room that was identical with the one that she had left and then plopped herself down upon an identical white iron bed.

There was silence on the verandah.

Without rising she reached above her to pull the cord of the light-bulb. Its watery glow was replaced by the crisp white flood of moonlight through the gauze-netted window and through the screen of the door.

She lay flat on her back with her arms lying rigidly along her sides and every nerve tingling with excitement over the spontaneous execution of a piece of strategy carried out more expertly than it would have been after days of preparation.

For a while the silence outside her new room continued.

Then the voice of the younger writer pronounced the word 'Goldilocks!'

Two shouts of laughter rose from the verandah. It continued without restraint till Miss Jelkes could feel her ears burning in the dark as if rays of intense light were concentrated on them.

Miss Jelkes was badly hurt, worse than she had been hurt the previous afternoon, when she had complained about the young man's immodesty on the beach. As she lay there upon the severe white bed that smelled of ammonia she could feel coming toward her one of those annihilating spells of neurasthenia which had led to her breakdown six years ago. She was too weak to cope with it, it would have its way with her and bring her God knows how close to the verge of lunacy and even possibly over! What an intolerable burden, and why did she have to bear it, she who was so humane and gentle by nature that even the sufferings of a lizard could hurt her! She turned her face to the cold white pillow and wept. She wished that she were a writer. If she were a writer it would be possible to say things that only Picasso had ever put into paint. But if she said them would anybody believe them? Was her sense of the enormous grotesquerie of the world communicable to any other person? And why should it be told if it could be? And why, most of all, did she make such a fool of herself in her frantic need to find comfort in people!

She felt that the morning was going to be pitilessly hot and bright and she turned over in her mind the list of neuroses that might fasten upon her. Everything that is thoughtless and automatic in healthy organisms might take on for her an air of preposterous novelty. The act of breathing and the heat of her heart and the very process of thinking would be self-conscious if this worst-of-all neuroses should take hold of her – and take hold of her it would, because she was so afraid of it! The precarious balance of her nerves would be all overthrown. Her entire being would turn into a feverish little machine for the production of fears, fears that could not be put into words because of their all-encompassing immensity, and even supposing that they could be put into language and so be susceptible to the comfort of telling – who was there at the Costa Verde, this shadowless rock by the ocean, that she could turn to except the two young writers who seemed to despise her? How awful to be at the mercy of merciless people!

Now I'm indulging in self-pity, she thought.

She turned on her side and fished among articles on the bed-table for the little cardboard box of sedative tablets. They would get her through the night, but tomorrow – oh, tomorrow! She lay there senselessly crying, hearing even at this distance the efforts of the captive Iguana to break from its rope and scramble into the bushes . . .

2

When Miss Jelkes awoke it was still a while before morning. The moon, however, had disappeared from the sky and she was lying in blackness that would have been total except for tiny cracks of light that came through the wall of the adjoining bedroom, the one that was occupied by the younger writer.

It did not take her long to discover that the younger writer was not alone in his room. There was no speech but the quality of sounds that came at intervals through the partition made her certain the room had two people in it.

If she could have risen from bed and peered through one of the cracks without betraying herself she might have done so, but knowing that any move would be overheard, she remained on the bed and her mind was now alert with suspicions which had before been only a formless wonder.

At last she heard someone speak.

'You'd better turn out the light,' said the voice of the younger writer.

'Why?'

'There are cracks in the wall.'

'So much the better. I'm sure that's why she moved down here.'

The younger one raised his voice.

'You don't think she moved because of the Iguana?'

'Hell, no, that was just an excuse. Didn't you notice how pleased she was with herself, as if she had pulled off something downright brilliant?'

'I bet she's eavesdropping on us right this minute,' said the younger.

'Undoubtedly she is. But what can she do about it?'

'Go to the Patrona.'

Both of them laughed.

'The Patrona wants to get rid of her,' said the younger.

'Does she?'

'Yep. She's crazy to have her move out. She's even given the cook instructions to put too much salt in her food.'

They both laughed.

Miss Jelkes discovered that she had risen from the bed. She was standing uncertainly on the cold floor for a moment and then she was rushing out of the screen door and up to the door of the younger writer's bedroom.

She knocked on the door, carefully keeping her eyes away from the lighted interior.

'Come in,' said a voice.

'I'd rather not,' said Miss Jelkes. 'Will you come here for a minute?'

'Sure,' said the younger writer. He stepped to the door, wearing only the trousers of his pyjamas.

'Oh,' he said. 'It's you!'

She stared at him without any idea of what she had come to say or had hoped to accomplish.

'Well?' he demanded brutally.

'I – I heard you!' she stammered.

'So?'

'I don't understand it!'

'What?'

'Cruelty! I never could understand it!'

'But you do understand spying, don't you?'

'I wasn't spying!' she cried.

He muttered a shocking word and shoved past her on to the porch.

The older writer called his name: 'Mike!' But he only repeated
the shocking word more loudly and walked away from them.
Miss Jelkes and the older writer faced each other. The violence
just past had calmed Miss Jelkes a little. She found herself
uncoiling inside and comforting tears beginning to moisten her
eyes. Outside the night was changing. A wind had sprung up and
the surf that broke on the other side of the land-locked bay called
Coleta could now be heard.

'It's going to storm,' said the writer.

'Is it? I'm glad!' said Miss Jelkes.

'Won't you come in?'

'I'm not at all properly dressed.'

'I'm not either.'

'Oh, well—'

She came in. Under the naked light-bulb and without the dark
glasses his face looked older and the eyes, which she had not seen
before, had a look that often goes with incurable illness.

She noticed that he was looking about for something.

'Tablets,' he muttered.

She caught sight of them first, among a litter of papers.

She handed them to him.

'Thank you. Will you have one?'

'I've had one already.'

'What kind are yours?'

'Secconal. Yours?'

'Barbital. Are yours good?'

'Wonderful.'

'How do they make you feel? Like a water-lily?'

'Yes, like a water-lily on a Chinese lagoon!'

Miss Jelkes laughed with real gaiety but the writer responded
only with a faint smile. His attention was drifting away from her
again. He stood at the screen door like a worried child awaiting
the return of a parent.

'Perhaps I should—'

Her voice faltered. She did not want to leave. She wanted to stay
there. She felt herself upon the verge of saying incommunicable
things to this man whose singularity was so like her own in many
essential respects, but his turned back did not invite her to stay.
He shouted the name of his friend. There was no response. The
writer turned back from the door with a worried muttering but his
attention did not return to Miss Jelkes.

'Your friend—' she faltered.

'Mike?'

'Is he the – right person for you?'

'Mike is helpless and I am always attracted by helpless people.'

'But you,' she said awkwardly. 'How about you? Don't you need somebody's help?'

'The help of God!' said the writer. 'Failing that, I have to depend on myself.'

'But isn't it possible that with somebody else, somebody with more understanding, more like *yourself*—!'

'You mean *you*?' he asked bluntly.

Miss Jelkes was spared the necessity of answering one way or another, for at that moment a great violence was unleashed outside the screen door. The storm that had hovered uncertainly on the horizon was now plunging toward them. Not continually but in sudden thrusts and withdrawals, like a giant bird lunging up and down on its terrestrial quarry, a bird with immense white wings and beak of godlike fury, the attack was delivered against the jut of rock on which the Costa Verde was planted. Time and again the whole night blanched and trembled, but there was something frustrate in the attack of the storm. It seemed to be one that came from a thwarted will. Otherwise surely the frame structure would have been smashed. But the giant white bird did not know where it was striking. Its beak of fury was blind, or perhaps the beak—

It may have been that Miss Jelkes was right on the verge of divining more about God than a mortal ought to – when suddenly the writer leaned forward and thrust his knees between hers. She noticed that he had removed the towel about him and now was quite naked. She did not have time to wonder nor even to feel much surprise for in the next few moments, and for the first time in her thirty years of pre-ordained spinsterhood, she was enacting a fierce little comedy of defence. He thrust at her like the bird of blind white fury. His one hand attempted to draw up the skirt of her robe while his other tore at the flimsy goods at her bosom. The upper cloth tore. She cried out with pain as the predatory fingers dug into her flesh. But she did not give in. Not she herself resisted but some demon of virginity that occupied her flesh fought off the assailant more furiously than he attacked her. And the demon won, for all at once the man let go of her gown and his fingers released her bruised bosom. A sobbing sound in his throat, he collapsed against her. She felt a wing-like throbbing against her belly, and then a scalding wetness. Then he let go of her altogether. She sank into her chair which had remained demurely upright throughout the struggle, as unsuitably, as ridiculously, as she herself had maintained her upright position. The man was sobbing. And then the screen door opened and the younger writer came in. Automatically Miss Jelkes freed herself from the damp embrace of her unsuccessful assailant.

'What is it?' asked the younger writer.

He repeated his question several times, senselessly but angrily, while he shook his older friend who could not stop crying.

I don't belong here, thought Miss Jelkes, and suiting action to thought, she slipped quietly out the screen door. She did not turn back into the room immediately adjoining but ran down the verandah to the room she had occupied before. She threw herself on to the bed which was now as cool as if she had never lain on it. She was grateful for that and for the abrupt cessation of fury outside. The white bird had gone away and the Costa Verde had survived its assault. There was nothing but the rain now, pattering without much energy, and the far away sound of the ocean only a little more distinct than it had been before the giant bird struck. She remembered the Iguana.

Oh, yes, the Iguana! She lay there with ears pricked for the painful sound of its scuffling, but there was no sound but the effortless flowing of water. Miss Jelkes could not contain her curiosity so at last she got out of bed and looked over the edge of the verandah. She saw the rope. She saw the whole length of the rope lying there in a relaxed coil, but not the Iguana. Somehow or other the creature tied by the rope had gotten away. Was it an act of God that had effected this deliverance? Or was it not more reasonable to suppose that only Mike, the beautiful and helpless and cruel, had cut the Iguana loose? No matter. No matter who did it, the Iguana was gone, had scrambled back into its native bushes and, oh, how gratefully it must be breathing now! And she was grateful, too, for in some equally mysterious way the strangling rope of her loneliness had also been severed by what had happened tonight on this barren rock above the moaning waters.

Now she was sleepy. But just before falling asleep she remembered and felt again the spot of dampness, now turning cool but still adhering to the flesh of her belly as a light but persistent kiss. Her fingers approached it timidly. They expected to draw back with revulsion but were not so affected. They touched it curiously and even pityingly and did not draw back for a while. *Ah, Life,* she thought to herself and was about to smile at the originality of this thought when darkness lapped over the outward gaze of her mind.

THREE PLAYERS OF A SUMMER GAME

Croquet is a summer game that seems, in a curious way, to be composed of images the way that a painter's abstraction of summer or one of its games would be built of them. The delicate wire wickets set in a lawn of smooth emerald that flickers fierily at some points and rests under violet shadow in others, the wooden poles gaudily painted as moments that stand out in a season that was a struggle for something of unspeakable importance to someone passing through it, the clean and hard wooden spheres of different colours and the strong rigid shape of the mallets that drive the balls through the wickets, the formal design of those wickets and poles upon the croquet lawn – all of these are like a painter's abstraction of a summer and a game played in it. And I cannot think of croquet without hearing a sound like the faraway boom of a cannon fired to announce a white ship coming into a harbour which had expected it anxiously for a long while. The faraway booming sound is that of a green-and-white striped awning coming down over a gallery of a white frame house. The house is of Victorian design carried to an extreme of improvisation, an almost grotesque pile of galleries and turrets and cupolas and eaves, all freshly painted white, so white and so fresh that it has the blue-white glitter of a block of ice in the sun. The house is like a new resolution not yet tainted by any defection from it. And I associate the summer game with players coming out of this house, out of the mysteries of a walled place, with the buoyant air of persons just released from a suffocating enclosure, as if they had spent the fierce day bound in a closet, were breathing freely at last in fresh atmosphere and able to move without hindrance. Their clothes are as light in weight and colour as the flattering clothes of dancers. There are three players – a woman, a man, and a child.

The voice of the woman player is not at all a loud one; yet it has a pleasantly resonant quality that carries it farther than most voices go and it is interspersed with peals of treble laughter, pitched much higher than the voice itself, which are cool-sounding as particles of ice in a tall shaken glass. This woman player, even more than her male opponent in the game, has the grateful quickness of motion of someone let out of a suffocating enclosure; her motion has the quickness of breath released just after a moment of terror, of fingers unclenched when panic is suddenly past or of a cry that subsides into laughter. She seems unable to speak or move about moderately; she moves in convulsive rushes, whipping her skirts with long strides that quicken to running. The whipped skirts are white ones. They make a faint crackling sound as her pumping thighs whip them open, the sound that comes to you, greatly diminished by distance, when fitful fair-weather gusts belly out and slacken the faraway sails of a yawl. That agreeably cool summer sound is accompanied by another which is even cooler, the ceaseless tiny chatter of beads hung in long loops from her throat. They are not pearls but they have a milky lustre, they are small faintly speckled white ovals, polished bird's eggs turned solid and strung upon glittery filaments of silver. This woman player is never still for a moment; sometimes she exhausts herself and collapses on the grass in the conscious attitudes of a dancer. She is a thin woman with long bones and skin of a silky lustre and her eyes are only a shade or two darker than the blue-tinted bird's egg beads about her long throat. She is never still, not even when she has fallen in exhaustion on the grass. The neighbours think she's gone mad but they feel no pity for her, and that, of course, is because of her male opponent in the game.

This player is Brick Pollitt, a man so tall with such a fiery thatch of hair on top of him that I never see a flagpole on an expanse of green lawn or even a particularly brilliant cross or weather vane on a steeple without thinking suddenly of that long-ago summer and Brick Pollitt and begin to assert again the baffling bits and pieces that make his legend. These bits and pieces, these assorted images, they are like the paraphernalia for a game of croquet, gathered up from the lawn when the game is over and packed carefully into an oblong wooden box which they just exactly fit and fill. There they all are, the bits and pieces, the images, the apparently incongruous paraphernalia of a summer that was the last one of my childhood, and now I take them out of the oblong box and arrange them once more in the formal design on the lawn. It would be absurd to pretend that this is altogether the way it was, and yet it may be closer than a literal history could be to the hidden truth of it. Brick Pollitt is the male player of this summer game, and he is a drinker who has not yet completely fallen beneath the savage axe blows of his liquor. He is not so young any more but he has not yet lost the slim grace of his youth. He is a head taller than the tall woman player of the game. He is such a tall man that, even in those sections of the lawn dimmed under violet shadow, his head continues to catch fiery rays of the descending sun, the way that the heavenward pointing index finger of that huge gilded hand atop a Protestant steeple in Meridian goes on drawing the sun's flame for a good while after the lower surfaces of the town have sunk into lingering dusk.

The third player of the summer game is the daughter of the woman, a plump twelve-year-old child named Mary Louise. This little girl had made herself distinctly unpopular among the children of the neighbourhood by imitating too perfectly the elegant manners and cultivated eastern voice of her mother. She sat in the electric automobile on the sort of a fat silk pillow that expensive lap dogs sit on, uttering treble peals of ladylike laughter, tossing her curls, using grown-up expressions such as, 'Oh, how delightful' and 'Isn't that just lovely.' She would sit in the electric automobile sometimes all afternoon by herself as if she were on display in a glass box, only now and then raising a plaintive voice to call her mother and ask if it was all right to come in now or if she could drive the electric around the block, which she was sometimes then permitted to do.

I was her only close friend and she was mine. Sometimes she called me over to play croquet with her but that was only when her mother and Brick Pollitt had disappeared into the house too early to play the game. Mary Louise had a passion for croquet; she played it for herself, without any more shadowy and important connotations.

What the game meant to Brick Pollitt calls for some further account of Brick's life before that summer. He was a young Delta planter who had been a celebrated athlete at Sewanee, who had married a New Orleans debutante who was a Mardi Gras queen and whose father owned a fleet of banana boats. It had seemed a brilliant marriage, with lots of wealth and prestige on both sides, but only two years later Brick had started falling in love with his liquor and Margaret, his wife, began to be praised for her patience and loyalty to him. Brick seemed to be throwing his life away as if it were something disgusting that he had suddenly found in his hands. This self-disgust came upon him with the abruptness and violence of a crash on a highway. But what had Brick crashed into? Nothing that anybody was able to surmise, for he seemed to have everything that young men like Brick might hope or desire to have. What else is there? There must have been something else that he wanted and lacked, or what reason was there for dropping his life and taking hold of a glass which he never let go of for more than one waking hour? His wife, Margaret, took hold of Brick's ten-thousand-acre plantation as firmly and surely as if she had always existed for that and no other purpose. She had Brick's power of attorney and she managed all of his business affairs with celebrated astuteness. 'He'll come out of it,' she said. 'Brick is passing through something that he'll come out of.' She always said the right thing; she took the conventionally right attitude and expressed it to the world that admired her for it. She had never committed any apostasy from the social faith she was born to and everybody admired her as a remarkably fine and brave little woman who had too much to put up with. Two sections of an hour glass could not drain and fill more evenly than Brick and Margaret changed places after he took to drink. It was as though she had her lips fastened to some invisible wound in his body through which drained out of him and flowed into her the assurance and vitality that he had owned before marriage. Margaret Pollitt lost her pale, feminine prettiness and assumed in its place something more impressive – a firm and rough-textured sort of handsomeness that came out of her indefinite chrysalis as mysteriously as one of those metamorphoses that occur in insect life. Once very pretty but indistinct, a graceful sketch that was done with a very light pencil, she became vivid as Brick disappeared behind the veil of his liquor. She came out of a mist. She rose into clarity as Brick descended. She abruptly stopped being quiet and dainty. She was now apt to have dirty fingernails which she covered with scarlet enamel. When the enamel chipped off, the grey showed underneath. Her hair was now cut short so that she didn't have to 'mess with it'. It was wind-blown and full of sparkle; she jerked a comb through it to make it crackle. She had white teeth that were a little too large for her thin lips, and when she threw her head back in laughter, strong cords of muscle stood out in her smooth brown throat. She had a booming laugh that she might have stolen from Brick while he was drunk or asleep beside her at night. She had a practice of releasing the clutch on a car and shooting off in high gear at the exact instant that her laughter boomed out, not calling goodbye but thrusting out one bare strong arm, straight out as a piston with fingers clenched into a fist, as the car whipped up and disappeared into a cloud of yellow dust. She didn't drive her own little runabout nowadays so much as she did Brick's Pierce-Arrow touring car, for Brick's driver's licence had been revoked. She frequently broke the speed limit on the highway. The patrolmen would stop her, but she had such an affability, such a disarming way with her, that they would have a good laugh together, she and the highway patrolman, and he would tear up the ticket.

Somebody in her family died in Memphis that spring, and she went there to attend the funeral and collect her inheritance, and while she was gone on that profitable journey, Brick Pollitt slipped out from under her thumb a bit. Another death occurred during her absence. That nice young doctor who took care of Brick when he had to be carried to the hospital, he suddenly took sick in a shocking way. An awful flower grew in his brain like a fierce geranium that shattered its pot. All of a sudden the wrong words came out of his mouth; he seemed to be speaking in an unknown tongue; he couldn't find things with his hands; he made troubled signs over his forehead. His wife led him about the house by one hand, yet he stumbled and fell flat; the breath was knocked out of him, and he had to be put to bed by his wife and the Negro yardman; and he lay there laughing weakly, incredulously, trying to find his wife's hand with both of his while she looked at him with eyes that she couldn't keep from blazing with terror. He stayed under drugs for a week, and it was during that time that Brick Pollitt came to see her. Brick came and sat with Isabel Grey by her dying husband's bed and she couldn't speak, she could only shake her head, incessantly as a metronome, with no lips visible in her white face, but two pressed narrow bands of a dimmer whiteness that shook as if some white liquid flowed beneath them with an incredible rapidity and violence which made them quiver . . .

God was the only word she was able to say; but Brick Pollitt somehow understood what she meant by that word, as if it were in a language that she and he, alone of all people, could speak and understand; and when the dying man's eyes forcibly opened on something they couldn't bear to look at, it was Brick, his hands suddenly quite sure and steady, who filled the hypodermic needle for her and pumped its contents fiercely into her husband's hard young arm. And it was over. There was another bed at the back of the house and he and Isabel lay beside each other on that bed for a couple of hours before they let the town know that her husband's agony was completed, and the only movement between them was the intermittent, spasmodic digging of their finger-nails into each other's clenched palm while their bodies lay stiffly separate, deliberately not touching at any other points as if they abhorred any other contact with each other, while this intolerable thing was ringing like an iron bell through them.

And so you see what the summer game on the violet-shadowed lawn was — it was a running together out of something unbearably hot and bright into something obscure and cool . . .

The young widow was left with nothing in the way of material possessions except the house and an electric automobile, but by the time Brick's wife, Margaret, had returned from her profitable journey to Memphis, Brick had taken over the post-catastrophic details of the widow's life. For a week or two, people thought it was very kind of him, and then all at once public opinion changed and they decided that Brick's reason for kindness was by no means noble. It appeared to observers that the widow was now his mistress, and this was true. It was true in the limited way that most such opinions are true. It is only the outside of each other's world that is visible to others, and all opinions are false ones, especially public opinions of individual cases. She was his mistress, but that was not Brick's reason. His reason had something to do with that chaste interlocking of hands their first time together, after the hypodermic; it had to do with those hours, now receding and fading behind them as all such hours must, but neither of them could have said what it was aside from that. Neither of them was able to think very clearly. But Brick was able to pull himself together for a while and take command of those post-catastrophic details in the young widow's life and her daughter's.

The daughter, Mary Louise, was a plump child of twelve. She was my friend that summer. Mary Louise and I caught lightning bugs and put them in Mason jars to make flickering lanterns, and we played the game of croquet when her mother and Brick Pollitt were not inclined to play it. It was Mary Louise that summer who taught me how to deal with mosquito bites. She was plagued by

mosquitoes and so was I. She warned me that scratching the bites
would leave scars on my skin, which was as tender as hers. I said
that I didn't care. 'Someday you will,' she told me. She carried
with her constantly that summer a lump of ice in a handkerchief.
Whenever a mosquito bit her, instead of scratching the bite she
rubbed it gently with the handkerchief-wrapped lump of ice until
the sting was frozen to numbness. Of course, in five minutes it
would come back and have to be frozen again, but eventually it
would disappear and leave no scar. Mary Louise's skin, where it
was not temporarily mutilated by a mosquito bite or a slight rash
that sometimes appeared after eating strawberry icecream, was
ravishingly smooth and tender. The association is not at all a
proper one, but how can you recall a summer in childhood
without some touches of impropriety? I can't remember Mary
Louise's plump bare legs and arms, fragrant with sweet-pea
powder, without also thinking of an afternoon drive we took in
the electric automobile to the little museum that had recently been
established in the town. We went there just before the five o'clock
closing time, and straight as a bee, Mary Louise led me into a
room that was devoted to replicas of famous antique sculptures.
There was a reclining male nude (the 'Dying Gaul', I believe) and
it was straight to this statue that she led me. I began to blush
before we arrived there. It was naked except for a fig leaf, which
was of a different-coloured metal from the bronze of the prostrate
figure, and to my astonished horror, that afternoon, Mary Louise,
after a quick, sly look in all directions, picked the fig leaf up,
removed it from what it covered, and then turned her totally
unembarrassed and innocent eyes upon mine and inquired
smiling very brightly, 'Is yours like that?'

My answer was idiotic; I said, 'I don't know!' and I think I was
blushing long after we left the museum . . .

The Greys' house in the spring when the doctor died of brain
cancer was very run down. But soon after Brick Pollitt started
coming over to see the young widow, the house was painted; it
was painted so white that it was almost a very pale blue; it had the
blue-white glitter of a block of ice in the sun. Coolness of
appearance seemed to be the most desired of all things that
summer. In spite of his red hair, Brick Pollitt had a cool
appearance because he was still young and thin, as thin as the
widow, and he dressed as she did in clothes of light weight and
colour. His white shirts looked faintly pink because of his skin

underneath them. Once I saw him through an upstairs window of the widow's house just a moment before he pulled the shade down. I was in an upstairs room of my house and I saw that Brick Pollitt was divided into two colours as distinct as two stripes of a flag, the upper part of him, which had been exposed to the sun, almost crimson and the lower part of him white as this piece of paper.

While the widow's house was being repainted (at Brick Pollitt's expense), she and her daughter lived at the Alcazar Hotel, also at Brick's expense. Brick supervised the renovation of the widow's house. He drove in from his plantation every morning to watch the house painters and gardeners at work. Brick's driving licence had been restored to him, and it was an important step forward in his personal renovation – being able to drive his own car again. He drove it with elaborate caution and formality, coming to a dead stop at every cross street in the town, sounding the silver trumpet at every corner, inviting pedestrians to precede him, with smiles and bows and great circular gestures of his hands. But observers did not approve of what Brick Pollitt was doing. They sympathized with his wife, Margaret, that brave little woman who had to put up with so much. As for Dr Grey's widow, she had not been very long in the town; the doctor had married her while he was an interne at a big hospital in Baltimore. Nobody had formed a definite opinion of her before the doctor died, so it was no effort, now, to simply condemn her, without any qualification, as a common strumpet.

Brick Pollitt, when he talked to the house painters, shouted to them as if they were deaf, so that all the neighbours could hear what he had to say. He was explaining things to the world, especially the matter of his drinking.

'It's something,' he shouted, 'that you can't cut out completely right away. That's the big mistake that most drinkers make – they try to cut it out completely, and you can't do that. You can do it for maybe a month or two months, but all at once you go back on it worse than before you went off it, and then the discouragement is awful – you lose all faith in yourself and just give up. The thing to do, the way to handle the problem, is like a bullfighter handles a bull in a ring. Wear it down little by little, get control of it gradually. That's how I'm handling this thing! Yep. Now, let's say that you get up wanting a drink in the morning. Say it's ten o'clock, maybe. Well, you say to yourself, "Just wait half an hour,

old boy, and then you can have one." Well, at half-past ten you
still want that drink, and you want it a little bit worse then you did
at ten, but you say to yourself, "Boy, you could do without it half
an hour ago so you can do without it now." You see, that's how
you got to argue about it with yourself, because a drinking man is
not one person — a man that drinks is two people, one grabbing
the bottle, the other one fighting him off it, not one but two people
fighting each other to get control of a bottle. Well, sir, if you can
talk yourself out of a drink at ten, you can still talk yourself out of
a drink at *half-past* ten! But at *eleven* o'clock the need for the
drink is greater. Now *here's* the important thing to remember
about this struggle. You got to watch those scales, and when they
tip too far against your power to resist, you got to give in a little.
That's not weakness. *That's strategy!* Because don't forget what I
told you. A drinking man is not one person but two, and it's a
battle of wits going on between them. And so I say at eleven,
"Well, *have* your drink at that hour, *go on*, and *have* it! One drink
at eleven won't hurt you!"

'What time is it, now? Yep! Eleven . . . All right, I'm going to
have me that one drink. I could do without it, I don't crave it, but
the important thing is . . .'

His voice would trail off as he entered the widow's house. He
would stay in there longer than it took to have one drink, and
when he came out, there was a change in his voice as definite as a
change of weather or season, the strong and vigorous tone would
be a bit filmed over.

Then he would usually talk about his wife. 'I don't say my wife
Margaret's not an intelligent woman. She is, and both of us know
it, but she don't have a good head for property values. Now, you
know Dr Grey, who used to live here before that brain thing killed
him. Well, he was my physician, he pulled me through some bad
times when I had that liquor problem. I felt I owed him a lot. Now,
that was a terrible thing the way he went, but it was terrible for his
widow, too; she was left with this house and that electric
automobile and that's all, and this house was put up for sale to
pay off her debts, and – well, I bought it. I bought it, and now I'm
giving it back to her. Now, my wife Margaret, she. And a lot of
other folks, too. Don't understand about this . . .

'What time is it? Twelve? High noon! . . . This ice is melted . . .'

He'd drift back into the house and stay there half an hour, and
when he came back out, it was rather shyly with a sad and

uncertain creaking of the screen door pushed by the hand not holding the tall glass, but after resting a little while on the steps, he would resume his talk to the house painters.

'Yes,' he would say, as if he had only paused a moment before, 'it's the most precious thing that a woman can give to a man – his lost respect for himself – and the meanest thing one human being can do to another human being is take his respect for himself away from him. I. I had it took away from me . . .'

The glass would tilt slowly up and jerkily down, and he'd have to wipe his chin dry.

'I had it took away from me! I won't tell you how, but maybe, being men about my age, you're able to guess it. That was how. Some of them don't want it. They cut if off. They cut it right off a man, and half the time he don't even know when they cut it off him. Well, I knew all right. I could feel it being cut off me. Do you know what I mean? . . . That's right . . .

'But once in a while there's one – and they don't come often – that wants for a man to keep it, and those are the women that God made and put on this earth. The other kind come out of hell, or out of . . . I don't know what. I'm talking too much. Sure. I know I'm talking too much about private matters. But that's all right. This property is mine. I'm talking on my own property and I don't give a s—— who hears me! I'm not shouting about it, but I'm not sneaking around about it neither. Whatever I do, I do it without any shame, and I've got a right to do it. I've been through a hell of a lot that nobody knows. But I'm coming out of it now. God damn it, yes, I am! I can't take all the credit. And yet I'm proud. I'm goddam proud of myself, because I was in a pitiful condition with that liquor problem of mine, but now the worst is over. I've got it just about licked. That's my car out there and I drove up here myself. It's no short drive, it's almost a hundred miles, and I drive it each morning and drive it back each night. I've got back my driver's licence, and I fired the man that was working for my wife, looking after our place. I fired that man and not only fired him but give him a kick in the britches that'll make him eat standing up for the next week or two. It wasn't because I thought he was fooling around. It wasn't that. But him and her both took about the same attitude toward me, and I didn't like the attitude they took. They would talk about me right in front of me, as if I wasn't there. "Is it time for his medicine?" Yes, they were giving me dope! So one day I played possum. I was lying out there on the sofa and she said to him, "I guess he's passed out now." And he said, "Jesus, dead drunk at half-past one in the afternoon!" Well. I got up slowly. I wasn't drunk at that hour, I wasn't even half drunk. I stood up straight and walked slowly toward him. I walked straight up to them both, and you should of seen the eyes of them both bug out! "Yes, Jesus," I said, "at half-past one!" And I grabbed him by his collar and by the seat of his britches and turkey-trotted him right on out of the house and pitched him on his face in a big mud puddle at the foot of the steps to the front verandah. And as far as I know or care, maybe he's still laying there and she's still screaming, "Stop, Brick!" But I believe I did hit her. Yes, I did. I did hit her. There's times when you got to hit them, and that was one of those times. I ain't been to the house since. I moved in the little place we lived in before the big one was built, on the other side of the bayou, and ain't crossed over there since . . .

'Well, sir, that's all over with now. I got back my power of attorney which I'd give to that woman and I got back my driver's licence and I bought this piece of property in town and signed my own cheque for it and I'm having it completely done over to make it as handsome a piece of residential property as you can find in this town, and I'm having that lawn out there prepared for the game of croquet.'

Then he'd look at the glass in his hands as if he had just then noticed that he was holding it; he'd give it a look of slightly pained surprise, as if he had cut his hand and just now noticed that it was cut and bleeding. Then he would sigh like an old-time actor in a tragic role. He would put the tall glass down on the balustrade with great, great care, look back at it to make sure that it wasn't going to fall over, and walk very straight and steady to the porch steps and just as steady but with more concentration down them. When he arrived at the foot of the steps, he would laugh as if someone had made a comical remark; he would duck his head genially and shout to the house painters something like this: 'Well, I'm not making any predictions because I'm no fortune-teller, but I've got a strong idea that I'm going to lick my liquor problem this summer, ha ha, I'm going to lick it this summer! I'm not going to take no cure and I'm not going to take no pledge, I'm just going to prove I'm a man with his balls back on him! I'm going to do it step by little step, the way that people play the game of croquet. You know how you play that game. You hit the ball through one wicket and then you drive it through the next one.

You hit it through that wicket and then you drive on to another. You go from wicket to wicket, and it's a game of precision – it's a game that takes concentration and precision, and that's what makes it a wonderful game for a drinker. It takes a sober man to play the game of precision. It's better than shooting pool, because a pool hall is always next door to a gin mill, and you never see a pool player that don't have his liquor glass on the edge of the table or somewhere pretty near it, and croquet is also a better game than golf, because in golf you've always got that nineteenth hole waiting for you. Nope, for a man with a liquor problem, croquet is a summer game and it may seem a little bit sissy, but let me tell you, it's a game of precision. You go from wicket to wicket until you arrive at that big final pole, and then, bang, you've hit it, the game is finished, you're there! And then, and not until then, you can go up here to the porch and have you a cool gin drink, a buck or a Collins – Hey! Where did I leave that glass? Aw! Yeah, hand it down to me, will you? Ha ha – thanks.'

He would take a birdlike sip, make a fiercely wry face, and shake his head violently as if somebody had drenched it with scalding water.

'*This God damn stuff!*' He would look round to find a safe place to set the glass down again. He would select a bare spot of earth between the hydrangea bushes, deposit the glass there as carefully as if he were planting a memorial tree, and then he would straighten up with a great air of relief and expand his chest and flex his arms. 'Ha, ha, yep, croquet is a summer game for widows and drinkers, ha ha!'

For a few moments, standing there in the sun, he would seem as sure and powerful as the sun itself; but then some little shadow of uncertainty would touch him again, get through the wall of his liquor, some tricky little shadow of a thought, as sly as a mouse, quick, dark, too sly to be caught and without his moving enough for it to be noticed, his still fine body would fall as violently as a giant tree crashes down beneath a final axe stroke, taking with it all the wheeling seasons of sun and stars, whole centuries of them, crashing suddenly into oblivion and rot. He would make this enormous fall without a perceptible movement of his body. At the most, it would show in the faint flicker of something across his face, whose colour gave him the name people knew him by. Something flickered across his flame-coloured face. Possibly one knee sagged a little forward. Then slowly, slowly, the way a bull trots uncertainly back from its first wild, challenging plunge into the ring, he would fasten one hand over his belt and raise the other one hesitantly to his head, feeling the scalp and the hard round bowl of the skull underneath it, as if he simply imagined that by feeling that dome he might be able to guess what was hidden inside it, the dark and wondering stuff beneath that dome of calcium, facing, now, the intricate wickets of the summer to come . . .

2

For one reason or another, Mary Louise Grey was locked out of the house a great deal of the time that summer, and since she was a lonely child with little or no imagination, apparently unable to amuse herself with solitary games – except the endless one of copying her mother – the afternoons that she was excluded from the house 'because Mother has a headache' were periods of great affliction. There were several galleries with outside stairs between them, and she patrolled the galleries and wandered forlornly about the lawn, and from time to time, she went down the front walk and sat in the glass box of the electric. She would vary her steps, sometimes walking sedately, sometimes skipping, sometimes hopping and humming, one plump hand always clutching the handkerchief that contained the lump of ice. This lump of ice to rub her mosquito bites had to be replaced at frequent intervals. 'Oh, iceman,' the widow would call sweetly from an upstairs window, 'don't forget to leave some extra pieces for little Mary Louise to rub her mosquito bites with!'

Each time a new bite was suffered Mary Louise would utter a soft cry in a voice that had her mother's trick of carrying a great distance without being loud.

'Oh, Mother,' she would moan, 'I'm simply being devoured by mosquitoes!'

'Darling,' her mother would answer, 'that's dreadful, but you know that Mother can't help it; she didn't create the mosquitoes and she can't destroy them for you!'

'You could let me come in the house, Mama.'

'No, I can't let you come in, precious. Not yet.'

'Why not, Mother?'

'Because Mother has a sick headache.'

'I will be quiet.'

'You say that you will, but you won't. You must learn to amuse yourself, precious; you mustn't depend on Mother to amuse you. Nobody can depend on anyone else forever. I'll tell you what you can do till Mother's headache is better. You can drive the electric out of the garage. You can drive it around the block, but don't go into the business district with it, and then you can stop in the shady part of the drive and sit there perfectly comfortably till Mother feels better and can get dressed and come out. And then I think Mr Pollitt may come over for a game of croquet. Won't that be lovely?'

'Do you think he will get here in time to play?'

'I hope so, precious. It does him so much good to play croquet.'

'Oh, I think it does all of us good to play croquet,' said Mary Louise in a voice that trembled just at the vision of it.

Before Brick Pollitt arrived — sometimes half an hour before his coming, as though she could hear his automobile on the highway thirty miles from the house — Mary Louise would bound plumply off the gallery and begin setting up the poles and wickets of the longed-for game. While she was doing this, her plump little buttocks and her beginning breasts and her shoulder-length copper curls would all bob up and down in perfect unison.

I would watch her from the steps of my house on the diagonally opposite corner of the street. She worked feverishly against time, for experience had taught her the sooner she completed the preparations for the game the greater would be the chance of getting her mother and Mr Pollitt to play it. Frequently she was not fast enough, or they were too fast for her. By the time she had finished her perspiring job, the verandah was often deserted. Her wailing cries would begin, punctuating the dusk at intervals only a little less frequent than the passing of cars of people going out for evening drives to cool off.

'Mama! Mama! The croquet set is ready!'

Usually there would be a long, long wait for any response to come from the upstairs window toward which the calls were directed. But one time there wasn't. Almost immediately after the wailing voice was lifted begging for the commencement of the game, Mary Louise's thin pretty mother showed herself at the window. She came to the window like a white bird flying into some unnoticed obstruction. That was the time when I saw, between the dividing gauze of the bedroom curtains, her naked breasts, small and beautiful, shaken like two angry fists by her violent motion. She leaned between the curtains to answer Mary

Louise not in her usual tone of gentle remonstrance but in a shocking cry of rage: 'Oh, be still, for God's sake, you fat little monster!'

Mary Louise was shocked into petrified silence that must have lasted for a quarter of an hour. It was probably the word 'fat' that struck her so overwhelmingly, for Mary Louise had once told me, when we were circling the block in the electric, that her mother had told her that she was *not* fat, that she was only plump, and that these cushions of flesh were going to dissolve in two or three more years and then she would be just as thin and pretty as her mother.

Sometimes Mary Louise would call me over to play croquet with her, but she was not at all satisfied with my game. I had had so little practice and she so much, and besides, more importantly, it was the company of the grown-up people she wanted. She would call me over only when they had disappeared irretrievably into the lightless house or when the game had collapsed owing to Mr Brick Pollitt's refusal to take it seriously. When he played seriously, he was even better at it than Mary Louise, who practised her strokes sometimes all afternoon in preparation for a game. But there were evenings when he would not leave his drink on the porch but would carry it down on to the lawn with him and would play with one hand, more and more capriciously, while in the other hand he carried the tall glass. Then the lawn would become a great stage on which he performed all the immemorial antics of the clown, to the exasperation of Mary Louise and her thin, pretty mother, both of whom would become very severe and dignified on these occasions. They would retire from the croquet lawn and stand off at a little distance, calling softly, 'Brick, Brick' and 'Mr Pollitt', like a pair of complaining doves, both in the same ladylike tones of remonstrance. He was not a middle-aged-looking man – that is, he was not at all big around the middle – and he could leap and run like a boy. He could turn cartwheels and walk on his hands, and sometimes he would grunt and lunge like a wrestler or make long crouching runs like a football player, weaving in and out among the wickets and gaudily painted poles of the croquet lawn. The acrobatics and sports of his youth seemed to haunt him. He called out hoarsely to invisible team-mates and adversaries – muffled shouts of defiance and anger and triumph, to which an incongruous counterpoint was continually provided by the faint, cooing voice of the widow, 'Brick, Brick, stop now, please stop. The child is crying. People will think you've gone crazy.' For Mary Louise's mother, despite the extreme ambiguity of her station in life, was a woman with a keener than ordinary sense of propriety. She knew why the lights had gone out on all the screened summer porches and why the automobiles drove past the house at the speed of a funeral procession while Mr Brick Pollitt was making a circus ring of the croquet lawn.

Late one evening when he was making one of his crazy dashes across the lawn with an imaginary football hugged against his belly, he tripped over a wicket and sprawled on the lawn, and he pretended to be too gravely injured to get back on his feet. His loud groans brought Mary Louise and her mother running from behind the vine-screened end of the verandah and out upon the lawn to assist him. They took him by each hand and tried to haul him up, but with a sudden shout of laughter he pulled them both down on top of him and held them there till both of them were sobbing. He got up, finally, that evening, but it was only to replenish his glass of iced gin, and then returned to the lawn. That evening was a fearfully hot one, and Brick decided to cool and refresh himself with the sprinkler hose while he enjoyed his drink. He turned it on and pulled it out to the centre of the lawn. There he rolled about the grass under its leisurely revolving arch of water, and as he rolled about, he began to wriggle out of his clothes. He kicked off his white shoes and one of his pale-green socks, tore off his drenched white shirt and grass-stained linen pants, but he never succeeded in getting off his necktie. Finally, he was sprawled, like some grotesque fountain figure, in underwear and necktie and the one remaining pale-green sock, while the revolving arch of water moved with cool whispers about him. The arch of water had a faint crystalline iridescence, a mist of delicate colours, as it wheeled under the moon, for the moon had by that time begun to poke with an air of slow astonishment over the roof of the little building that housed the electric. And still the complaining doves of the widow and her daughter cooed at him from various windows of the house, and you could tell their voices apart only by the fact that the mother murmured 'Brick, Brick' and Mary Louise called him Mr Pollitt. 'Oh, Mr Pollitt, Mother is so unhappy, Mother is crying!'

That night he talked to himself or to invisible figures on the lawn. One of them was his wife, Margaret. He kept saying, 'I'm sorry, Margaret, I'm sorry, Margaret, I'm so sorry, so sorry, Margaret. I'm sorry I'm no good, I'm sorry, Margaret, I'm so sorry, so sorry I'm no good, sorry I'm drunk, sorry I'm no good, I'm so sorry it all had to turn out like this . . .'

Later on, much later, after the remarkably slow procession of touring cars stopped passing the house, a little black sedan that belonged to the police came rushing up to the front walk and sat there for a while. In it was the chief of police himself. He called 'Brick, Brick', almost as gently and softly as Mary Louise's mother had called him from the lightless windows. 'Brick, Brick, old boy. Brick, fellow', till finally the inert fountain figure in underwear and green sock and unremovable necktie staggered out from under the rotating arch of water and stumbled down to the walk and stood there negligently and quietly conversing with the chief of police under the no longer at all astonished, now quite large and indifferent great yellow stare of the August moon. They began to laugh softly together, Mr Brick Pollitt and the chief of police, and finally the door of the little black car opened and Mr Brick Pollitt got in beside the chief of police while the common officer got out to collect the clothes, flabby as drenched towels, on the croquet lawn. Then they drove away, and the summer night's show was over . . .

It was not quite over for me, for I had been watching it all that time with unabated interest. And about an hour after the little black car of the very polite officers had driven away, I saw the mother of Mary Louise come out into the lawn; she stood there with an air of desolation for quite a while. Then she went into the small building in back of the house and drove out the electric. The electric went sedately out into the summer night, with its buzzing no louder than a summer insect's, and perhaps an hour later, for this was a very long night, it came back again containing in its glass show box not only the young and thin and pretty widow but a quiet and chastened Mr Pollitt. She curved an arm about his immensely tall figure as they went up the front walk, and I heard him say only one word distinctly. It was the name of his wife.

Early that autumn, which was different from summer in nothing except the quicker coming of dusk, the visits of Mr Brick Pollitt began to have the spasmodic irregularity of a stricken heart muscle. That faraway boom of a cannon at five o'clock was now the announcement that two ladies in white dresses were waiting on a white gallery for someone who was each time a little more likely to disappoint them than the time before. But disappointment was not a thing that Mary Louise was inured to; it was a country that she was passing through not as an old inhabitant but as a bewildered explorer, and each afternoon she removed the oblong yellow wood box, lugged it out of the little building in which it lived with the electric, ceremoniously opened it upon the centre of the silken green lawn, and began to arrange the wickets in their formal pattern between the two gaudily painted poles that meant beginning, middle and end. And the widow, her mother, talked to her from the gallery, under the awning, as if there had been no important alteration in their lives or their prospects. Their almost duplicate voices as they talked back and forth between gallery and lawn rang out as clearly as if the enormous corner lot were enclosed at this hour by a still more enormous and perfectly translucent glass bell which picked up and carried through space whatever was uttered beneath it, and this was true not only when they were talking across the lawn but when they were seated side by side in the white wicker chairs on the gallery. Phrases from these conversations became catch-words, repeated and mocked by the neighbours, for whom the widow and her daughter and Mr Brick Pollitt had been three players in a sensational drama which had shocked and angered them for two acts but which now, as it approached a conclusion, was declining into unintentional farce, which they could laugh at. It was not difficult to find something ludicrous in the talks between the two ladies or the high-pitched elegance of their voices.

Mary Louise would ask, 'Will Mr Pollitt get here in time for croquet?'

'I hope so, precious. It does him so much good.'

'He'll have to come soon or it will be too dark to see the wickets.'

'That's true, precious.'

'Mother, why is it dark so early now?'

'Honey, you know why. The sun goes south.'

'But why does it go south?'

'Precious, Mother cannot explain the movements of the heavenly bodies, you know that as well as Mother knows it. Those things are controlled by certain mysterious laws that people on earth don't know or understand.'

'Mother, are we going east?'

'When, precious?'

'Before school starts.'

'Honey, you know it's impossible for Mother to make any definite plans.'

'I hope we do. I don't want to go to school here.'

'Why not, precious? Are you afraid of the children?'

'No, Mother, but they don't like me, they make fun of me.'

'How do they make fun of you?'

'They mimic the way I talk and they walk in front of me with their stomachs pushed out and giggle.'

'That's because they're children and children are cruel.'

'Will they stop being cruel when they grow up?'

'Why, I suppose some of them will and some of them won't.'

'Well, I hope we go east before school opens.'

'Mother can't make any plans or promises, honey.'

'No, but Mr Brick Pollitt—'

'Honey, lower your voice! Ladies talk softly.'

'Oh, my goodness!'

'What is it, precious?'

'A mosquito just bit me!'

'That's too bad, but don't scratch it. Scratching can leave a permanent scar on the skin.'

'I'm not scratching it. I'm just sucking it, Mother.'

'Honey, Mother has told you time and again that the thing to do when you have a mosquito bite is to get a small piece of ice and wrap it up in a handkerchief and rub the bite gently with it until the sting is removed.'

'That's what I do, but my lump of ice is melted!'

'Get you another piece, honey. You know where the icebox is!'

'There's not much left. You put so much in the ice bag for your headache.'

'There must be some left, honey.'

'There's just enough left for Mr Pollitt's drinks.'

'Never mind that . . .'

'He needs it for his drinks, Mother.'

'Yes, Mother knows what he wants the ice for, precious.'

'There's only a little piece left. It's hardly enough to rub a mosquito bite with.'

'Well, use it for that purpose, that purpose is better, and anyhow when Mr Pollitt comes over as late as this, he doesn't deserve to have any ice saved for him.'

'Mother?'

'Yes, precious?'

'I love ice and sugar!'

'What did you say, precious?'

'I said I loved ice and sugar.'

'Ice and sugar, precious?'

'Yes, I love the ice and sugar in the bottom of Mr Pollitt's glass when he's through with it.'

'Honey, you mustn't eat the ice in the bottom of Mr Pollitt's glass!'

'Why not, Mother?'

'Because it's got liquor in it!'

'Oh, no, Mother, it's just ice and sugar when Mr Pollitt's through with it.'

'Honey, there's always a little liquor left in it.'

'Oh, no, not a drop's left when Mr Pollitt's through with it!'

'But you say there's sugar left in it, and, honey, you know that sugar is very absorbent.'

'It's what, Mummy?'

'It absorbs some liquor and that's a good way to cultivate a taste for it, and, honey, you know what dreadful consequences a taste for liquor can have. It's bad enough for a man, but for a woman it's fatal. So when you want ice and sugar, let Mother know and she'll prepare some for you, but don't ever let me catch you eating what's left in Mr Pollitt's glass!'

'Mama?'

'Yes, precious?'

'It's almost completely dark now. Everybody is turning on their lights or driving out on the river road to cool off. Can't we go out riding in the electric?'

'No, honey, we can't till we know Mr Pollitt's not—'

'Do you still think he will come?'

'Precious, how can I say? Is Mother a fortune-teller?'

'*Oh, here comes the Pierce, Mummy, here comes the Pierce!*'

'*Is it? Is it the Pierce?*'

'Oh, no. No, it isn't. It's a Hudson Super Six. Mummy, I'm going to pull up the wickets now, and water the lawn, because if Mr Pollitt does come, he'll have people with him or won't be in a condition to play croquet. And when I've finished, I want to drive the electric around the block.'

'Drive it around the block, honey, but don't go into the business district with it.'

'Are you going with me, Mummy?'

'No, precious, I'm going to sit here.'

'It's cooler in the electric.'

'I don't think so. The electric goes too slowly to make much breeze.'

If Mr Pollitt did finally arrive those evenings, it was likely to be with a caravan of cars that came from Memphis, and then Mrs Grey would have to receive a raffish assortment of strangers as if she herself had invited them to a party. The party would not confine itself to the downstairs rooms and galleries but would explode quickly and brilliantly as a rocket in all directions, overflowing both floors of the house, spilling out upon the lawn and sometimes even penetrating the little building that housed the electric automobile and the oblong box that held the packed-away croquet set. On those party nights, the fantastically balustraded and gabled and turreted white building would glitter all over, like one of those huge night-excursion boats that came downriver from Memphis, and it would be full of ragtime music and laughter. But at some point in the evening there would be, almost invariably, a startling disturbance. Some male guest would utter a savage roar, a woman would scream, you would hear a shattering of glass. Almost immediately afterward, the lights would go out in the house, as if it really were a boat that had collided fatally with a shoal underwater. From all the doors and galleries and stairs, people would come rushing forth, and the dispersion would be more rapid than the arrival had been. A little while later, the police car would pull up in front of the house. The thin, pretty widow would come out on the front gallery to receive the chief of police, and you could hear her light voice tinkling like glass chimes. 'Why, it was nothing, it was nothing at all, just somebody who drank a little too much and lost his temper. You know how that Memphis crowd is, Mr Duggan, there's always one gentleman in it who can't hold his liquor. I know it's late, but we have such a huge lawn – it occupies half the block – that I shouldn't think anybody who wasn't overcome with curiosity would have to know that a party had been going on!'

And then something must have happened that made no sound at all.

It wasn't an actual death, but it had nearly all the external evidence of one. When death occurs in a house, the house is unnaturally quiet for a day or two before the occurrence is finished. During that interval, the enormous, translucent glass bell that seems to enclose and separate one house from those that surround it does not transmit any noise to those who are watching but seems to have thickened invisibly so that very little can be heard through it. That was the way it had been five months ago, when the pleasant young doctor had died of that fierce flower grown in his skull. It had been unnaturally quiet for several days, and then a peculiar grey car with frosted windows had crashed through the bell of silence and the young doctor had emerged from the house in a very curious way, as if he were giving a public demonstration of how to go to sleep on a narrow bed in atmosphere blazing with light and while in motion.

That was five months ago, and it was now early October.

The summer had spelled out a word that had no meaning, and the word was now spelled out and, with or without any meaning, there it was, inscribed with as heavy a touch as the signature of a miser on a cheque or a boy with chalk on a fence.

One afternoon, a fat and pleasantly smiling man, whom I had seen times without number loitering around in front of the used-car lot which adjoined the Paramount movie, came up the front walk of the Greys' with the excessive nonchalance of a man who is about to commit a robbery. He pushed the bell, waited awhile, pushed it again for a longer moment, and then was admitted through an opening that seemed to be hardly wide enough for his fingers. He came back out almost immediately with something caught in his fist. It was the key to the little building that contained the croquet set and the electric automobile. He entered that building and drew its folding doors all the way open to disclose the ladylike electric sitting there with its usual manner of a lady putting on or taking off her gloves at the entrance to a reception. He stared at it a moment, as if its elegance were momentarily baffling. But then he got in it and he drove it out of the garage holding the polished black pilot stick with a look on his round face that was like the look of an adult who is a little embarrassed to find himself being amused by a game that was meant for children. He drove it serenely out into the wide, shady street and at an upstairs window of the house there was some kind of quick movement, as if a figure looking out had been startled by something it watched and then had retreated in haste . . .

Later, after the Greys had left town, I saw the elegant square vehicle, which appeared to be made out of glass and patent leather, standing with an air of haughty self-consciousness among

·a dozen or so other cars for sale on a lot called 'Hi-Class Values' next door to the town's best movie, and as far as I know, it may be still sitting there, but many degrees less glittering by now.

The Greys were gone from Meridian all in one quick season: the young doctor whom everyone had liked in a hesitant, early way and had said would do well in the town with his understanding eyes and quiet voice; the thin, pretty woman, whom no one had really known except Brick Pollitt; and the plump little girl, who might someday be as pretty and slender as her mother. They had come and gone in one season, yes, like one of those tent shows that suddenly appear in a vacant lot in a southern town and cross the sky at night with mysteriously wheeling lights and unearthly music, and then are gone, and the summer goes on without them, as if they had never come there.

As for Mr Brick Pollitt, I can remember seeing him only once after the Greys left town, for my time there was also of brief duration. This last time that I saw him was a brilliant fall morning. It was a Saturday morning in October. Brick's driver's licence had been revoked again for some misadventure on the highway due to insufficient control of the wheel, and it was his legal wife, Margaret, who sat in the driver's seat of the Pierce-Arrow touring car. Brick did not sit beside her. He was on the back seat of the car, pitching this way and that way with the car's jolting motion, like a loosely wrapped package being delivered somewhere. Margaret Pollitt handled the car with a wonderful male assurance, her bare arms brown and muscular as a Negro field hand's, and the car's canvas top had been lowered the better to expose on its back seat the sheepishly grinning and nodding figure of Brick Pollitt. He was clothed and barbered with his usual immaculacy, so that he looked from some great distance like the president of a good social fraternity in a gentleman's college of the South. The knot of his polka-dot tie was drawn as tight as strong and eager fingers could knot a tie for an important occasion. One of his large red hands protruded, clasping over the outside of the door to steady his motion, and on it glittered two bands of gold, a small one about a finger, a large one about the wrist. His cream-coloured coat was neatly folded on the seat beside him and he wore a shirt of thin white material that was tinted faintly pink by his skin beneath it. He was a man who had been, and even at that time still was, the handsomest you were likely to remember, physical beauty being of all human attributes the most incontinently used and wasted, as if whoever made it despised it, since it is made so often only to be disgraced by painful degrees and drawn through the streets in chains.

Margaret blew the car's silver trumpet at every intersection. She leaned this way and that way, elevating or thrusting out an arm as she shouted gay greetings to people on porches, merchants beside store entrances, people she barely knew along the walks, calling them all by their familiar names, as if she were running for office in the town, while Brick nodded and grinned with senseless amiability behind her. It was exactly the way that some ancient conqueror, such as Caesar or Alexander the Great or Hannibal, might have led in chains through a capital city the prince of a state newly conquered.

THE IMPORTANT THING

They met at the spring dance by the Baptist Female College which Flora was attending that year. The college was in the same town as the State University at which John was completing his sophomore year. He knew only one girl at the college and wasn't able to find her in the ballroom. It was hot and crowded in there and had that feverish, glaring effect which usually prevails at a spring dance given by a sectarian girls' school. The room was lighted by four or five blazing chandeliers and the walls were covered with long mirrors. Between dances the couples stood about stiffly in their unaccustomed formal dress and glanced uneasily at their reflections in the highly polished glass, shifted their weight from foot to foot, nervously twisted or flipped their programme cards. None of them seemed to know each other very well. They talked in loud, unnatural voices, shrieked with laughter or stood sullenly quiet. The teachers flitted among them with bird-like alacrity, intently frowning or beaming, introducing, prompting, encouraging. It was not like a social affair. It was more like an important military manœuvre.

John walked around the edge of the floor several times and was rather relieved at not finding the one girl he knew. When he arrived at the palm-flanked entrance he turned to go out, but just then his arm was violently plucked by one of the teachers, a middle-aged woman with frowzy grey hair, sharp nose and large yellow teeth. She looked so wild and Harpy-like that John involuntarily squirmed from her grasp.

'Are you alone?' she shrieked in his ear.

The band was thumping out a terrifically loud foxtrot. John rubbed his ear and pointed vaguely toward the door. She tightened her grasp on his arm and propelled him across the floor by a series of jerks that careened him from one dancing couple to another till they reached a corner where stood an apparently stranded group of young Baptist Females beneath the protective fronds of an enormous boxed palm.

The Harpy gave his arm a final twist and John found himself facing a tall, thin girl in a pink taffeta dress who stood slightly apart from her fellow refugees. He caught the name Flora shrieked through the increasing din. He didn't notice the girl's face. He was too furious at being roped in like this to even look at her. They advanced awkwardly toward each other. John slid his arm around her unbelievably slender waist. Through the silk he could feel the hard ridge of her spine. There was no weight in her body. She floated before him so lightly that it was almost like dancing by himself, except that the cord of bone kept moving beneath his warm, sweating fingers and her fine, loose hair plastered itself against his damp cheek.

The foxtrot had reached a crescendo. Cymbals were clashing and drums beating out double time. The girl's lips moved against his throat. Her breath tickled his skin but he couldn't hear a word she was saying. He looked helplessly down at her. Suddenly she broke away from him. She stood slightly off from him, her eyes crinkling with laughter and one hand clutched to her mouth. The music stopped.

'What're you laughing at?' John asked.

'The whole situation,' said Flora. 'You no more wanted to dance than I did!'

'Didn't you want to?'

'Of course not. When I think of dancing I think of Isadora Duncan who said she wanted to teach the whole world how to dance, but this wasn't what she meant – do you think it was?'

She had a way of looking up that made her face very brilliant and for a few moments obscured the fact that she was by no means pretty. But there was something about her, something which already excited him a little, and so he said:

'Let's go outside.'

They spent practically all the rest of the evening in the oak grove between the gymnasium and the chapel, strolling around and smoking his cigarettes. While smoking the girl would flatten herself against a tree trunk for smoking was forbidden on the campus.

'This is the advantage of being a fence-pole,' she told him. 'You can hide behind anything with the slightest diameter.'

Everything that she said had a wry, humorous twist and even when it wasn't humorous she would laugh slightly and John had the impression that she was unusually clever. They went into the empty chapel for a while and sat in a back pew and talked about religion.

'It is all so archaic,' Flora said. 'It is all a museum piece!'

John had recently become an agnostic himself. They agreed that Christian religion and Hebrew, in fact nearly all religions were based on a concept of guilt.

'*Mea culpa!*' said John, thinking that she would say, 'What's that?' But she didn't. She nodded her head. And he was excited to discover that she, too, was interested in writing. She had won a literary prize in high-school and she was now editor of the college literary magazine. The teacher who had brought them together was Flora's English instructor.

'She thinks I'm very talented,' said Flora. 'She wants me to send one of my stories to Harper's.'

'Why don't you?' asked John.

'Oh, I don't know,' said Flora. 'I think the main thing is just expressing yourself as honestly as you can. I am not interested in style,' she went on, 'it's such a waste of time to do things over and get the right cadence and always just the right word. I'd rather just scramble through one thing and then rush into another, until I have said everything that I have to say!'

How extraordinary it was that she and John should feel exactly the same way about this! He confessed that he was himself a writer and that two or three of his stories were coming out in the University's literary magazine – and when Flora heard this she was almost absurdly moved.

'I'd love to see them, I've got to see them!' she cried.

'I'll bring them over,' he promised.

'When?'

'As soon as they come out!'

'I don't care how the style is as long as they're honest. They've got to be honest!' she pleaded. 'Are they?'

'I hope so,' he answered uneasily.

She had taken his arm and was squeezing it in a grip that was almost as tight as a wrestler's and with every excited inflection in her speech she squeezed it tighter. There was no relaxation in Flora, none of the softness and languor which he had found physically interesting in girls. He could not imagine her lying passively still and quietly submitting the way he thought a girl should to a man's embraces.

'What do you think about human relations?' she asked him

just at the moment when this disturbing image was in his mind.

'That's a large subject,' said John.

'Oh, what a large, large subject! And it is the one I will never be able to cope with!'

'Why?' asked John.

'I'm equal to anything else, but not human relations! I'll always be moving when other people are still, and still when they're moving,' said Flora, 'and it will be a terrible mess and a mix-up from start to finish!'

'You shouldn't feel that way about it,' he told her lamely, astonished at the way her words fitted exactly what he had been thinking.

She looked up at John. 'You'll have the same trouble!' she told him. 'We'll never be happy but we'll have lots of excitement and if we hold on to our personal integrity everything won't be lost!'

He wasn't quite sure what Flora was talking about, and personal integrity seemed the vaguest of terms. Was it something like what she meant by 'honest' writing?

'Yes, something,' said Flora, 'but ever so much more difficult, because writing is ideal reality and living is not ideal . . .'

At the window of the gymnasium they stood for a while and watched the dancers who had reached what appeared to be nearly the point of exhaustion. Faces that had been flushed and perspiring when they had left the room were now quite desperate-looking and the men in the jazz-band seemed to be playing now out of sheer inability to break an old habit. Some of the paper streamers had come unfastened and fallen upon the floor, others hung limply from the ceiling and in one corner a small crowd, mostly teachers, were clustered about a girl who had fainted.

'Don't they look silly!' said Flora.

'Who?'

'Dancers — everybody?'

'What isn't silly, in your opinion?' asked John.

'Give me a little while to answer that question!'

'How long shall I give you?'

'I'll tell you right now — The Important Thing isn't silly!'

'What Important Thing?' John asked.

'I don't know yet,' said Flora. 'Why do you think I'm living, except to discover what The Important Thing is?'

John didn't see her again that spring. Final examinations came soon after the dance, and besides he was not altogether sure that she was the sort he would get along with. She was not good-looking and her intensity which was so charming while he was with her seemed afterwards a little – fantastic!

Very soon after he returned to school that fall he ran into her on the campus. She was now enrolled as a sophomore in the State University. He barely recognized her. It had been so dark in the oak grove, where they spent most of their time at the spring dance, that he hadn't gotten a very clear impression of her face. She was at once homelier and more attractive than he remembered. Her face was very wide at the top and narrow at the bottom: almost an inverted pyramid. Her eyes were large and rather oblique, hazel brown with startling flecks of blue or green in them. Her nose was long and pointed and the tip covered with freckles. She had a way of smiling and blinking her eyes very rapidly as she talked. She talked so fast and shrilly that he felt a little embarrassed. He noticed a group of girls staring at her and giggling. Fools! he thought, and was angry at himself for having felt embarrassed.

It was noon when they met and she was on her way to the boarding-house where she was staying. She hadn't pledged a sorority. She announced the fact with an air of proud defiance that John liked.

'I could see that I wouldn't fit into any of them,' she said. 'I'd rather be independent, wouldn't you? The trouble with this world is that everybody has to compromise and conform. Oh, I'm sick of it! I won't do it! I shall live my own life just the way that I please!'

John had felt the same way about joining a fraternity and he told her so.

'Ah, we're a couple of Barbs!' she shrieked. 'Isn't that marvellous? The other girls at the boarding-house simply detest being called Barbs – but I adore it! I think it's really thrilling to be called a barbican! It makes you feel like you could strip off your clothes and dance naked in the streets if you felt like doing it!'

John felt a warm glow as though he'd been drinking. It was the way he'd felt in the oak grove, talking to her last spring. It seemed suddenly that he had a great deal to say. He became excited and started talking rapidly about a one-act play that he was writing. It was full of involved symbolism and hard to explain. But Flora nodded her head with quick, eager jerks and supplied words wherever he stumbled. She seemed to know intuitively what he was trying to say.

'Oh, I think that's marvellous, marvellous!' she kept repeating.

He was thinking of submitting it to the one-act play contest. His room-mate had urged him to do so.

'My goodness, why don't you?' exclaimed Flora.

'Oh, I don't know,' John said. 'I think the main thing is just expressing one's self, don't you?'

Immediately afterwards they both laughed, remembering that Flora had said the same thing about the story her English teacher had wanted her to send to Harper's. 'Was it accepted?' John asked.

'No, it came back with a printed card,' she admitted ruefully. 'But I don't care. I'm writing poetry now. They say that you should write poetry while you're young and feel things keenly.'

She laughed and caught John's arm.

'I feel things very keenly, don't you?'

They sat down on the front steps of the boarding-house and talked until the bell tolled for one o'clock classes. Both of them had missed their lunch.

They saw a great deal of each other after that. They had many interests in common. They were both on the staff of the University's literary magazine and belonged to the Poetry and French Clubs. It was the year of the national election and John became twenty-one just in time to vote. Flora spent hours arguing with him about politics and finally convinced him that he must vote for Norman Thomas. Later they both joined the Young Communists' League. John became a very enthusiastic radical. He helped operate a secret printing press and distribute pamphlets about the campus attacking fraternities, political control of the University, academic conservatism, and so forth. He was once called before the Dean of Men and threatened with expulsion. Flora thought this was terribly thrilling.

'If you get expelled,' she promised, 'I'll quit school too!'

But it all blew over and they both remained in the University.

All of these things served to draw them closer together. But for some reason they were not altogether at ease with each other. John always had the feeling that something very important was going to happen between them. He could not have explained why he felt that way. Perhaps it was the contagion of Flora's intensity. When he was with her he felt the kind of suppressed excitement a scientist might feel upon the verge of an important discovery. A constant expectation or suspense. Was Flora conscious of the same thing? Sometimes he felt sure that she was. But her enthusiasm was so diffuse that he could never be sure. One thing after another caught her interest. She was like a precocious child just discovering the world, taking nothing in it for granted, receiving each impression with the fresh wonder of a child but an adult's mature understanding. About most things she talked very frankly. But once in a while she would become oddly reticent.

Once he asked her where she came from.

'Kansas,' she told him.

'I know, but what place in Kansas?'

He was surprised to see her face colouring. They were in the reference room of the library that evening, studying together at one of the yellow oak tables. She opened her notebook and ignored his question.

'What place?' he insisted, wondering why she flushed.

Abruptly she slammed the notebook shut and faced him with a laugh.

'What does it matter what place?'

'I just wanted to know.'

'Well, I won't tell you!'

'Why not?'

'Because it doesn't matter where you come from. It only matters where you're going!'

'Where are you going, then?'

'I don't know!'

She leaned back in the straight yellow oak chair and shook with laughter.

'How on earth should I know where I'm going?'

The librarian approached them with a warning frown.

'Please not so loud. This room's for study.'

'Where are you going?' John repeated under his breath.

Flora hid her face in the notebook and continued laughing.

'Where are you going, where are you going, where are you going!' John whispered. He did it to tease her. She looked so funny with the black leather notebook covering her face, only her braided hair showing and her throat flushed Turkey red.

All at once she jumped up from the table and he saw that her face was contorted with crying. She rushed out of the room and he couldn't get her to speak a word to him all the way back to her boarding-house.

Some time later he found the name of her home town on the envelope of a letter which she'd forgotten to remove from a book of poems she'd loaned him. The envelope was postmarked from

Hardwood, Kansas. John grinned. It was a hick town in the north-western part of the state and probably the deadest spot on earth . . .

Despising himself for doing so, he opened the letter and read it. It was from Flora's mother and was a classic of its kind. It complained of the money Flora was having to spend on board and books, urged her to spend less time writing nonsense and buckle down to hard work so that she could get a teaching job when she got through with her schooling because times were getting to be very bad . . .

'The ground and the people and the business and everything is dried up around here,' wrote her mother. 'I don't know what things are coming to. It must be God's judgement, I guess. Three solid years of drought. Looks like this time God is planning to dry the wickedness out of the world instead of drowning it out!'

That spring John bought a used car for thirty-five dollars and every free afternoon he and Flora drove around the lovely country roads and had picnic lunches which Flora prepared. He was getting used to Flora's odd appearance and her absurd animation, but other people weren't. She had become something of a 'character' on the campus. John was at this time being rushed by a professional fraternity and he was told that some of the fellows thought that Flora was a very queer person for him to be seen around with. Now and again his mind would go back to their first conversation in the oak grove of the Baptist Female College, the talk about human relations and her inability to cope with them, and it appeared to him that she was not even going half way in attempting to. There was no reason for her to talk so loudly on such eclectic subjects whenever they passed along a crowded corridor of a university building, there was surely no reason for her to be so rude to people she wasn't interested in, walking abruptly away without an excuse when talk turned to things she classified as inane – which was almost everything John's other friends talked about.

Other girls on the campus he could look at and imagine in the future, settled down into average middle-class life, becoming teachers or entering other professions. But when he looked at Flora he could not see her future, he could not imagine her becoming or doing any known thing, or going back to Hardwood, Kansas, or going anywhere else. She did not fit happily or comfortably into the university cosmos but in what other place or circumstances – he asked himself – could she have found any refuge whatsoever? Perhaps he was no more like other people than she was, but his case was different. He was more adaptable, he demanded a good deal less of people and things. Come up against a barrier, he was of a nature to look for a way around it. But Flora—

Flora had decided that the English department of the University was hopelessly reactionary and the only course she took an interest in, now, was geology. Their favourite spot, that spring, was an abandoned rock quarry where Flora searched for fossils. She danced around the quarry like a bright, attractive little monkey on a wire, her green smock fluttering in the wind and her voice constantly flowing up to him, sometimes shrill with excitement and sometimes muted with intense absorption.

'Don't you ever want to be still?' John asked her.

'Never till I have to!'

John would get tired of waiting and would open the lunch-box. She would finally join him on the hill-top, too tired to eat, and would spread her fossils around her and pore delightedly over them while John munched sandwiches of peanut butter and jelly or swiss cheese on rye. The rest of the afternoon they would spend talking about literature and life, art and civilization. They both had tremendous admiration for the ancient Greeks and the modern Russians. Greece is the world's past, said Flora, and Russia is the future – which John thought a brilliant statement, though it sounded a little familiar as if he had come across it somewhere before in a book.

Their discussions would continue unflaggingly till sundown, but as dusk began to settle they would become a little nervous and constrained, for some reason, and there would be long pauses in their talk, during which it was curiously difficult for them to look at each other. After a while, when it was getting really dark, Flora would abruptly jump up from the grass and brush off her smock.

'I guess we'd better be going,' she would say. Her voice would sound with the dull, defeated tone of someone who has argued a long time about something very important without making any impression upon the other's mind. John would feel strangely miserable as he followed her down the hill to where they had parked the old roadster. He would also feel that something had been left unsaid or undone, a feeling of incompletion . . .

*

It was the last Saturday before the end of the spring term. They were going to spend the whole day out in the country, studying for a final examination in a French course which they were taking together. Flora had prepared sandwiches and devilled eggs. And John, with some trepidation, had purchased a quart of red wine. He put the bottle in the side pocket of the roadster and didn't mention it until after they'd finished eating because he knew Flora didn't like drinking. She had no moral objections, she said, but thought it was a senseless, wasteful practice. She refused to drink any of the wine. 'But you may, if you wish,' she added with a primness that made John laugh.

They were seated as usual on the grassy hill above the rock quarry. It was called Lover's Leap. Flora held the notebook which they had prepared together and was quizzing John. She was leaning against one of the large white boulders scattered about the hill-top and John was stretched at her feet. He held the wine bottle between his knees and drank out of the thermos cup. Flora's constraint at first sight of the bottle wore off. She called him Bacchus.

'I wish I had time to make you a wreath,' she said. 'You'd look too adorable with a wreath of green leaves!'

'Why don't you be a nymph?' John asked. 'Take off your clothes and be a wood nymph! I'll chase you through the birch trees!'

The idea pleased John very much. He laughed loudly. But Flora was embarrassed. She cleared her throat and held the notebook in front of her face, but he could see by the base of her throat that she was blushing. He stopped laughing, feeling somewhat embarrassed himself. He knew what she was thinking. She was thinking what might happen if he should catch her among the birch trees with all her clothes off . . .

John drank another cupful of wine. He felt very good. He had removed his jacket and unbuttoned the collar of his shirt and rolled up the sleeves. The sun shone dazzlingly in his eyes, made rainbows in his eyelashes, warmed the bare flesh of his throat and arms. A comfortable glow passed through him. He was newly conscious of the life in his body; flexed his legs, rubbed his stomach and arched his thighs. He no longer listened to the questions that Flora was asking him out of the notebook. She had to repeat them two or three times before they were clear.

At last she became disgusted and tossed the notebook aside.
'I believe you're getting intoxicated!' she told him sharply.
He looked indolently up at her.
'Maybe I am! What of it?'
He noticed that she was not very pretty. Especially not when she drew her brows together and squinted her eyes like that. Her face was irregular and bony-looking. Rather outlandish. So broad at the top and narrow at the bottom. Long pointed nose, and eyes, flecked with different colours, which were too large for the rest of her and always so filled with superfluous brightness. Reminded him of an undersized child he once knew in grammar school. For some reason they called him Peekie and threw rocks at him after school. A timid, ridiculous creature with a high, squeaky voice that everyone mocked. The large boys caught him after school and asked him the meaning of obscene words or pulled the buttons off his knickers. She was like that. A queer person. But there was something exciting about her just as there'd been something exciting about Peekie that made the larger boys want to amuse themselves with him. There was something about her that he wanted to set his hands on in a rough way – twist and pull and tease! Her skin was the most attractive thing about her. It was very fine and smooth and white . . .

John's eyes travelled down her body. She wore a black sweater and a black and white checked skirt. As he looked at her legs a brisk wind tossed the skirt up and he could see the bare flesh above where the stockings ended. He rolled over on his stomach and placed both hands on her thighs. He'd never touched her so intimately before but somehow it seemed a perfectly natural thing to do. She made a startled movement away from him. Suddenly he thought he knew what the important thing was that was going to happen between them. He caught her by the shoulders and tried to pull her down in the grass, but she fought against him wildly. Neither of them said anything. They just fought together like two wild animals, rolling in the grass and clawing at each other. Flora clawed at John's face and John clawed at Flora's body. They accepted this thing, this desperate battle between them, as though they'd known all along it was coming, as though it had been inevitable from the start. Neither of them spoke a word until they were at last exhausted and lay still on the grass, breathing heavily and looking up at the slowly darkening sky.

John's face was scratched and bleeding in several places. Flora pressed her hands against her stomach and groaned. He had kicked her with his knee trying to make her lie still.

'It's all over now!' he said. 'I'm not going to hurt you.' But she continued moaning.

The sun had gone down and dusk gathered. There was a big purplish red blotch in the western sky that looked like a bruised place.

John got up to his feet and stood silently staring at the angry afterglow. A way off to the left was the university town, beginning to emerge through its leafy clouds with the sparkling animation of a Saturday night in late spring. There would be many gay parties and dances that night. Girls in dresses that seemed to be woven of flowers would whirl about polished dance-floors and couples would whisper and laugh behind clumps of ghostly spirea. These were the natural celebrations of youth. He and this girl had been searching for something else. What was it? Again and again later on the search would be made, the effort to find something outside of common experience, digging and rooting among the formless rubble of things for the one lost thing that was altogether lovely – and perhaps every time a repetition of this, violence and ugliness of desire turned to rage . . .

He spoke aloud to himself. 'We didn't have anything – we were fooling ourselves.'

He turned from the dark, haunting beauty of the town and looked down at Flora. She blinked her eyes and drew her breath sharply. She looked almost ugly, her face covered with sweat and grass stain. She was not like a girl. He wondered that he had never noticed before how anonymous was her gender, for this was the very central fact of her nature. She belonged nowhere, she fitted in no place at all, she had no home, no shell, no place of comfort or refuge, she was a fugitive with no place to run to. Others in her position might make some adjustment. The best of whatever is offered, however not right. But Flora would not accept it, none of the ways and means. The most imperfect part of her was the most pure. And that meant—

'Flora . . .'

He held out his hand and put his heart in his eyes. She felt the sudden turning of understanding and took his hand and he pulled her gently to her feet.

For the first time they stood together in the dark without any fear of each other, their hands loosely clasped and returning each other's look with sorrowful understanding, unable to help each other except through knowing, each completely separate and alone – but no longer strangers . . .

ONE ARM

In New Orleans in the winter of '39 there were three male hustlers usually to be found hanging out on a certain corner of Canal Street and one of those streets that dive narrowly into the ancient part of the city. Two of them were just kids of about seventeen and worth only passing attention, but the oldest of the three was an unforgettable youth. His name was Oliver Winemiller and he had been the light heavyweight champion boxer of the Pacific fleet before he lost an arm. Now he looked like a broken statue of Apollo, and he had also the coolness and impassivity of a stone figure.

While the two younger boys exhibited the anxious energy of sparrows, darting in and out of bars, flitting across streets and around corners in pursuit of some likely quarry, Oliver would remain in one spot and wait to be spoken to. He never spoke first, nor solicited with a look. He seemed to be staring above the heads of passers-by with an indifference which was not put on, or surly and vain, but had its root in a genuine lack of concern. He paid almost no attention to weather. When the cold rains swept in from the Gulf the two younger boys stood hunched and shuddering in shabby coats that effaced them altogether. But Oliver remained in his skivvy shirt and his dungarees which had faded nearly white from long wear and much washing, and held to his body as smooth as the clothes of sculpture.

Conversations like this would occur on the corner.

'Aren't you afraid of catching cold, young fellow?'

'No, I don't catch cold.'

'Well, there's a first time for everything.'

'Sure is.'

'You ought to go in somewhere and get warmed up.'

'Where?'

'I have an apartment.'

'Which way is it?'

'A few blocks down in the Quarter. We'll take a cab.'

'Let's walk and you give me the cab-fare.'

Oliver had been in his crippled condition for just two years. The injury had been suffered in the seaport of San Diego when he and a group of shipmates had collided with the wall of an underpass while driving a rented car at seventy-five miles an hour. Two of the sailors in the car had been killed outright, a third had received a spinal injury that would keep him in a wheel chair for the rest of his life. Oliver got off lightest with just the loss of an arm. He was eighteen then and his experience had been limited. He came from the cotton fields of Arkansas, where he had known only hard work in the sun and such emotional adventures as farm boys have on Saturday nights and Sunday afternoons, a tentative knowledge of girls that suddenly exploded into a coarse and startling affair with a married woman whose husband he had hauled lumber for. She was the first to make him aware of the uncommon excitement he was able to stir. It was to break off this affair that he left home and entered the navy at a base in Texas. During his period of training he had taken up boxing and while he was still a 'boot' he became an outstanding contender for the navy championship. The life was good fun and no thinking. All that he had to deal with was the flesh and its feelings. But then the arm had been lost, and with it he was abruptly cut off from his development as an athlete and a young man wholly adequate to the physical world he grew into.

Oliver couldn't have put into words the psychic change which came with his mutilation. He knew that he had lost his right arm, but didn't consciously know that with it had gone the centre of his being. But the self that doesn't form words nor even thoughts had come to a realization that whirled darkly up from its hidden laboratory and changed him altogether in less time than it took new skin to cover the stump of the arm he had lost. He never said to himself, I'm lost. But the speechless self knew it and in submission to its unthinking control the youth had begun as soon as he left the hospital to look about for destruction.

He took to knocking about the country, going first to New York. It was there that Oliver learned the ropes of what became his calling. He fell in with another young vagrant who wised him up to his commodity value and how to cash in on it. Within a week the one-armed youth was fully inured to the practices and the culture of the underworld that seethed around Times Square and the Broadway bars and the bench-lined walks of the park, and foreign as it was, the shock that it gave him was slight. The loss of the arm had apparently dulled his senses. With it had gone the wholesome propriety that had made him leave home when the coarse older woman had introduced him to acts of unnatural ardour. Now he could feel no shame that green soap and water did not remove well enough to satisfy him.

When summer had passed, he joined the southern migration. He lived in Miami a while. He struck it rich down there. He made the acquaintance of some wealthy sportsmen and all that season he passed from one to another with money that piled up faster than he could spend it on clothes and amusement. Then one night he got drunk on a broker's yacht in the harbour at Palm Beach and, for no reason that was afterwards sure to him, he struck the man's inclined head eight times with a copper book-end, the final stroke splitting the skull. He swam to shore, collected his things and beat it out of the State. This ended the more affluent chapter of Oliver's existence. From that time on he moved for protection in less conspicuous channels, losing himself in the swarm of his fugitive kind wherever a town was large enough for such traffic to pass without too much attention.

Then, one evening during this winter in New Orleans, shortly after the Mardi Gras season and when he was beginning to think of heading back North, Oliver was picked up by a plain-clothesman and driven to jail, not on an ordinary charge of lewd vagrancy, but for questioning in connection with the murder of the wealthy broker in the harbour at Palm Beach. They got a full confession from him in fifteen minutes.

He hardly made any effort to dodge their questions.

They gave him half a tumbler of whiskey to loosen his tongue and he gave them a lurid account of the party the broker had given on his yacht. Oliver and a girl prostitute had been given a hundred dollars each to perform in what is called a blue movie, that is, a privately made film of licentious behaviour among two or more persons, usually with some crude sort of narrative sequence. He and the girl had undressed by drunken stages before the camera and the yacht party, and had gone through a sequence of such embraces and intimacies as only four walls and a locked door usually witness. The film was not finished. To his own astonishment, Oliver had suddenly revolted, struck the girl and kicked the camera over and fled to the upper deck. Up there he had guessed that if he remained on the yacht he would do something still more violent. But when the others finally went ashore in a launch, Oliver had remained because the host had wheedled him with money and the promise of more.

'I knew when they left him alone with me that he would be sorry,' Oliver said in his statement to the police. It was this admission which the prosecutor used to establish premeditation in the case.

Everything went against him at the trial. His testimony was ineffectual against the prestige of the other witnesses, all of whom swore that nothing irregular had occurred on the yacht. [No one remembered anything about the blue movie except Oliver, the girl prostitute was equally unheard of.] And the fact that Oliver had removed from the victim's body a diamond ring and a wallet assured the youth's conviction and doomed him to the chair.

The arrest of the broker's killer was given space in papers all over the country. The face of the one-armed youth was shot from newspapers into the startled eyes of men who had known him in all those places Oliver had passed through in his aimless travels. None of these men who had known him had found his image one that faded readily out of mind. The great blond youth who had been a boxer until he had lost his arm had stood as a planet among the moons of their longing, fixed in his orbit while they circled about him. Now he was caught somewhere, he had crashed into ruin. And in a sense this ruin had returned him to them. He was no longer on highways or tracks going further, but penned in a corner and waiting only for death.

He began to receive letters from them. Each morning the jailer thrust more envelopes through the bars of his cell. The letters were usually signed by fictitious names and if they requested an answer, the address given would be general delivery in one of those larger cities where Oliver's calling was plied. They were written on fine white paper, some of them were faintly scented, and some enclosed paper money. The messages were similarly phrased. All of them spoke of their shock at his dilemma, they couldn't believe it was true, it was like a bad dream, and so forth. They made allusions to the nights which he had spent with them, or the few hours which they almost invariably pronounced to be the richest of their entire experience. There was something about him, they wrote, not only the physical thing, important as that was, which had made him haunt their minds since.

What they were alluding to was the charm of the defeated which Oliver had possessed, a quality which acts as a poultice upon the inflamed nerves of those who are still in active contention. This quality is seldom linked with youth and physical charm, but in Oliver's case it had been, and it was this rare combination which had made him a person impossible to forget. And because he was sentenced to death, Oliver had for these correspondents the curtained and abstract quality of the priest who listens without being visible to confessions of guilt. The usual restraints upon the unconscious were accordingly lifted and the dark joys of *mea culpa* were freely indulged in. The litanies of their sorrows were poured on to paper like water from broken dams. To some he became the archetype of the Saviour Upon The Cross who had taken upon himself the sins of their world to be washed and purified in his blood and passion. Letters of this sort enraged the imprisoned boy and he clamped them under one foot and tore them to pieces and tossed the pieces in his slop bucket.

With the mechanical cruelty of the law, the execution of Oliver's sentence had given him several months in which to expect it and they were the months of summer. In his stifling cubicle there was very little to do while waiting for death and time enough with the impetus of disaster for the boy's malleable nature to be remoulded still again, and the instrument of this process became the letters.

He sat on a folding chair or sprawled on his cot those first few weeks in the death house in a way that was not unlike the way in which he had stood against a brick wall in rain-soaked dungarees and skivvy shirt on the New Orleans corner till someone had asked him for the time or a light. He was given a deck of cards with stains of candy bars on them and tattered books of comic and adventure cartoons to pass away the time with. And there was a radio at the end of the corridor. But Oliver was cut off from the world that blared through the mouth of the radio and from that world of one-dimensional clownery and heroism in the raw colours of childhood's spectrum which the cartoon strips celebrated. All of these rushed by him instead of with him, and only the letters remained in connection with him.

After a while he not only read all of the letters, but folded them back in their envelopes and began to accumulate them in rubber bands on a shelf. One night without thinking he took them down from the shelf and placed them beneath his pillow, and he went to sleep with his one hand resting on them.

A few weeks before the time for his execution Oliver began to write out replies to those men who had begged to hear from him. He used a soft lead pencil that dwindled rapidly to a stub beneath his awkward pressure. He wrote on manila paper and mailed the replies in government-stamped envelopes to all of those cities that he had formerly haunted.

Having no surviving family to write to, this was Oliver's first attempt at writing letters. He wrote at first with a laborious stiffness. The composition of the simplest sentence would knot up the muscles in his one powerful arm, but as the writing went on a greater laxity developed in a wonderfully short time. Soon the sentences gathered momentum as springs that clear out a channel and they began to flow out almost expressively after a while and to ring with the crudely eloquent backwoods speech of the South, to which had been added salty idioms of the underworld he had moved in, and the road, and the sea. Into them went the warm and vivid talk that liquor and generous dealing had brought from his lips on certain occasions, the *chansons de geste* which American tongues throw away so casually in bars and hotel bedrooms. The cartoon symbol of laughter was often employed, that heavily drawn HA-HA with its tail of exclamatory punctuation, its stars and spirals, and setting that down on paper was what gave him most relief, for it had the feel of the boiling intensity in him. He would often include a rough illustration, a sketch of the chair that he was condemned to sit in.

The letters would go like this.

'Yes, I remember you plainly. I met you in the park in back of the public library, or was it the men's room in the Greyhound depot. I met so many they sometimes get mixed up. However you stand out plainly. You asked for the time or a light and we got to talking and first thing I knew we was in your apartment drinking. And how is Chicago now that it's summer again? I sure would appreciate feeling those cool lake breezes or pouring down shots of that wonderful Five Star Connyack where we shacked up that day. I tell you it's hot in this cooler. Cooler is good. Ha-ha! One thing I can sure count on is it's going to get hotter before it gets cooler again. If you get what I mean. I mean the chair on the wire that is patiently waiting for me to sit down in it. The date is the tenth of August and you are invited except that you could not get in. It is very exclusive. I guess you would like to know if I am afraid. The answer is Yes. I do not look forward to it. I was a boxer until I lost my arm and after that happened I seemed to go through a change which I cannot account for except I was very disgusted with all of the world. I guess I stopped caring about what happened to me. That is to say I had lost my self-respect.

'I went all over the country without any plans except to keep on moving. I picked up strangers in every city I went to. I had experience with them which only meant money to me and a place to shack up for the night and liquor and food. I never thought it could mean very much to them. Now all of these letters like yours have proven it did. I meant something very important to hundreds of people whose faces and names had slipped clean out of my mind as soon as I left them. I feel as if I had run up a debt of some kind. Not money but feelings. I treated some of them badly. Went off without even so much as saying goodbye in spite of all their generosity to me and even took things which hadn't been given to me. I cannot imagine how some of these men could forgive me. If I had known then, I mean when I was outside, that such true feelings could even be found in strangers, I mean the kind that I picked up for a living, I guess I might have felt there was more to live for. Anyhow now the situation is hopeless. All will be over for me in a very short while. Ha-ha!

'You probably didn't know that I was an artist as well as being a one-armed champion boxer and therefore I'm going to draw you a wonderful picture!'

This writing of letters became his one occupation, and as a stone gathers heat when lain among coals, the doomed man's brain grew warmer and warmer with a sense of communion. Coming prior to disaster, this change might have been a salvation. It might have offered a centre for personal integration which the boy had not had since the mandala dream of the prize ring had gone with the arm. A personality without a centre throws up a wall and lives in a state of siege. So Oliver had cultivated his cold and absolute insularity behind which had lain the ruined city of the crippled champion. Within those battlements had been little or nothing to put up a fight for survival. Now something was stirring within.

But this coming to life was unmerciful, coming so late. The indifference had passed off when it should have remained to make death easier for him. And time passed quicker. In the changeless enclosure of his cell the time that stood between the youth and his death wore away like the soft lead pencil that he wrote with, until only a stub too small for his grasp was left him.

But how alive he still was!

Before imprisonment he had thought of his maimed body as something that, being broken, was only fit for abuse. You God-damned cripple, he used to groan to himself. The excitement he stirred in others had been incomprehensible and disgusting to him. But lately the torrent of letters from men whom he had forgotten who couldn't stop thinking of him had begun to revive his self-interest. Auto-erotic sensations began to flower in him. He felt the sorrowful pleasure that stirred his groin in response to manipulation. Lying nude on the cot in the southern July, his one large hand made joyless love to his body, exploring all of those erogenous zones that the fingers of others, hundreds of strangers' fingers, had clasped with a hunger that now was beginning to be understandable to him. Too late, this resurrection. Better for all those rainbows of the flesh to have stayed with the arm cut off in San Diego.

During the earlier period of his confinement Oliver had not particularly noticed or cared about the spatial limitations of his cell. Then he had been satisfied to sit on the edge of his cot and move no more than was necessary for bodily functions. That had been merciful. However, it was gone and every morning he seemed to wake up in a space that had mysteriously diminished while he slept. The inner repressions took this way of screaming for their release. The restlessness became a phobia and the phobia was turning into panic.

He could not remain still for a moment. His heavy footpads sounded from the end of the hall like an ape's, for he walked barefooted with rapid, shuffling strides around and around the little space of his cage. He talked to himself in a monotonous undertone that grew louder, as the days passed, until it began to compete with the endless chatter and blare of the guards' radio. At first he would hush up when he was ordered to, but later his panic deafened him to the guard's voices, until they shouted threats at him. Then he would grip the bars of his cage door and shout back at them names and curses more violent than their own. The doomed boy's behaviour cut off whatever acts of humanity these hard men might have shown him as he drew close to his death. Finally, on the third day before his execution, they punished one of his tantrums by turning the fire-hose on him, until he was crushed to the floor in a strangling heap. He lay there and sobbed and cursed with his brain spinning through a dizzy spiral of nightmares.

By this time, the writing of letters was altogether cut off, but during his quieter intervals he drew wild pictures in his manila tablet and printed out the violent comic-strip symbols, especially the immense HA-HA with its screaming punctuation. Sedatives were put in his food in the last few days, but the drugs were burned up in the furnace of his nerves and the little sleep they gave him would plunge him in worse nightmares than the ones of waking.

The day before he would die Oliver received a visitor in the death cell.

The visitor was a young Lutheran minister who had just come out of the seminary and had not yet received an appointment to a church. Oliver had refused to see the prison chaplain. This had been mentioned in the local newspapers with a picture of Oliver and a caption, Condemned Youth Refuses Consolation of Faith. It had spoken also of the hard and unrepentant nature of the boy who was to die very soon and of his violent behaviour in the prison. But the picture was incongruous to these facts, the face of the blond youth having a virile but tender beauty of the sort that some painter of the Renaissance might have slyly attributed to a juvenile saint, a look which had sometimes inspired commentators to call him 'the baby-faced killer'.

From the moment that he had seen this photograph the Lutheran minister had been following out a series of compulsions so strong that he appeared to himself to be surrendering to an outside power. His earnestness was so apparent that he had no trouble convincing the warden that his mission to the youth was divinely inspired, but by the time the pass was issued, the force of his compulsions had so exhausted the young minister that he fell into a state of nervous panic and would have fled from the building if he had not been attended by a guard.

He found Oliver seated on the edge of his cot senselessly rubbing the sole of a bare foot. He wore only a pair of shorts and his sweating body radiated a warmth that struck the visitor like a powerful spotlight. The appearance of the boy had not been falsely reported. At his first glance the minister's mind shot back to an obsession of his childhood when he had gone all of one summer daily to the zoo to look at a golden panther. The animal was supposed to be particularly savage and a sign on its cage had admonished visitors to keep their distance. But the look in the animal's eyes was so radiant with innocence that the child, who was very timid and harassed by reasonless anxieties, had found a mysterious comfort in meeting their gaze and had come to see them staring benignly out of the darkness when his own eyes were closed before sleeping. Then he would cry himself to sleep for pity of the animal's imprisonment and an unfathomable longing that moved through all of his body.

But one night he dreamed of the panther in a shameful way. The immense clear eyes had appeared to him in a forest and he had thought, if I lie down very quietly the panther will come near me and I am not afraid of him because of our long communions through the bars. He took off his clothes before lying down in the forest. A chill wind began to stir and he felt himself shivering. Then a little fear started in his nerves. He began to doubt his security with the panther and he was afraid to open his eyes again, but he reached out and slowly and noiselessly as possible gathered some leaves about his shuddering nudity and lay under them in a tightly curled position trying to breathe as softly as possible and hoping that now the panther would not discover him. But the chill little wind grew stronger and the leaves blew away. Then all at once he was warm in spite of the windy darkness about him and he realized that the warmth was that of the golden panther coming near him. It was no longer any use trying to conceal himself and it was too late to make an attempt at flight, and so with a sigh the dreamer uncurled his body from its tight position and lay outstretched and spread-eagled in an attitude of absolute trust and submission. Something began to stroke him and presently because of its liquid heat he realized that it was the tongue of the beast bathing him as such animals bathe their young, starting at his feet but progressing slowly up the length of his legs until the narcotic touch arrived at his loins, and then the dream had taken the shameful turn and he had awakened burning with shame beneath the damp and aching initial of Eros.

He had visited the golden panther only once after that and had found himself unable to meet the radiant scrutiny of the beast without mortification. And so the idyll had ended, or had seemed to end. But here was the look of the golden panther again, the innocence in the danger, an exact parallel so unmistakably clear that the minister knew it and felt the childish instinct to curl into a protective circle and cover his body with leaves.

Instead, he reached into his pocket and took out a box of tablets.

The very clear gaze of the boy was now fixed on him, but neither of them had spoken and the guard had closed the door of the cell and withdrawn to his station at the end of the corridor, which was out of their sight.

'What is that?' asked the boy.

'Barbital tablets. I am not very well,' the minister whispered.

'What is the matter with you?'

'A little functional trouble of the heart.'

He had put the tablet on his tongue, but the tongue was utterly dry. He could not swallow.

'Water?' he whispered.

Oliver got up and went to the tap. He filled an enamelled tin cup with tepid water and handed it to his caller.

'What have you come here for?' he asked the young man.

'Just for a talk.'

'I have got nothing to say but the deal is rugged.'

'Then let me read something to you?'

'What's something?'

'The twenty-first psalm.'

'I told them I didn't want no chaplain in here.'

'I am not a chaplain, I am just—'

'Just what?'

'A stranger with sympathy for the misunderstood.'

Oliver shrugged and went on rubbing the sole of his foot. The minister sighed and coughed.

'Are you prepared,' he whispered.

'I'm not prepared for the hot seat, if that's what you mean. But the seat is prepared for me, so what is the difference?'

'I am taking about Eternity,' said the minister. 'This world of ours, this transitory existence, is just a threshold to something Immense beyond.'

'Bull,' said Oliver.

'You don't believe me?'

'Why should I?'

'Because you are face to face with the last adventure!'

This answer had shot from his tongue with a sort of exultant power. He was embarrassed by the boy's steady look. He turned away from it as he finally had from the golden panther's the last time he had gone to him.

'Ha-ha!' said Oliver.

'I'm only trying to help you realize—'

Oliver cut in.

'I was a boxer. I lost my arm. Why was that?'

'Because you persisted in error.'

'Bull,' said Oliver. 'I was not the driver of the car. I yelled at the son of a bitch, slow down, you fucker. Then came the crash. A boxer, my arm comes off. Explain that to me.'

'It gave you the chance of a lifetime.'

'A chance for what?'

'To grow your spiritual arms and reach for God.' He leaned toward Oliver and gripped the prisoner's knees. 'Don't think of me as a man, but as a connection!'

'Huh?'

'A wire that is plugged in your heart and charged with a message from God.'

The curiously ambient look of the condemned youth was fixed on his visitor's face for several seconds.

Then he said, 'Wet that towel.'

'What towel?'

'The one that is over the chair you're sitting in.'

'It's not very clean.'

'I guess it is clean enough to use on Ollie.'

'What do you want to do with it?'

'Rub the sweat off my back.'

The minister dampened the crumpled and stiffened cloth and handed it to the boy.

'You do it for me.'

'Do what?'

'Rub the sweat off my back.'

He rolled on his stomach with a long-drawn sigh, an exhalation that brought again to his frightened visitor's mind the golden panther of fifteen years ago. The rubbing went on for a minute.

'Do I smell?' asked Oliver.

'No. Why?'

'I am clean,' said the boy. 'I took a bath after breakfast.'

'Yes.'

'I have always been careful to keep myself clean. I was a very clean fighter — and a very clean whore!'

He said, 'Ha-ha! Did you know that I was a whore?'

'No,' said the other.

'Well, that's what I was all right. That was my second profession.'

The rubbing continued for another minute, during which an

invisible drummer had seemed to the minister to be advancing from the end of the corridor to the door of the cell and then to come through the bars and stand directly above them.

It was his heartbeat. Now it was becoming irregular and his breath whistled. He dropped the towel and dug in his white shirt pocket for the box of sedatives, but when he removed it he found that the cardboard was pulpy with sweat and the tablets had oozed together in a white paste.

'Go on,' said Oliver. 'It feels good.'

He arched his body and pulled his shorts further down. The narrow and sculptural flanks of the youth were exposed.

'Now,' said Oliver softly, 'rub with your hands.'

The Lutheran sprang from the cot.

'No!'

'Don't be a fool. There's a door at the end of the hall. It makes a noise when anybody comes in it.'

The minister retreated.

The boy reached out and caught him by the wrist.

'You see that pile of letters on the shelf? They're bills from people I owe. Not money, but feelings. For three whole years I went all over the country stirring up feelings without feeling nothing myself. Now that's all changed and I have feelings, too. I am lonely and bottled up the same as you are. I know your type. Everything is artistic or else it's religious, but that's all a bunch of bullshit and I don't buy it. All that you need's to be given a push on the head!'

He moved toward the man as if he would give him the push.

The caller cried out. The guard came running to let him out of the cell. He had to be lifted and half carried down the corridor and before he had reached the end of it, he started to retch as if his whole insides were being torn out.

Oliver heard him.

'Maybe he'll come back tonight,' the doomed boy thought. But he didn't come back and then Oliver died with all of his debts unpaid. However, he died with a good deal more dignity than he had given his jailers to expect of him.

During the last few hours his attention returned to the letters. He read them over and over, whispering them aloud. And when the warden came to conduct him to the death chamber, he said, 'I would like to take these here along with me.' He carried them into the death chamber with him as a child takes a doll or a toy into a dentist's office to give the protection of the familiar and loved.

The letters were resting companionably in the fork of his thighs when he sat down in the chair. At the last moment a guard reached out to remove them. But Oliver's thighs closed on them in a desperate vice that could not have been easily broken. The warden gave a signal to let them remain. Then the moment came, the atmosphere hummed and darkened. Bolts from across the frontiers of the unknown, the practically named and employed but illimitably mysterious power that first invested a static infinitude of space with heat and brilliance and motion, were channelled through Oliver's nerve cells for an instant and then shot back across those immense frontiers, having claimed and withdrawn whatever was theirs in the boy whose lost right arm had been known as 'lightning in leather'.

The body, unclaimed after death, was turned over to a medical college to be used in a class-room laboratory. The men who performed the dissection were somewhat abashed by the body under their knives. It seemed intended for some more august purpose, to stand in a gallery of antique sculpture, touched only by light through stillness and contemplation, for it had the nobility of some broken Apollo that no one was likely to carve so purely again.

But death has never been much in the way of completion.

PORTRAIT OF A GIRL IN GLASS

We lived in a third-floor apartment on Maple Street in Saint Louis, on a block which also contained the Ever-ready Garage, a Chinese laundry, and a bookie shop disguised as a cigar store.

Mine was an anomalous character, one that appeared to be slated for radical change or disaster, for I was a poet who had a job in a warehouse. As for my sister Laura, she could be classified even less readily than I. She made no positive motion toward the world but stood at the edge of the water, so to speak, with feet that anticipated too much cold to move. She'd never have budged an inch, I'm pretty sure, if my mother who was a relatively aggressive sort of woman had not shoved her roughly forward, when Laura was twenty years old, by enrolling her as a student in a nearby business college. Out of her 'magazine money' (she sold subscriptions to women's magazines), Mother had paid my sister's tuition for a term of six months. It did not work out. Laura tried to memorize the typewriter keyboard, she had a chart at home, she used to sit silently in front of it for hours, staring at it while she cleaned and polished her infinite number of little glass ornaments. She did this every evening after dinner. Mother would caution me to be very quiet. 'Sister is looking at her typewriter chart!' I felt somehow that it would do her no good, and I was right. She would seem to know the positions of the keys until the weekly speed-drill got under way, and then they would fly from her mind like a bunch of startled birds.

At last she couldn't bring herself to enter the school any more. She kept this failure a secret for a while. She left the house each morning as before and spent six hours walking around the park. This was in February, and all the walking out-doors regardless of weather brought on influenza. She was in bed for a couple of weeks with a curiously happy little smile on her face. Of course Mother phoned the business college to let them know she was ill. Whoever was talking on the other end of the line had some trouble, it seems, in remembering who Laura was, which annoyed

my mother and she spoke up pretty sharply. 'Laura has been
attending that school of yours for two months, you certainly
ought to recognize her name!' Then came the stunning disclosure.
The person sharply retorted, after a moment or two, that now she
did remember the Wingfield girl, and that she had not been at the
business college *once* in about a month. Mother's voice became
strident. Another person was brought to the phone to verify the
statement of the first. Mother hung up and went to Laura's
bedroom where she lay with a tense and frightened look in place
of the faint little smile. Yes, admitted my sister, what they said was
true. 'I couldn't go any longer, it scared me too much, it made me
sick at the stomach!'

After this fiasco, my sister stayed at home and kept in her
bedroom mostly. This was a narrow room that had two windows
on a dusky areaway between two wings of the building. We called
this areaway Death Valley for a reason that seems worth telling.
There were a great many alleycats in the neighbourhood and one
particularly vicious dirty white Chow who stalked them continually. In the open or on the fire-escapes they could usually elude
him but now and again he cleverly contrived to run some
youngster among them into the cul-de-sac of this narrow areaway
at the far end of which, directly beneath my sister's bedroom
windows, they made the blinding discovery that what had
appeared to be an avenue of escape was really a locked arena, a
gloomy vault of concrete and brick with walls too high for any cat
to spring, in which they must suddenly turn to spit at their death
until it was hurled upon them. Hardly a week went by without a
repetition of this violent drama. The areaway had grown to be
hateful to Laura because she could not look out on it without
recalling the screams and the snarls of killing. She kept the shades
drawn down, and as Mother would not permit the use of electric
current except when needed, her days were spent almost in
perpetual twilight. There were three pieces of dingy ivory
furniture in the room, a bed, a bureau, a chair. Over the bed was a
remarkably bad religious painting, a very effeminate head of
Christ with tear-drops visible just below the eyes. The charm of
the room was produced by my sister's collection of glass. She
loved coloured glass and had covered the walls with shelves of
little glass articles, all of them light and delicate in colour. These
she washed and polished with endless care. When you entered the
room there was always this soft, transparent radiance in it which

came from the glass absorbing whatever faint light came through the shades on Death Valley. I have no idea how many articles there were of this delicate glass. There must have been hundreds of them. But Laura could tell you exactly. She loved each one.

She lived in a world of glass and also a world of music. The music came from a 1920 victrola and a bunch of records that dated from about the same period, pieces such as *Whispering* or *The Love Nest* or *Dardanella*. These records were souvenirs of our father, a man whom we barely remembered, whose name was spoken rarely. Before his sudden and unexplained disappearance from our lives, he had made this gift to the household, the phonograph and the records, whose music remained as a sort of apology for him. Once in a while, on pay-day at the warehouse, I would bring home a new record. But Laura seldom cared for these new records, maybe because they reminded her too much of the noisy tragedies in Death Valley or the speed-drills at the business college. The tunes she loved were the ones she had always heard. Often she sang to herself at night in her bedroom. Her voice was thin, it usually wandered off-key. Yet it had a curious childlike sweetness. At eight o'clock in the evening I sat down to write in my own mouse-trap of a room. Through the closed doors, through the walls, I would hear my sister singing to herself, a piece like *Whispering* or *I Love You* or *Sleepy Time Gal*, losing the tune now and then but always preserving the minor atmosphere of the music. I think that was why I always wrote such strange and sorrowful poems in those days. Because I had in my ears the wispy sound of my sister serenading her pieces of coloured glass, washing them while she sang or merely looking down at them with her vague blue eyes until the points of gem-like radiance in them gently drew the aching particles of reality from her mind and finally produced a state of hypnotic calm in which she even stopped singing or washing the glass and merely sat without motion until my mother knocked at the door and warned her against the waste of electric current.

I don't believe that my sister was actually foolish. I think the petals of her mind had simply closed through fear, and it's no telling how much they had closed upon in the way of secret wisdom. She never talked very much, not even to me, but once in a while she did pop out with something that took you by surprise.

After work at the warehouse or after I'd finished my writing in the evening, I'd drop in her room for a little visit because she had a restful and soothing effect on nerves that were worn rather thin from trying to ride two horses simultaneously in two opposite directions.

I usually found her seated in the straight-back ivory chair with a piece of glass cupped tenderly in her palm.

'What are you doing? Talking to it?' I asked.

'No,' she answered gravely, 'I was just looking at it.'

On the bureau were two pieces of fiction which she had received as Christmas or birthday presents. One was a novel called the *Rose-Garden Husband* by someone whose name escapes me. The other was *Freckles* by Gene Stratton Porter. I never saw her reading the *Rose-Garden Husband*, but the other book was one that she actually lived with. It had probably never occurred to Laura that a book was something you read straight through and then laid aside as finished. The character Freckles, a one-armed orphan youth who worked in a lumber-camp, was someone that she invited into her bedroom now and then for a friendly visit just as she did me. When I came in and found this novel open upon her lap, she would gravely remark that Freckles was having some trouble with the foreman of the lumber-camp or that he had just received an injury to his spine when a tree fell on him. She frowned with genuine sorrow when she reported these misadventures of her story-book hero, possibly not recalling how successfully he came through them all, that the injury to the spine fortuitously resulted in the discovery of rich parents and that the bad-tempered foreman had a heart of gold at the end of the book. Freckles became involved in romance with a girl he called The Angel, but my sister usually stopped reading when this girl became too prominent in the story. She closed the book or turned back to the lonelier periods in the orphan's story. I only remember her making one reference to this heroine of the novel. 'The Angel is nice,' she said, 'but seems to be kind of conceited about her looks.'

Then one time at Christmas, while she was trimming the artificial tree, she picked up the Star of Bethlehem that went on the topmost branch and held it gravely toward the chandelier.

'Do stars have five points really?' she enquired.

This was the sort of thing that you didn't believe and that made you stare at Laura with sorrow and confusion.

'No,' I told her, seeing she really meant it, 'they're round like the earth and most of them much bigger.'

She was gently surprised by this new information. She went to the window to look up at the sky which was, as usual during Saint Louis winters, completely shrouded by smoke.

'It's hard to tell,' she said, and returned to the tree.

So time passed on till my sister was twenty-three. Old enough to be married, but the fact of the matter was she had never even had a date with a boy. I don't believe this seemed as awful to her as it did to Mother.

At breakfast one morning Mother said to me, 'Why don't you cultivate some nice young friends? How about down at the warehouse? Aren't there some young men down there you could ask to dinner?'

This suggestion surprised me because there was seldom quite enough food on her table to satisfy three people. My mother was a terribly stringent housekeeper. God knows we were poor enough in actuality, but my mother had an almost obsessive dread of becoming even poorer. A not unreasonable fear since the man of the house was a poet who worked in a warehouse, but one which I thought played too important a part in all her calculations.

Almost immediately Mother explained herself.

'I think it might be nice,' she said, 'for your sister.'

I brought Jim home to dinner a few nights later. Jim was a big red-haired Irishman who had the scrubbed and polished look of well-kept chinaware. His big square hands seemed to have a direct and very innocent hunger for touching his friends. He was always clapping them on your arms or shoulders and they burned through the cloth of your shirt like plates taken out of an oven. He was the best-liked man in the warehouse and oddly enough he was the only one that I was on good terms with. He found me agreeably ridiculous I think. He knew of my secret practice of retiring to a cabinet in the lavatory and working on rhyme schemes when work was slack in the warehouse, and of sneaking up on the roof now and then to smoke my cigarette with a view across the river at the undulant open country of Illinois. No doubt I was classified as screwy in Jim's mind as much as in the others', but while their attitude was suspicious and hostile when they first knew me, Jim's was warmly tolerant from the beginning. He called me Slim, and gradually his cordial acceptance drew the others around, and while he remained the only one who actually had anything to do with me, the others had now begun to smile when they saw me as people smile at an oddly fashioned dog who crosses their path at some distance.

Nevertheless it took some courage for me to invite Jim to dinner. I thought about it all week and delayed the action till Friday noon, the last possible moment, as the dinner was set for that evening.

'What are you doing tonight?' I finally asked him.

'Not a God damn thing,' said Jim. 'I had a date but her Aunt took sick and she's hauled her freight to Centralia!'

'Well,' I said, 'why don't you come over for dinner?'

'Sure!' said Jim. He grinned with astonishing brightness.

I went outside to phone the news to Mother.

Her voice that was never tired responded with an energy that made the wires crackle.

'I suppose he's Catholic?' she said.

'Yes,' I told her, remembering the tiny silver cross on his freckled chest.

'Good!' she said. 'I'll bake a salmon loaf!'

And so we rode home together in his jalopy.

I had a curious feeling of guilt and apprehension as I led the lamb-like Irishman up three flights of cracked marble steps to the door of Apartment F, which was not thick enough to hold inside it the odour of baking salmon.

Never having a key, I pressed the bell.

'Laura!' came Mother's voice. 'That's Tom and Mr Delaney! Let them in!'

There was a long, long pause.

'Laura?' she called again. 'I'm busy in the kitchen, you answer the door!'

Then at last I heard my sister's footsteps. They went right past the door at which we were standing and into the parlour. I heard the creaking noise of the phonograph crank. Music commenced. One of the oldest records, a march of Sousa's, put on to give her the courage to let in a stranger.

The door came timidly open and there she stood in a dress from Mother's wardrobe, a black chiffon ankle-length and high-heeled slippers on which she balanced uncertainly like a tipsy crane of melancholy plumage. Her eyes stared back at us with a glass brightness and her delicate wing-like shoulders were hunched with nervousness.

'Hello!' said Jim, before I could introduce him.

He stretched out his hand. My sister touched it only for a second.

'Excuse me!' she whispered, and turned with a breathless rustle back to her bedroom door, the sanctuary beyond it briefly revealing itself with the tinkling, muted radiance of glass before the door closed rapidly but gently on her wraithlike figure.

Jim seemed to be incapable of surprise.

'Your sister?' he asked.

'Yes, that was her,' I admitted. 'She's terribly shy with strangers.'

'She looks like you,' said Jim, 'except she's pretty.'

Laura did not reappear till called to dinner. Her place was next to Jim at the drop-leaf table and all through the meal her figure was slightly tilted away from his. Her face was feverishly bright and one eyelid, the one on the side toward Jim, had developed a nervous wink. Three times in the course of the dinner she dropped her fork on her plate with a terrible clatter and she was continually raising the water-glass to her lips for hasty little gulps. She went on doing this even after the water was gone from the glass. And her handling of the silver became more awkward and hurried all the time.

I thought of nothing to say.

To Mother belonged the conversational honours, such as they were. She asked the caller about his home and family. She was delighted to learn that his father had a business of his own, a retail shoe store somewhere in Wyoming. The news that he went to night-school to study accounting was still more edifying. What was his heart set on beside the warehouse? Radio-engineering? My, my, my! It was easy to see that here was a very up-and-coming young man who was certainly going to make his place in the world!

Then she started to talk about her children. Laura, she said, was not cut out for business. She was domestic, however, and making a home was really a girl's best bet.

Jim agreed with this and seemed not to sense the ghost of an implication. I suffered through it dumbly, trying not to see Laura trembling more and more beneath the incredible unawareness of Mother.

And bad as it was, excruciating in fact, I thought with dread of the moment when dinner was going to be over, for then the diversion of food would be taken away, we would have to go into the little steam-heated parlour. I fancied the four of us having run out of talk, even Mother's seemingly endless store of questions about Jim's home and his job all used up finally – the four of us, then, just sitting there in the parlour, listening to the hiss of the radiator and nervously clearing our throats in the kind of self-consciousness that gets to be suffocating.

But when the blancmange was finished, a miracle happened.

Mother got up to clear the dishes away. Jim gave me a clap on the shoulders and said, 'Hey, Slim, let's go have a look at those old records in there!'

He sauntered carelessly into the front room and flopped down on the floor beside the victrola. He began sorting through the collection of worn-out records and reading their titles aloud in a voice so hearty that it shot like beams of sunlight through the vapours of self-consciousness engulfing my sister and me.

He was sitting directly under the floor-lamp and all at once my sister jumped up and said to him, 'Oh – you have freckles!'

Jim grinned. 'Sure, that's what my folks call me – Freckles!'

'Freckles?' Laura repeated. She looked toward me as if for the confirmation of some too wonderful hope. I looked away quickly, not knowing whether to feel relieved or alarmed at the turn that things were taking.

Jim wound the victrola and put on *Dardanella*.

He grinned at Laura.

'How about you an' me cutting the rug a little?'

'What?' said Laura breathlessly, smiling and smiling.

'Dance!' he said, drawing her into his arms.

As far as I knew she had never danced in her life. But to my everlasting wonder she slipped quite naturally into those huge arms of Jim's, and they danced round and around the small steam-heated parlour, bumping against the sofa and chairs and laughing loudly and happily together. Something opened up in my sister's face. To say it was love is not too hasty a judgment, for after all he had freckles and that was what his folks called him. Yes, he had undoubtedly assumed the identity – for all practical purposes – of the one-armed orphan youth who lived in the Limberlost, that tall and misty region to which she retreated whenever the walls of Apartment F became too close to endure.

Mother came back in with some lemonade. She stopped short as she entered the portiers.

'Good heavens! Laura? Dancing?'

Her look was absurdly grateful as well as startled.

'But isn't she stepping all over you, Mr Delaney?'

'What if she does?' said Jim, with bearish gallantry. 'I'm not made of eggs!'

'Well, well, well,' said Mother, senselessly beaming.

'She's light as a feather!' said Jim. 'With a little more practice she'd dance as good as Betty!'

There was a little pause of silence.

'Betty?' said Mother.

'The girl I go out with!' said Jim.

'Oh!' said Mother.

She set the pitcher of lemonade carefully down and with her back to the caller and her eyes on me, she asked him just how often he and the lucky lady went out together.

'Steady!' said Jim.

Mother's look, remaining on my face, turned into a glare of fury.

'Tom didn't mention that you went out with a girl!'

'Nope,' said Jim. 'I didn't mean to let the cat out of the bag. The boys at the warehouse'll kid me to death when Slim gives the news away.'

He laughed heartily but his laughter dropped heavily and awkwardly away as even his dull senses were gradually penetrated by the unpleasant sensation the news of Betty had made.

'Are you thinking of getting married?' said Mother.

'First of next month!' he told her.

It took her several moments to pull herself together. Then she said in a dismal tone, 'How nice! If Tom had only told us we could have asked you *both*!'

Jim had picked up his coat.

'Must you be going?' said Mother.

'I hope it don't seem like I'm rushing off,' said Jim, 'but Betty's gonna get back on the eight o'clock train an' by the time I get my jalopy down to the Wabash depot—'

'Oh, then, we mustn't keep you.'

Soon as he'd left, we all sat down, looking dazed.

Laura was the first to speak.

'Wasn't he nice?' she said. 'And all those freckles!'

'Yes,' said Mother. Then she turned on me.

'You didn't mention that he was engaged to be married!'

'Well, how did I know that he was engaged to be married?'

'I thought you called him your best friend down at the warehouse?'

'Yes, but I didn't know he was going to be married!'

'How peculiar!' said Mother. 'How very peculiar!'

'No,' said Laura gently, getting up from the sofa. 'There's nothing peculiar about it.'

She picked up one of the records and blew on its surface a little as if it were dusty, then set it softly back down.

'People in love,' she said, 'take everything for granted.'

What did she mean by that? I never knew.

She slipped quietly back to her room and closed the door.

Not very long after that I lost my job at the warehouse. I was fired for writing a poem on the lid of a shoe-box. I left Saint Louis and took to moving around. The cities swept about me like dead leaves, leaves that were brightly coloured but torn away from the branches. My nature changed. I grew to be firm and sufficient.

In five years' time I had nearly forgotten home. I had to forget it, I couldn't carry it with me. But once in a while, usually in a strange town before I have found companions, the shell of deliberate hardness is broken through. A door comes softly and irresistibly open. I hear the tired old music my unknown father left in the place he abandoned as faithlessly as I. I see the faint and sorrowful radiance of the glass, hundreds of little transparent pieces of it in very delicate colours. I hold my breath, for if my sister's face appears among them — the night is hers!

THE COMING OF SOMETHING TO THE
WIDOW HOLLY

The widow Isabel Holly was a rooming-house owner. How she had come to be one she hardly knew. It had crept up on her the same as everything else. She had an impression, however, that this was the house where she had lived as a bride. There had been, she also believed, a series of more or less tragic disappointments, the least of which had been Mr Holly's decease. In spite of the fact that the late Mr Holly, whose first name she could no longer remember, had left her with an adequate trust fund, she had somehow felt compelled at one time or another to open her house on Bourbon Street in New Orleans to persons regarding themselves as 'paying guests'. In times more recent the payments had dwindled away and now it seemed that the guests were really dependants. They had also dwindled in number. She had an idea that there had once been many, but now there were only three, two middle-aged spinsters and a bachelor in his eighties. They got along not well together. Whenever they met on the stairs or in the hall or at the door of the bathroom, there was invariably some kind of dispute. The bolt on the bathroom door was continually broken, repaired, and broken again. It was impossible to keep any glassware about the place. Mrs Holly had finally resorted to the use of nothing but aluminium in the way of portable fixtures. And while objects of this material withstood shocks better themselves, they also inflicted considerably more damage on whatever they struck. Time and again one of the terrible three tenants would appear in the morning with a bloodstained bandage about the head, a bruised and swollen mouth or a blackened eye. In view of the circumstances it was reasonable to suppose that they would, at least one of them, move out of the premises. Nothing, however, seemed further from their intention. They clung as leeches to their damp-smelling rooms. All were collectors of things, bottle caps or matchboxes or tin-foil wrappings, and the length of their tenancy was eloquently witnessed by the vast store of such articles stacked about the mouldy walls of their bedrooms. It would be hard to say which of the three was the least desirable tenant, but the bachelor in his eighties was certainly the one most embarrassing to a woman of gentle birth and breeding as Isabel Holly unquestionably had been and was.

This octogenarian recluse had run up a great many debts. The last few years he had seemed to be holding an almost continual audience with his creditors. They stamped in and out of the house, in and out, not only during the day but sometimes at the most unlikely hours of the night. The widow Holly's establishment was located in that part of the old French Quarter given over mostly to honky-tonks and bars. The old man's creditors were heavy drinkers, most of them, and when the bars closed against them at night, the liquor having inflamed their tempers, they would stop off at Mrs Holly's to renew their relentless siege of her tenant, and if he declined to answer the loud ringing and banging at the door, missiles of various kinds were thrown through the panes of the windows wherever the shutters were fallen off or unfastened. In New Orleans the weather is sometimes remarkably good. When this was the case, the creditors of the old man were less obnoxious, at times merely presenting their bills at the door and marching quietly away. But when it was bad outside, when the weather was nasty, the language the creditors used in making demands was indescribably awful. Poor Mrs Holly had formed the habit of holding her hands to her ears on days when the sun wasn't out. There was one particular tradesman, a man named Cobb who represented some mortician's establishment, who had the habit of using the worst epithet in the English language at the top of his voice, over and over again with increasing frenzy. Only the middle-aged women, Florence and Susie, could cope with the tradesman Cobb. When they acted together, he could be driven away, but only at the sacrifice of broken banisters.

The widow Holly had only once made an allusion to these painful scenes between the tradesman Cobb and her bachelor tenant. On that occasion, after a particularly disagreeable session in the downstairs hall, she had timidly inquired of the old man if some kind of settlement couldn't be reached with his friend from the undertakers.

Not till I'm dead, he told her.

And then he went on to explain, while bandaging his head, that he had ordered a casket, the finest casket procurable, that it had been especially designed and built for him – now the unreasonable Mr Cobb wished him to pay for it, even before his decease.

This son of an illegitimate child, said the roomer, suspects me of being immortal! I wish it were true, he sighed, but my doctor assures me that my life expectancy is barely another eighty-seven years!

Oh, said poor Mrs Holly.

Mild as her nature was, she was nearly ready to ask him if he expected to stay in the rooming house all that time – but just at this moment, one of the two indistinguishable female tenants, Florence or Susie, opened the door of her bedroom and stuck her head out.

This awful disturbance has got to stop! she yelled.

To emphasize her demand, she tossed an aluminium washbasin in their direction. It glanced off the head of the man who had ordered his casket and struck Mrs Holly a terrible blow in the bosom. The octogenarian's head was bandaged with flannel, several layers of it, and padded with damp cardboard, so the blow did not hurt him nor even catch him off guard. But as Isabel Holly fled in pain down the stairs to the cellar – her usual sanctuary – she glanced behind her to see the powerful old gentleman yanking a wooden post from the balustrade and shouting at Florence or Susie the very same unrepeatable word that the undertaker had used.

FOR PROBLEMS CONFER WITH
A. ROSE, METAPHYSICIAN!

This was the legend which Isabel Holly found on a business card stuck under her door facing Bourbon.

She went at once to the address of the consultant and found him seemingly waiting to receive her.

My dear Mrs Holly, he said, you seem to be troubled.

Troubled? she said, Oh, yes, I'm terribly troubled. There seems to be something important left out of the picture.

What picture? he asked her gently.

My life, she told him.

And what is the element which appears to be missing?

An explanation.

Oh – an explanation! Not many people ask for *that* anymore.

Why? Why don't they? she asked.

Well, you see— Ah, but it's useless to tell you!

Then why did you wish me to come here?

The old man took off his glasses and closed a ledger.

My dear Mrs Holly, he said, the fact of the matter is that you have a very unusual destiny in store. You are the first of your kind and character ever to be transplanted to this earth from a certain star in another universe!

And what is that going to result in?

Be patient, my dear. Endure your present trials as well as you can. A change is coming, a very momentous change, not only for you but for practically all others confined to this lunatic sphere!

Mrs Holly went home and, before long, this interview, like everything else in the past, had faded almost completely out of her mind. The days behind her were like an un-clear, fuzzy negative of a film that faded when exposed to the present. They were like a dull piece of thread she would like to cut and be done with. Yes, to be done with forever, like a thread from a ravelled hem that catches on things when you walk. But where had she put the scissors? Where had she put away everything sharp in her life, everything which was capable of incision? Sometimes she searched about her for something that had an edge that she could cut with. But everything about her was rounded or soft.

The trouble in the house went on and on.

Florence Domingo and Susie Patten had quarrelled. Jealousy was the reason.

Florence Domingo had an aged female relative who came to pay her a call about once a month, bringing an empty paper bag in the usually vain hope that Florence would give her something of relative value to take away in it. This indigent old cousin was extremely deaf, as deaf, you might say, as a fence pole, and consequently her conversations with Florence Domingo had to be carried on at the top of both their lungs, and since these conversations were almost entirely concerned with the other roomers at Mrs Holly's, whatever degree of peace had prevailed under the roof before one of these visits was very drastically reduced right after one took place and sometimes even during its progress. Now Susie Patten never received a visitor and this comparative unpopularity of Susie's was not allowed to pass without comment by Florence and her caller.

How is old Susie Patten? the cousin would shriek.

Terrible. Same as ever, Florence would shout back.

Does she ever go out anywhere to pay a call? the cousin would yell.

Never, never! Florence would reply at the top of her lungs, and nobody comes to see her! She is a friendless soul, completely alone in the world.

Nobody comes to her?

Nobody!

Never?

Never! Absolutely *never!*

When the cousin got up to go, Florence Domingo would say to her, Now close your eyes and hold out your paper bag and see what you find in it when you get downstairs. This was her playful fashion of making a gift, and the old cousin was forbidden to look in the bag till she had left the house, and so great was her curiosity and her greed that she'd nearly break her neck in her rush to get out after the gift was presented. Usually it turned out to be a remnant of food of some kind, such as a half-eaten apple with the bitten places turned brown and withered about the edges where Florence had left her tooth marks, but once when the conversation had not gone to suit Miss Domingo, it was the corpse of a rat that she had dropped in the held-out paper bag and the visits had been suspended for three months. But now the visits were going on again and the vexation of Susie Patten was well-nigh indescribable. Then an idea came to her. She launched a counter-offensive and a very clever one, too. Susie invented a caller of her own. Susie was very good at speaking in two voices: that is, she would speak in her own voice and then she would answer in a different one as if she were carrying on a conversation with someone. This invented caller of Susie's, moreover, was not an old woman. It was a gentleman who addressed her as Madam.

Madam, the invented caller would say, You are wearing your beautiful dotted Swiss today!

Oh, do you like it? Susie would cry out.

Yes, it goes with your eyes, the caller would tell her.

Then Susie would make kissing sounds with her mouth, first soft ones, then very loud ones, and then she would rock back and forth rapidly in her rocking-chair and go, Huff, huff, huff! And after a suitable interval she would cry out to herself, *Oh, no!* Then she would rock some more and go, Huff, huff, again, and presently, after another suitable pause, the conversation would be resumed and in due course it would turn to the subject of Florence

Domingo. Disparaging comments would be made on the subject and also upon the subject of the Domingo collection of tin-foil wrappings and the Domingo's female relative with the paper bag held out for a gift when she left.

Madam, cried Susie's caller, that woman is not fit to live in a respectable house!

No, indeed, she is not, Susie would agree with him loudly, and all this while Florence Domingo would be listening to every word that was spoken and every sound produced in the course of the long social call. Florence was only half sure that the caller existed, but she could not be completely sure that he didn't, and her doubt and uncertainty on this subject was extremely nerve-racking, and something really had to be done about it.

Something was done about it.

Isabel Holly, the widow who owned the building and suffered this – what shall we call it? – knew there was going to be trouble in the house when she saw Miss Domingo come in the front door one evening with a medium-sized box labelled EXPLOSIVES.

The widow Holly did not wait for eventualities that night. She went right out on the street, dressed as she was, in a pair of rayon bloomers and a brassière. She had hardly gotten round the corner when the whole block shook with a terrible detonation. She kept on running, shuddering in the cold, till she came to the park, the one beside the Cabildo, and there she knelt and prayed for several hours before she dared to turn back toward her home.

When Isabel Holly crept back to the house on Bourbon, she found it a shambles. The rooms were silent. But as she tiptoed past them, she saw here and there the bloody, inert, and hoarsely panting figures of easily twenty tradesmen including the ruffian Cobb. All over the floors and the treads of the stairs were little glittering objects which first she mistook for fragments of glass, but when she picked one up she found it to be a coin. Apparently money had been forthcoming from some quarter of the establishment, it had been cast around everywhere, but the creditors of the old man were still in no condition to gather it up. There must have been a great deal of violence preceding the money's disbursal.

Isabel Holly tried to think about this, but her brain was like a cracked vessel that won't hold water, and she was staggering with weariness. So she gave it up and dragged herself to her bedroom. In an envelope half thrust under the door she found a message which only increased the widow's mystification.

The message went as follows:

'My dear Mrs Holly, I think that with my persuasion the ghastly disturbance has stopped. I am sorry I cannot wait till you return home as I am sure that you must feel a good deal of sorrow and confusion over conditions here. However I shall see you personally soon, and stay a good deal longer. Sincerely, Christopher D. Cosmos.'

The weeks that followed were remarkably tranquil. All three of the incorrigible tenants remained locked in their rooms apparently in a state of intimidation. The violently paid-off creditors called at the house no more. The carpenters came and patched things up in silence. Telegraph messengers tiptoed up the stairs and rapped discreetly at the roomers' doors. Boxes began to be carried in and out – It soon appeared to Mrs Holly's hardly believing mind that general preparations were being made by the terrible two and one to move from the premises.

As a matter of fact a bulletin corroborating this hopeful suspicion appeared in the downstairs hall not very long afterwards.

'We have decided,' said this bulletin, 'in view of your cousin's behaviour, not to maintain our residence here any longer. This decision is absolutely inalterable and we would prefer not to discuss it. Signed: Florence Domingo, Susie Patten, Regis de Winter.' (The signatures of the roomers.)

After her roomers' departure Isabel Holly found it harder than ever to concentrate on things. Often during the day she would sit down worriedly at the kitchen table or on her unmade bed and clasp her forehead and murmur to herself, I've got to think, I've simply *got* to think! But it did no good, it did no good at all. Oh, yes, for a while she would *seem* to be thinking of something. But in the end it was always pretty much like a lump of sugar making strenuous efforts to preserve its integrity in a steamingly warm cup of tea. The cubic shape of a thought would not keep. It relaxed and dissolved and spread out flat on the bottom or drifted away.

At last one day she paid another visit to the house of the metaphysician. On his door was nailed a notice: 'I've gone to Florida to stay young forever. Dear Love to all my enemies. Goodbye.' She stared at it hopelessly for a moment and started to turn away. But just in the nick of time, a small white rodent squeezed from beneath the door and dropped at her feet an envelope sealed as the one that Christopher Cosmos had left at her house the time of the last disturbance. She tore it open and read the following message: 'I have returned and am sleeping in your bedroom. Do not wake me up till after seven o'clock. We've had a long hard trip around the cape of the sun and need much rest before we start back again. Sincerely, Christopher D. Cosmos.'

When Isabel Holly returned, there was, indeed, a sleeping man in her bedroom. She stood in the door and nearly stopped breathing with wonder. Oh, how handsome he was! He had on the uniform of a naval commander. The cloth was crisp and lustrous as deeply banked winter snow: the shoulders of the coat were braided; the braids were clasped to the garment with ruby studs. The buttons were aquamarine. And the chest of the man, exposed by the unbuttoned jacket, was burnished as fine, pale gold with diamond-like beads of perspiration on it.

He opened one eye and winked and murmured 'hello' and lazily rolled on his stomach and went back to sleep.

She couldn't decide what action she ought to take. She wandered vaguely about the house for a while, observing the changes which had occurred in her absence.

Everything was now put straight. It was all spick and span as if a regiment of servants had worked industriously for days, scrubbing and polishing, exacting a radiance from the dullest objects. Kitchen utensils worn away with rust and various other truck which could not, be renovated had been thrown into or heaped beside an incinerator. GET RID OF THIS NONSENSE was scrawled on a laundry cardboard in the Commander's handwriting. Also among the stuff which her marvellous visitor had ordained for destruction were various relics of the late Mr Holly, his stomach pump, the formidable bearded photograph of his mother in her daredevil outfit, the bucket of mutton tallow he greased himself with thrice weekly in lieu of bathing, the 970-page musical composition called *Punitive Measures* which he had striven tirelessly to master upon a brass instrument of his own invention – all of this reliquary truck was now heaped inside or beside the giant incinerator.

Wonders will never cease! the widow murmured as she returned upstairs.

A state of irresolution was not unfamiliar to the widow Holly, but this was the first time that it had made her lightfooted as well as lightheaded. She rose to the chambers above with no effort of climbing, as a vapour rises from water into first morning light. There was not much light, not even in the parlour that fronted Bourbon Street, there was hardly more light than might have emanated from the uncovered chest of the slumbering young Commander in her bedroom. There was just light enough to show the face of the clock if she leaned toward it as if to invite a kiss. It was seven o'clock — so soon!

The widow did not have a cold, but as she folded some garments over a nest of pine cones in the parlour fireplace, she began to sniff. She sniffed again and again; all of the muscles under the surface of her chilly young skin began to quiver, for somewhere in the house, tremulous with moments coming and going as almost bodiless creatures might rush through a room made of nothing but doors, someone was surely holding a sugar-coated apple on a forked metal stick above a flame's rapid tongue, until the skin of it hissed and crackled and finally split open, spilling out sweet juices, spitting them into the flame and filling the whole house, now, all of the chill and dim chambers, upstairs and down, with an odour of celebration in the season of Advent.

TWO ON A PARTY

He couldn't really guess the age of the woman, Cora, but she was certainly not any younger than he, and he was almost thirty-five. There were some mornings when he thought she looked, if he wasn't flattering himself, almost old enough to be his mother, but there were evenings when the liquor was hitting her right, when her eyes were lustrous and her face becomingly flushed, and then she looked younger than he. As you get to know people, if you grow to like them, they begin to seem younger to you. The cruelty or damaging candour of the first impression is washed away like the lines in a doctored photograph, and Billy no longer remembered that the first night he met her he had thought of her as 'an old bag'. Of course, that night when he first met her she was not looking her best. It was in a Broadway bar; she was occupying the stool next to Billy and she had lost a diamond ear-clip and was complaining excitedly about it to the barman. She kept ducking down like a diving seal to look for it among the disgusting refuse under the brass rail, bobbing up and down and grunting and complaining, her face inflamed and swollen by the exertion, her rather heavy figure doubled into ludicrous positions. Billy had the uncomfortable feeling that she suspected him of stealing the diamond ear-clip. Each time she glanced at him his face turned hot. He always had that guilty feeling when anything valuable was lost, and it made him angry; he thought of her as an irritating old bag. Actually she wasn't accusing anybody of stealing the diamond ear-clip; in fact she kept assuring the barman that the clasp on the ear-clip was loose and she was a goddamn fool to put it on.

Then Billy found the thing for her, just as he was about to leave the bar, embarrassed and annoyed beyond endurance; he noticed the sparkle of it almost under his shoe, the one on the opposite side from the ducking and puffing 'old bag'. With the sort of school-teacherish austerity that he assumed when annoyed, when righteously indignant over something, an air that he had picked

up during his short, much earlier, career as an English instructor
at a midwestern university, he picked up the clip and slammed it
wordlessly down on the bar in front of her and started to walk
away. Two things happened to detain him. Three sailors off a
Norwegian vessel came one, two, three through the revolving
door of the bar and headed straight for the vacant stools just
beyond where he had been sitting, and at the same instant, the
woman, Cora, grabbed hold of his arm, shouting, Oh, don't go,
don't go, the least you can do is let me buy you a drink! And so he
had turned right around, as quickly and precisely as the revolving
door through which the glittering trio of Norsemen had entered.
Okay, why not? He resumed his seat beside her, she bought him a
drink, he bought her a drink, inside of five minutes they were
buying beer for the sailors and it was just as if the place was
suddenly lit up by a dozen big chandeliers.

Quickly she looked different to him, not an old bag at all but
really sort of attractive and obviously more to the taste of the
dazzling Norsemen than Billy could be. Observing the two of
them in the long bar mirror, himself and Cora, he saw that they
looked good together, they made a good pair, they were mutually
advantageous as a team for cruising the Broadway bars. She was a
good deal darker than he and more heavily built. Billy was slight
and he had very blond skin that the sun turned pink. Unfortunately for Billy, the pink also showed through the silky, thin
yellow hair on the crown of his head where the baldness, so
fiercely but impotently resisted, was now becoming a fact that he
couldn't disown. Of course, the crown of the head doesn't show in
the mirror unless you bow to your image in the glass, but there is
no denying that the top of a queen's head is a conspicuous area on
certain occasions which are not unimportant. That was how he
put it, laughing about it to Cora. She said, Honey, I swear to Jesus
I think you're more self-conscious about your looks and your age
than I am! She said it kindly, in fact, she said everything kindly.
Cora was a kind person. She was the kindest person that Billy had
ever met. She said and meant everything kindly, literally everything; she hadn't a single malicious bone in her body, not a
particle of jealousy or suspicion or evil in her nature, and that was
what made it so sad that Cora was a lush. Yes, after he stopped
thinking of her as 'an old bag', which was almost immediately
after they got acquainted, he started thinking of Cora as a lush,
kindly, yes, but not as kindly as Cora thought about him, for Billy

was not, by nature, as kind as Cora. Nobody else could be. Her
kindness was monumental, the sort that simply doesn't exist any
more, at least not in the queen world.

Fortunately for Billy, Billy was fairly tall. He had formed the
defensive habit of holding his head rather high so that the crown
of it wouldn't be so noticeable in bars, but unfortunately for Billy,
he had what doctors had told him was a calcium deposit in the
ears which made him hard of hearing and which could only be
corrected by a delicate and expensive operation – boring a hole in
the bone. He didn't have much money; he had just saved enough
to live, not frugally but carefully, for two or three more years
before he would have to go back to work at something. If he had
the ear operation, he would have to go back to work right away
and so abandon his sybaritic existence which suited him better
than the dubious glory of being a somewhat better than hack
writer of Hollywood film scenarios and so forth. Yes, and so
forth!

Being hard of hearing, in fact, progressively so, he would have
to crouch over, and bend sidewise a little to hold a conversation in
a bar, that is, if he wanted to understand what the other party was
saying. In a bar it's dangerous not to listen to the other party,
because the way of speaking is just as important as the look of the
face in distinguishing between good trade and dirt, and Billy did
not at all enjoy being beaten as some queens do. So he would have
to bend sidewise and expose the almost baldness on the crown of
his blond head, and he would cringe and turn red instead of pink
with embarrassment as he did so. He knew that it was ridiculous
of him to be that sensitive about it. But as he said to Cora, age does
worse things to a queen than it does to a woman.

She disagreed about that and they had great arguments about it.
But it was a subject on which Billy could hold forth as eloquently
as a southern Senator making a filibuster against the repeal of the
poll tax, and Cora would lose the argument by default, simply not
able to continue it any longer, for Cora did not like gloomy topics
of conversation so much as Billy liked them.

About her own defects of appearance, however, Cora was
equally distressed and humble.

You see, she would tell him, I'm really a queen myself. I mean
it's the same difference, honey, I like and do the same things,
sometimes I think in bed if they're drunk enough they don't even
know I'm a woman, at least they don't act like they do, and I don't

blame them. Look at me, I'm a mess. I'm getting so heavy in the hips and I've got these big udders on me!

Nonsense, Billy would protest, you have a healthy and beautiful female body, and you mustn't low-rate yourself all the time that way, I won't allow it!

And he would place his arm about her warm and Florida-sun-browned shoulders, exposed by her backless white gown (the little woolly-looking canary yellow jacket being deposited on a vacant bar stool beside her), for it was usually quite late, almost time for the bars to close, when they began to discuss what the years had done to them, the attritions of time. Beside Billy, too, there would be a vacant bar stool on which he had placed the hat that concealed his thinning hair from the streets. It would be one of those evenings that gradually wear out the exhilaration you start with. It would be one of these evenings when lady luck showed the bitchy streak in her nature. They would have had one or two promising encounters which had fizzled out, coming to a big fat zero at three A.M. In the game they played, the true refinement of torture is to almost pull in a catch and then the line breaks, and when that happens, each not pitying himself as much as he did the other, they would sit out the final hour before closing, talking about the wicked things time had done to them, the gradual loss of his hearing and his hair, the fatty expansion of her breasts and buttocks, forgetting that they were still fairly attractive people and still not old.

Actually, in the long run their luck broke about fifty-fifty. Just about every other night one or the other of them would be successful in the pursuit of what Billy called 'the lyric quarry'. One or the other or both might be successful on the good nights, and if it was a really good night, then both would be. Good nights, that is, really good nights, were by no means as rare as hen's teeth nor were they as frequent as streetcars, but they knew very well, both of them, that they did better together than they had done separately in the past. They set off something warm and good in each other that strangers responded to with something warm and good in themselves. Loneliness dissolved any reserve and suspicion, the night was a great warm comfortable meeting of people, it shone, it radiated, it had the effect of a dozen big chandeliers, oh, it was great, it was grand, you simply couldn't describe it, you got the coloured lights going, and there it all was, the final pattern of it and the original pattern, all put together, made to fit exactly, no, there were simply no words good enough to describe it. And if the worst happened, if someone who looked like a Botticelli angel drew a knife, or if the law descended suddenly on you, and those were eventualities the possibility of which a queen must always consider, you still could say you'd had a good run for your money.

Like everyone whose life is conditioned by luck, they had some brilliant streaks of it and some that were dismal. For instance, that first week they operated together in Manhattan. That was really a freak; you couldn't expect a thing like that to happen twice in a lifetime. The trade was running as spawning salmon up those narrow cataracts in the Rockies. Head to tail, tail to head, crowding, swarming together, seemingly driven along by some immoderate instinct. It was not a question of catching; it was simply a question of deciding which ones to keep and which to throw back in the stream, all glittering, all swift, all flowing one way which was toward you!

That week was in Manhattan, where they teamed up. It was, to be exact, in Emerald Joe's at the corner of Forty-second and Broadway that they had met each other the night of the lost diamond clip that Billy had found. It was the week of the big blizzard and the big Chinese Red offensive in North Korea. The combination seemed to make for a wildness in the air, and trade is always best when the atmosphere of a city is excited whether it be over a national election or New Year's or a championship prizefight or the World Series baseball games; anything that stirs up the whole population makes it better for cruising.

Yes, it was a lucky combination of circumstances, and that first week together had been brilliant. It was before they started actually living together. At that time, she had a room at the Hotel Pennsylvania and he had one at the Astor. But at the end of that week, the one of their first acquaintance, they gave up separate establishments and took a place together at a small East Side hotel in the Fifties, because of the fact that Cora had an old friend from her hometown in Louisiana employed there as the night clerk. This one was a gay one that she had known long ago and innocently expected to be still the same. Cora did not understand how some people turn bitter. She had never turned bitchy and it was not understandable to her that others might. She said this friend on the desk was a perfect setup; he'd be delighted to see them bringing in trade. But that was the way in which it failed to work out . . .

That second week in New York was not a good one. Cora had been exceeding her usual quota of double ryes on the rocks and it began all at once to tell on her appearance. Her system couldn't absorb any more; she had reached the saturation point, and it was no longer possible for her to pick herself up in the evenings. Her face had a bloated look and her eyes remained bloodshot all the time. They looked, as she said, like a couple of poached eggs in a sea of blood, and Billy had to agree with her that they did. She started looking her oldest and she had the shakes.

Then about Friday of that week the gay one at the desk turned bitchy on them. Billy had expected him to turn, but Cora hadn't. Sooner or later, Billy knew, that frustrated queen was bound to get a severe attack of jaundice over the fairly continual coming and going of so much close-fitting blue wool, and Billy was not mistaken. When they brought their trade in, he would slam down the key without looking at them or speaking a word of greeting. Then one night they brought in a perfectly divine-looking pharmacist's mate of Italian extraction and his almost equally attractive buddy. The old friend of Cora's exploded, went off like a spit-devil.

I'm sorry, he hissed, but this is *not* a flea-bag! You should have stayed on Times Square where you started.

There was a scene. He refused to give them their room-key unless the two sailors withdrew from the lobby. Cora said, Fuck you, Mary, and reached across the desk and grabbed the key from the hook. The old friend seized her wrist and tried to make her let go.

Put that key down, he shrieked, or you'll be sorry!

He started twisting her wrist; then Billy hit him; he vaulted right over the desk and knocked the son-of-a-bitch into the switchboard.

Call the police, call the police, the clerk screamed to the porter.

Drunk as she was, Cora suddenly pulled herself together. She took as much command of the situation as could be taken.

You boys wait outside, she said to the sailors, there's no use in you all getting into S.P. trouble.

One of them, the Italian, wanted to stay and join in the roughhouse, but his buddy, who was the bigger one, forcibly removed him to the sidewalk. (Cora and Billy never saw them again.) By that time, Billy had the night clerk by the collar and was giving him slaps that bobbed his head right and left like something rubber, as if that night clerk was everything that he loathed in a hostile world. Cora stopped him. She had that wonderful, that really invaluable faculty of sobering up in a crisis. She pulled Billy off her old friend and tipped the coloured porter ten dollars not to call in the law. She turned on all her southern charm and sweetness, trying to straighten things out. You darling, she said, you poor darling, to the bruised night clerk. The law was not called, but the outcome of the situation was far from pleasant. They had to check out, of course, and the hysterical old friend said he was going to write Cora's family in Alexandria, Louisiana, and give them a factual report on how she was living here in New York and how he supposed she was living anywhere else since she'd left home and he knew her.

At that time Billy knew almost nothing about Cora's background and former life, and he was surprised at her being so upset over this hysterical threat, which seemed unimportant to him. But all the next day Cora kept alluding to it, speculating whether or not the bitch would really do it, and it was probably on account of this threat that Cora made up her mind to leave New York. It was the only time, while they were living together, that Cora ever made a decision, at least about places to go and when to go to them. She had none of that desire to manage and dominate which is a typically American perversion of the female nature. As Billy said to himself, she was like a big piece of seaweed. Sometimes he said it irritably to himself, just like a big piece of seaweed washing this way and that way. It isn't healthy or normal to be so passive, Billy thought.

Where do you want to eat?

I don't care.

No, tell me, Cora, what place would you prefer?

I really don't care, she'd insist, it makes no difference to me.

Sometimes out of exasperation he would say, All right, let's eat at the Automat.

Only then would Cora demur.

Of course, if you want to, honey, but couldn't we eat some place with a liquor licence?

She was agreeable to anything and everything; she seemed to be grateful for any decision made for her, but this one time, when they left New York, when they made their first trip together, it was Cora's decision to go. This was before Billy began to be terribly fond of Cora, and at first, when Cora said, Honey, I've got

to leave this town or Hugo (the hotel queen) will bring up Bobo
(her brother who was a lawyer in Alexandria and who had played
some very unbrotherly legal trick on her when a certain inheritance was settled) and there will be hell to pay, he will freeze up
my income – then, at this point, Billy assumed that they would go
separate ways. But at the last moment Billy discovered that he
didn't want to go back to a stag existence. He discovered that
solitary cruising had been lonely, that there were spiritual
comforts as well as material advantages in their double arrange-
ment. No matter how bad luck was, there was no longer such a
thing as going home by himself to the horrors of a second- or
third-class hotel bedroom. Then there *were* the material
advantages, the fact they actually did better operating together,
and the fact that it was more economical. Billy had to be
somewhat mean about money since he was living on savings that
he wanted to stretch as far as he could, and Cora more than
carried her own weight in the expense department. She was only
too eager to pick up a check and Billy was all too willing to let her
do it. She spoke of her income but she was vague about what it
was or came from. Sometimes looking into her handbag she had a
fleeting expression of worry that made Billy wonder uncomfort-
ably if her finances, like his, might not be continually dwindling
toward an eventual point of eclipse. But neither of them had a
provident nature or dared to stop and consider much of the
future.

Billy was a light traveller, all he carried with him was a three-
suiter, a single piece of hand luggage and his portable typewriter.
When difficulties developed at a hotel, he could clear out in five
minutes or less. He rubbed his chin for a minute, then he said,
Cora, how about me going with you?

They shared a compartment in the Sunshine Special to Florida.
Why to Florida? One of Cora's very few pretensions was a little
command of French; she was fond of using little French phrases
which she pronounced badly. Honey, she said, I have a little *pied-
à-terre* in Florida.

Pied-à-terre was one of those little French phrases that she was
proud of using, and she kept talking about it, her little *pied-à-terre*
in the Sunshine State.

Whereabouts is it, Billy asked her.

No place fashionable, she told him, but just you wait and see
and you might be surprised and like it.

That night in the shared compartment of the Pullman was the first time they had sex together. It happened casually, it was not important and it was not very satisfactory, perhaps because they were each too anxious to please the other, each too afraid the other would be disappointed. Sex has to be slightly selfish to have real excitement. Start worrying about the other party's reactions and the big charge just isn't there, and you've got to do it a number of times together before it becomes natural enough to be a completely satisfactory thing. The first time between strangers can be like a blaze of light, but when it happens between people who know each other well and have an established affection, it's likely to be selfconscious and even a little embarrassing, most of all afterwards.

Afterwards they talked about it with a slight sense of strain. They felt they had gotten that sort of thing squared away and would not have to think about it between them again. But perhaps, in a way, it did add a little something to the intimacy of their living together; at least it had, as they put it, squared things away a bit. And they talked about it shyly, each one trying too hard to flatter the other.

Gee, honey, said Cora, you're a wonderful lay, you've got wonderful skin, smooth as a baby's, gee, it sure was wonderful, honey, I enjoyed it so much, I wish you had. But I know you didn't like it and it was selfish of me to start it with you.

You didn't like it, he said.

I swear I *loved* it, she said, but I knew that *you* didn't like it, so we won't do it again.

He told Cora that she was a wonderful lay and that he had loved it every bit as much as she did and maybe more but he agreed they'd better not do it again.

Friends can't be lovers, he said.

No, they can't, she agreed with a note of sadness.

Then jealousy enters in.

Yes, they get jealous and bitchy . . .

They never did it again, at least not that completely, not any time during that year and two months since they started living together. Of course, there were some very drunk, *blind* drunk nights when they weren't quite sure what happened between them after they fell into bed, but you could be pretty certain it wasn't a sixty-six in that condition. Sixty-six was Cora's own slightly inexact term for a normal lay, that is, a lay that occurred in the ordinary position.

What happened? Billy would ask when she'd had a party.

Oh, it was wonderful, she would exclaim, a sixty-six!

Good Jesus, drunk as he was?

Oh, I sobered him up, she'd laugh.

And what did you do, Billy? Take the sheets? Ha ha, you'll have to leave this town with a board nailed over your ass!

Sometimes they had a serious conversation, though most of the time they tried to keep the talk on a frivolous plane. It troubled Cora to talk about serious matters, probably because matters were too serious to be talked about with comfort. And for the first month or so neither of them knew that the other one actually had a mind that you could talk to. Gradually they discovered about each other the other things, and although it was always their mutual pursuit, endless and indefatigable, of 'the lyric quarry' that was the mainstay of their relationship, at least upon its surface, the other things, the timid and tender values that can exist between people, began to come shyly out and they had a respect for each other, not merely to like and enjoy, as neither had ever respected another person.

It was a rare sort of moral anarchy, doubtless, that held them together, a really fearful shared hatred of everything that was restrictive and which they felt to be false in the society they lived in and against the grain of which they continually operated. They did not dislike what they called 'squares'. They loathed and despised them, and for the best of reasons. Their existence was a never-ending contest with the squares of the world, the squares who have such a virulent rage at everything not in their book. Getting around the squares, evading, defying the phony rules of convention, that was maybe responsible for half their pleasure in their outlaw existence. They were a pair of kids playing cops and robbers; except for that element, the thrill of something lawless, they probably would have gotten bored with cruising. Maybe not, maybe so. Who can tell? But hotel clerks and house dicks and people in adjoining hotel bedrooms, the spectre of Cora's family in Alexandria, Louisiana, the spectre of Billy's family in Montgomery, Alabama, the various people involved in the niggardly control of funds, almost everybody that you passed when you were drunk and hilariously gay on the street, especially all those bull-like middle-aged couples that stood off sharply and glared at you as you swept through a hotel lobby with your blushing trade – all, all, all of those were natural enemies to them, as well as the one great terrible, worst of all enemies, which is the fork-tailed, cloven-hoofed, pitchfork-bearing devil of Time!

Time, of course, was the greatest enemy of all, and they knew that each day and each night was cutting down a little on the distance between the two of them running together and that demon pursuer. And knowing it, knowing that nightmarish fact, gave a wild sort of sweetness of despair to their two-ring circus.

And then, of course, there was also the fact that Billy was, or had been at one time, a sort of artist *manqué* and still had a touch of homesickness for what that was.

Sometime, said Cora, you're going to get off the party.

Why should I get off the party?

Because you're a serious person. You are fundamentally a serious sort of person.

I'm not a serious person any more than you are. I'm a goddam remittance man and you know it.

No, I don't know it, said Cora. Remittance men get letters enclosing cheques, but you don't even get letters.

Billy rubbed his chin.

Then how do you think I live?

Ha ha, she said.

What does 'Ha, Ha' mean?

It means I know that I know!

Balls, said Billy, you know no more about me than I do about you.

I know, said Cora, that you used to write for a living, and that for two years you haven't been writing but you're still living on the money you made as a writer, and sooner or later, you're going to get off the party and go back to working again and being a serious person. What do you imagine I think of that portable typewriter you drag around with you everywhere we go, and that big fat portfolio full of papers you tote underneath your shirts in your three-suiter? I wasn't born yesterday or the day before yesterday, baby, and I know that you're going to get off the party some day and leave me on it.

If I get off the party, we'll get off it together, said Billy.

And me do *what*? she'd ask him, realistically.

And he would not be able to answer that question. For she knew and he knew, both of them knew it together, that they would remain together only so long as they stayed on the party, and not any longer than that. And in his heart he knew, much as he might deny it, that it would be pretty much as Cora predicted in her Cassandra moods. One of those days or nights it was bound to happen. He would get off the party, yes, he would certainly be the one of them to get off it, because there was really nothing for Cora to do but stay on it. Of course, if she broke down, that would take her off it. Usually or almost always it's only a breakdown that takes you off a party. A party is like a fast-moving train – you can't jump off it, it thunders past the stations you might get off at, very few people have the courage to leap from a thing that is moving that fast, they have to stay with it no matter where it takes them. It only stops when it crashes, the ticker wears out, a blood vessel bursts, the liver or kidneys quit working. But Cora was tough. Her system had absorbed a lot of punishment, but from present appearances it was going to absorb a lot more. She was too tough to crack up any time soon, but she was not tough enough to make the clean break, the daring jump off, that Billy knew, or felt that he knew, that he was still able to make when he was ready to make it. Cora was five or maybe even ten years older than Billy. She rarely looked it, but she was that much older and time is one of the biggest differences between two people.

I've got news for you, baby, and you had better believe it.

What news?

This news, Cora would say. You're going to get off the party and leave me on it!

Well, it was probably true, as true as anything is, and what a pity it was that Cora was such a grand person. If she had not been such a nice person, so nice that at first you thought it must be phony and only gradually came to see it was real, it wouldn't matter so much. For usually queens fall out like a couple of thieves quarrelling over the split of the loot. Billy remembered the one in Baton Rouge who was so annoyed when he confiscated a piece she had a lech for that she made of Billy an effigy of candle wax and stuck pins in it with dreadful imprecations, kept the candle-wax effigy on her mantel and performed black rites before it. But Cora was not like that. She didn't have a jealous bone in her body. She took as much pleasure in Billy's luck as her own. Sometimes he suspected she was more interested in Billy having good luck than having it herself.

Sometimes Billy would wonder. Why do we do it?

We're lonely people, she said, I guess it's as simple as that . . .

But nothing is ever quite so simple as it appears when you are comfortably loaded.

Take this occasion, for instance.

Billy and Cora are travelling by motor. The automobile is a joint possession which they acquired from a used-car dealer in Galveston. It is a '47 Buick convertible with a brilliant new scarlet paint-job. Cora and Billy are outfitted with corresponding brilliance; she has on a pair of black and white checked slacks, a cowboy shirt with a bucking broncho over one large breast and a roped steer over the other, and she has on harlequin sun-glasses with false diamonds encrusting the rims. Her freshly peroxided hair is bound girlishly on top of her head with a diaphanous scarf of magenta chiffon; she has on her diamond ear-clips and her multiple slave-bracelets, three of them real gold and two of them only gold-plated, and hundreds of little tinkling gold attachments, such as tiny footballs, liberty bells, hearts, mandolins, choo-choos, sleds, tennis rackets, and so forth. Billy thinks she has overdone it a little. It must be admitted, however, that she is a noticeable person, especially at the wheel of this glittering scarlet Roadmaster. They have swept down the Camino Real, the Old Spanish Trail, from El Paso eastward instead of westward, having decided at the last moment to resist the allure of Southern California on the other side of the Rockies and the desert, since it appears that the Buick has a little tendency to overheat and Cora notices that the oil pressure is not what it should be. So they have turned eastward instead of westward, with a little side trip to Corpus Christi to investigate the fact or fancy of those legendary seven connecting glory-holes in a certain tea-room there. It turned out to be fancy or could not be located. Says Cora: You queens know places but never know where places are!

A blowout going into New Orleans. That's to be expected, said Cora, they never give you good rubber. The spare is no good either. Two new tyres had to be bought in New Orleans and Cora paid for them by hocking some of her baubles. There was some money left over and she buys Billy a pair of cowboy boots. They are still on the Wild West kick. Billy also presents a colourful appearance in a pair of blue jeans that fit as if they had been painted on him, the fancily embossed cowboy boots and a sport shirt that is covered with leaping dolphins, Ha ha! They have never had so much fun in their life together, the coloured lights are going like pinwheels on the Fourth of July, everything is big and very bright celebration. The Buick appears to be a fairly solid investment, once it has good rubber on it and they get those automatic devices to working again . . .

It is a mechanical age that we live in, they keep saying.

They did Mobile, Pensacola, West Palm Beach and Miami in one continual happy breeze! The scoreboard is brilliant! Fifteen lays, all hitching rides on the highway, since they got the convertible. It's all we ever needed to hit the jackpot, Billy exults . . .

Then comes the badman into the picture!

They are on the Florida keys, just about midway between the objective, Key West, and the tip of the peninsula. Nothing is visible about them but sky and mangrove swamp. Then all of a sudden that used-car dealer in Galveston pulls the grinning joker out of his sleeve. Under the hood of the car comes a loud metallic noise as if steel blades are scraping. The fancy heap will not take the gas. It staggers gradually to a stop, and trying to start it again succeeds only in running the battery down. Moreover, the automatic top has ceased to function; it is the meridian of a day in early spring which is as hot as midsummer on the Florida keys . . .

Cora would prefer to make light of the situation, if Billy would let her do so. The compartment of the dashboard is filled with roadmaps, a flashlight and a thermos of dry martinis. The car has barely uttered its expiring rattle and gasp when Cora's intensely ornamented arm reaches out for this unfailing simplification of the human dilemma. For the first time in their life together, Billy interferes with her drinking, and out of pure meanness. He grabs her wrist and restrains her. He is suddenly conscious of how disgusted he is with what he calls her Oriental attitude toward life. The purchase of this hoax was her idea. Two-thirds of the investment was also her money. Moreover she had professed to be a pretty good judge of motors, Billy himself had frankly confessed that he couldn't tell a spark plug from a carburettor. So it was Cora who had examined and appraised the possible buys on the used-car lots of Galveston and come upon this 'bargain'! She had looked under the hoods and shimmied fatly under the chassis of dozens of cars before she arrived at this remarkably misguided choice. The car had been suspiciously cheap for a '47 Roadmaster with such a brilliantly smart appearance, but Cora said it was just as sound as the American dollar! She put a thousand dollars into the deal and Billy put in five hundred which had come in from the resale to pocket editions of a lurid potboiler he had written under a pseudonym a number of years ago when he was still an active member of the literary profession.

Now Cora was reaching into the dashboard compartment for a thermos of martinis because the car whose purchase was her responsibility had collapsed in the middle of nowhere . . .

Billy seizes her wrist and twists it.

Let go of that goddam thermos, you're not gonna get drunk!

She struggles with him a little, but soon she gives up and suddenly goes feminine and starts to cry.

After that a good while passes in which they sit side by side in silence in the leather-lined crematorium of the convertible.

A humming sound begins to be heard in the distance. Perhaps it's a motorboat on the other side of the mangroves, perhaps something on the highway . . .

Cora begins to jingle and jangle as she twists her ornamented person this way and that way with nervous henlike motions of the head and shoulder and torso, peering about on both sides and half-rising and flopping awkwardly back down again, and finally grunting eagerly and piling out of the car, losing her balance, sprawling into a ditch, ha ha, scrambling up again, taking the middle of the road and making frantic circles with her arm as a motorcycle approaches. If the cyclist had desired to pass them it would have been hardly possible. Later Billy will remind her that it was *she* who stopped it. But right now Billy is enchanted, not merely at the prospect of a rescue but much more by the looks of the potential instrument of rescue. The motorcyclist is surely something dispatched from a sympathetic region back of the sun. He has one of those blond and block-shaped heads set upon a throat which is as broad as the head itself and has the smooth and supple muscularity of the male organ in its early stage of tumescence. This bare throat and the blond head above it have never been in a country where the sun is distant. The hands are enormous square knobs to the golden doors of Paradise. And the legs that straddle the quiescent fury of the cycle (called Indian) could not have been better designed by the appreciative eyes and fingers of Michelangelo or Phidias or Rodin. It is in the direct and pure line of those who have witnessed and testified in stone what they have seen of a simple physical glory in mankind! The eyes are behind sun-glasses. Cora is a good judge of eyes but she has to see them to judge them. Sometimes she will say to a young man wearing sun-glasses, Will you kindly uncover the windows of your soul? She considers herself to be a better judge of good and bad trade than is Billy whose record contains a number of memorable errors. Later Cora will remember that from the moment she saw this youth on the motorcycle something whispered *Watch Out* in her ear. Honey, she will say, later, he had more Stop signs on him than you meet when you've got five minutes to get to the station! Perhaps this will be an exaggerated statement, but it is true that Cora had misgivings in exact proportion to Billy's undisguised enchantment.

As for right now, the kid seems fairly obliging. He swings his great legs off the cycle which he rests upon a metal support. He hardly says anything. He throws back the hood of the car and crouches into it for a couple of minutes, hardly more than that, then the expressionless blond cube comes back into view and announces without inflection, Bearings gone out.

What does that mean, asks Cora.

That means you have been screwed, he says.

What can we do about it?

Not a goddam thing. You better junk it.

What did he say, inquires Billy.

He said, Cora tells him, that the bearings have gone out.

What are bearings?

The cyclist utters a short barking laugh. He is back astraddle the frankly shaped leather seat of his Indian, but Cora has once more descended from the Buick and she has resorted to the type of flirtation that even most queens would think common. She has fastened her bejewelled right hand over the elevated and narrow front section of the saddle which the boy sits astride. There is not only proximity but contact between their two parties, and all at once the boy's blond look is both contemptuous and attentive, and his attitude toward their situation has undergone a drastic alteration. He is now engaged in it again.

There's a garage on Boca Raton, he tells them. I'll see if they got a tow truck. I think they got one.

Off he roars down the Keys!

One hour and forty-five minutes later the abdicated Road-master is towed into a garage on Boca Raton, and Cora and Billy plus their new-found acquaintance are checking, all three, into a tourist cabin at a camp called The Idle-wild, which is across the highway from the garage.

Cora has thought to remove her thermos of martinis from the

dashboard compartment, and this time Billy has not offered any objection. Billy is restored to good spirits. Cora still feels guilty, profoundly and abjectly guilty, about the purchase of the glittering fraud, but she is putting up a good front. She knows, however, that Billy will never quite forgive and forget and she does not understand why she made that silly profession of knowing so much about motors. It was, of course, to impress her beloved companion. He knows so much more than she about so many things, she has to pretend, now and then, to know *something* about *something*, even when she knows in her heart that she is a comprehensive and unabridged dictionary of human ignorance on nearly all things of importance. She sighs in her heart because she's become a pretender, and once you have pretended, is it ever possible to stop pretending?

Pretending to be a competent judge of a motor has placed her in the sad and embarrassing position of having cheated Billy out of five hundred dollars. How can she make it up to him?

A whisper in the heart of Cora: *I love him!*

Whom does she love?

There are three persons in the cabin, herself, Billy and the young man from the highway.

Cora despises herself and she has never been much attracted to men of an altogether physical type.

So there is the dreadful answer! She is in love with Billy.

I am in love with Billy, she whispers to herself.

That acknowledgment seems to call for a drink.

She gets up and pours herself another martini. Unfortunately someone, probably Cora herself, has forgotten to screw the cap back on the thermos bottle and the drinks are now tepid. No drink is better than an ice-cold martini, but no drink is worse than a martini getting warm. However, be that as it may, the discovery just made, the one about loving Billy, well, after *that* one the temperature of a drink is not so important so long as the stuff is still liquor!

She says to herself: I have admitted a fact! Well, the only thing to do with a fact is admit it, but once admitted, you don't have to keep harping on it.

Never again, so long as she stays on the party with her companion, will she put into words her feelings for him, not even in the privacy of her heart . . .

Le coeur a ses raisons que la raison ne connaît pas!

That is one of those little French sayings that Cora is proud of knowing and often repeats to herself as well as to others.

Sometimes she will translate it, to those who don't know the French language, as follows:

The heart knows the scoop when the brain is ignorant of it!

Ha ha!

Well, now she is back in the cabin after a mental excursion that must have lasted at least half an hour.

Things have progressed thus far.

Billy has stripped down to his shorts and he has persuaded the square-headed blond to do likewise.

Cora herself discovers that she has made concessions to the unseasonable warmth of the little frame building.

All she is wearing is her panties and bra.

She looks across without real interest at the square-headed stranger. Yes. A magnificent torso, as meaningless, now, to Cora, as a jigsaw puzzle which put together exhibits a cow munching grass in a typical one-tree pasture . . .

Excuse me, people, she remarks to Billy. I just remembered I promised to make a long-distance call to Atlanta.

A long-distance call to Atlanta is a code message between herself and Billy.

What it means is this: The field is yours to conquer!

Cora goes out, having thrown on a jacket and pulled on her checkerboard slacks.

Where does Cora go? Not far, not far at all.

She is leaning against a palm tree not more than five yards distant from the cabin. She is smoking a cigarette in a shadow.

Inside the cabin the field is Billy's to conquer.

Billy says to the cyclist: How do you like me?

Huh . . .

(That is the dubious answer to his question!)

Billy gives him a drink, another one, thinking that this may evoke a less equivocal type of response.

How do you like me, now?

You want to know how I like you?

Yes!

I like you the way that a cattleman loves a sheepherder!

I am not acquainted, says Billy, with the likes and dislikes of men who deal in cattle.

Well, says the square-headed blond, if you keep messing around I'm going to give you a demonstration of it!

A minute is a microscope view of eternity.

It is less than a minute before Cora hears a loud sound.

She knew what it was before she even heard it, and almost before she heard it, that thud of a body not falling but thrown to a floor, she is back at the door of the cabin and pushing it open and returning inside.

Hello! is what she says with apparent good humour.

She does not seem to notice Billy's position and bloody mouth on the floor . . .

Well, she says, I got my call through to Atlanta!

While she is saying this, she is getting out of her jacket and checkerboard slacks, and she is not stopping there.

Instant diversion is the doctor's order.

She is stripped bare in ten seconds, and on the bed.

Billy has gotten outside and she is enduring the most undesired embrace that she can remember in all her long history of desired and undesired and sometimes only patiently borne embraces . . .

Why do we do it?

We're lonely people. I guess it's simple as that . . .

But nothing is ever that simple! Don't you know it?

And so the story continues where it didn't leave off . . .

Trade ceased to have much distinction. One piece was fundamentally the same as another, and the nights were like waves rolling in and breaking and retreating again and leaving you washed up on the wet sands of morning.

Something continual and something changeless.

The sweetness of their living together persisted.

We're friends! said Cora.

She meant a lot more than that, but Billy is satisfied with this spoken definition, and there's no other that can safely be framed in language.

Sometimes they look about them, privately and together, and what they see is something like what you see through a powerful telescope trained upon the moon, flatly illuminated craters and treeless plains and a vacancy of light — much light, but an emptiness in it.

Calcium is the element of this world.

Each has held some private notion of death. Billy thinks his death is going to be violent. Cora thinks hers will be ungraciously slow. Something will surrender by painful inches . . .

Meanwhile they are together.

To Cora that's the one important thing left.

Cities!

You queens know places, but never know where places are!

No Mayor has ever handed them a gold key, nor have they entered under a silken banner of welcome, but they have gone to them all in the northern half of the western hemisphere, this side of the Arctic Circle! Ha ha, just about all . . .

Many cities!

Sometimes they wake up early to hear the awakening tumult of a city and to reflect upon it.

They're two on a party which has made a departure and a rather wide one.

Into brutality? No. It's not that simple.

Into vice? No. It isn't nearly that simple.

Into what, then?

Into something unlawful? Yes, of course!

But in the night, hands clasping and no questions asked.

In the morning, a sense of being together no matter what comes, and the knowledge of not having struck nor lied nor stolen.

A female lush and a fairy who travel together, who are two on a party, and the rush continues.

They wake up early, sometimes, and hear the city coming awake, the increase of traffic, the murmurous shuffle of crowds on their way to their work, the ordinary resumption of daytime life in a city, and they reflect upon it a little from their, shall we say, bird's-eye situation.

There's the radio, and the newspaper and there is TV, which Billy says means 'Tired Vaudeville', and everything that is known is known very fully and very fully stated.

But after all, when you reflect upon it at the only time that is suitable for reflection, what can you do but turn your other cheek to the pillow?

Two queens sleeping together with sometimes a stranger between them . . .

One morning a phone will ring.

Cora will answer, being the lighter sleeper and the quicker to rise.

Bad news!

Clapping a hand over the shrill mouthpiece, instinctive gesture of secrecy, she will cry to Billy.

Billy, Billy, wake up! They've raided the Flamingo! The heat is on! Get packed!

Almost gaily this message is delivered and the packing performed, for it's fun to fly away from a threat of danger.

(Most dreams are about it, one form of it or another, in which man remembers the distant mother with wings . . .)

Off they go, from Miami to Jacksonville, from Jacksonville to Savannah or Norfolk, all winter shuttling about the Dixie circuit, in spring going back to Manhattan, two birds flying together against the wind, nothing real but the party, and even that sort of dreamy.

In the morning, always Cora's voice addressing room service, huskily, softly, not to disturb his sleep before the coffee arrives, and then saying gently, Billy, Billy, your coffee . . .

Cup and teaspoon rattling like castanets as she hands it to him, often spilling a little on the bedclothes and saying, Oh, honey, excuse me, ha ha!

THE YELLOW BIRD

Alma was the daughter of a Protestant minister named Increase Tutwiler, the last of a string of Increase Tutwilers who had occupied pulpits since the Reformation came to England. The first American progenitor had settled in Salem, and around him and his wife, Goody Tutwiler, née Woodson, had revolved one of the most sensational of the Salem witch-trials. Goody Tutwiler was cried out against by the Circle Girls, a group of hysterical young ladies of Salem who were thrown into fits whenever a witch came near them. They claimed Goody Tutwiler afflicted them with pins and needles and made them sign their names in the devil's book, quite against their wishes. Also one of them declared that Goody Tutwiler had appeared to them with a yellow bird which she called by the name of Bobo and which served as interlocutor between herself and the devil to whom she was sworn. The Reverend Tutwiler was so impressed by these accusations, as well as by the fits of the Circle Girls when his wife entered their presence in court, that he himself finally cried out against her and testified that the yellow bird named Bobo had flown into his church one Sabbath and, visible only to himself, had perched on his pulpit and whispered indecent things to him about several younger women in the congregation. Goody Tutwiler was accordingly condemned and hanged, but this was by no means the last of the yellow bird named Bobo. It had manifested itself in one form or another, and its continual nagging had left the Puritan spirit fiercely aglow, from Salem to Hobbs, Arkansas, where the Increase Tutwiler of this story was preaching.

Increase Tutwiler was a long-winded preacher. His wife sat in the front pew of the church with a palm-leaf fan which she would agitate violently when her husband had preached too long for anybody's endurance. But it was not always easy to catch his attention, and Alma, the daughter, would finally have to break into the offertory hymn in order to turn him off. Alma played the organ, the primitive kind of organ that had to be supplied with air by an old Negro operating a pump in a stifling cubicle behind the wall. On one occasion the old Negro had fallen asleep, and no amount of discreet rapping availed to wake him up. The minister's wife had plucked nervously at the strings of her palm-leaf fan till it began to fall to pieces, but without the organ to stop him, Increase Tutwiler ranted on and on, exceeding the two-hour mark. It was by no means a cool summer day, and the interior of the church was yellow oak, a material that made you feel as if you were sitting in the middle of a fried egg.

At last Alma despaired of reviving the Negro and got to her feet. 'Papa,' she said. But the old man didn't look at her. 'Papa,' she repeated, but he went right on. The whole congregation was whispering and murmuring. One stout old lady seemed to have collapsed, because two people were fanning her from either side and holding a small bottle to her nostrils. Alma and her mother exchanged desperate glances. The mother half got out of her seat. Alma gave her a signal to remain seated. She picked up the hymn-book and brought it down with such terrible force on the bench that dust and fibre spurted in all directions. The minister stopped short. He turned a dazed look in Alma's direction, 'Papa,' she said, 'it's fifteen minutes after twelve and Henry's asleep and these folks have got to get to dinner, so for the love of God, quit preaching.'

Now Alma had the reputation of being a very quiet and shy girl, so this speech was nothing short of sensational. The news of it spread throughout the Delta, for Mr Tutwiler's sermons had achieved a sort of unhappy fame for many miles about. Perhaps Alma was somewhat pleased and impressed by this little celebration that she was accordingly given on people's tongues the next few months, for she was never quite the same shy girl afterwards. She had not very much fun out of being a minister's daughter. The boys had steered clear of the rectory, because when they got around there they were exposed to Mr Tutwiler's inquisitions. A boy and Alma would have no chance to talk in the Tutwiler porch or parlour while the old man was around. He was obsessed with the idea that Alma might get to smoking, which he thought was the initial and, once taken, irretrievable step towards perdition. 'If Alma gets to smoking,' he told his wife, 'I'm going to denounce her from the pulpit and put her out of the house.' Every time he said this Alma's mother would scream and go into a faint, as she knew that every girl who is driven out of her father's house goes right into a good-time house. She was unable to conceive of anything in between.

Now Alma was pushing thirty and still unmarried, but about six months after the episode in the church, things really starting popping around the minister's house. Alma had gotten to smoking in the attic, and her mother knew about it. Mrs Tutwiler's hair had been turning slowly grey for a number of years, but after Alma took to smoking in the attic, it turned snow-white almost overnight. Mrs Tutwiler concealed the terrible knowledge that Alma was smoking in the attic from her husband, and she didn't even dare raise her voice to Alma about it because the old man might hear. All she could do was stuff the attic door around with newspapers. Alma *would* smoke; she claimed it had gotten a hold of her and she couldn't stop it now. At first she only smoked twice a day, but she began to smoke more as the habit grew on her. Several times the old man had said he smelled smoke in the house, but so far he hadn't dreamed that his daughter would dare take up smoking. But his wife knew he would soon find out about it, and Alma knew he would too. The question was whether Alma cared. Once she came downstairs with a cigarette in her mouth, smoking it, and her mother barely snatched it out of her mouth before the old man saw her. Mrs Tutwiler went into a faint, but Alma paid no attention to her, just went on out of the house, lit another cigarette, and walked down the street to the drugstore.

It was unavoidable that sooner or later people who had seen Alma smoking outside the house, which she now began to do pretty regularly, would carry the news back to the preacher. There were plenty of old women who were ready and able to do it. They had seen her smoking in the White Star drugstore while she was having her afternoon Coke, puffing on the cigarette between sips of the Coke and carrying on a conversation with the soda-jerk, just like anyone from that set of notorious high school girls that the whole town had been talking about for several generations. So one day the minister came into his wife's bedroom and said to her, 'I have been told that Alma has taken to smoking.'

His manner was deceptively calm. The wife sensed that this was not an occasion for her to go into a faint, so she didn't. She had to keep her wits about her this time – that is, if she had any left after all she had been through with Alma's smoking.

'Well,' she said, 'I don't know what to do about it. It's true.'

'You know what I've always said,' her husband replied. 'If Alma gets to smoking, out she goes.'

'Do you want her to go into a good-time house?' inquired Mrs Tutwiler.

'If that's where she's going, she can go,' said the preacher, 'but not until I've given her something that she'll always remember.'

He was waiting for Alma when she came in from her afternoon smoke and Coke at the White Star drugstore. Soon as she walked into the door he gave her a good, hard slap with the palm of his hand on her mouth, so that her front teeth bit into her lip and it started bleeding. Alma didn't blink an eye, she just drew back her right arm and returned the slap with good measure. She had bought a bottle of something at the drugstore, and while her father stood there, stupefied, watching her, she went upstairs with the mysterious bottle in brown wrapping paper. And when she came back down they saw that she had peroxided her hair and put on lipstick. Alma's mother screamed and went into one of her faints, because it was evident to her that Alma was going right over to one of the good-time houses on Front Street. But all the iron had gone out of the minister's character then. He clung to Alma's arm. He begged and pleaded with her not to go there. Alma lit up a cigarette right there in front of him and said, 'Listen here, I'm going to do as I please around here from now on, and I don't want any more interference from you!'

Before this conversation was finished the mother came out of her faint. It was the worst faint she had ever gone into, particularly since nobody had bothered to pick her up off the floor. 'Alma,' she said weakly, 'Alma!' Then she said her husband's name several times, but neither of them paid any attention to her, so she got up without any assistance and began to take a part in the conversation. 'Alma,' she said, 'you can't go out of this house until that hair of yours grows in dark again.'

'That's what you think,' said Alma.

She put the cigarette back in her mouth and went out the screen door, puffing and drawing on it and breathing smoke out of her nostrils all the way down the front walk and down to the White Star drugstore, where she had another Coke and resumed her conversation with the boy at the soda-counter. His name was Stuff – that was what people called him – and it was he who had suggested to Alma that she would look good as a blonde. He was ten years younger than Alma but he had more girls than pimples.

It was astonishing the way Alma came up fast on the outside of Stuff's affections. With the new blonde hair you could hardly call her a dark horse, but she was certainly running away with the field. In two weeks' time after the peroxide she was going steady with Stuff; for Alma was smart enough to know there were plenty of good times to be had outside the good-time houses on Front Street, and Stuff knew that, too. Stuff was not to be in sole possession of her heart. There were other contenders, and Alma could choose among them. She started going out nights as rapidly as she had taken up smoking. She stole the keys to her father's Ford sedan and drove to such near-by towns as Lakewater, Sunset, and Lyons. She picked up men on the highway and went out 'juking' with them, making the rounds of the highway drinking places; never got home till three or four in the morning. It was impossible to see how one human constitution could stand up under the strain of so much running around to night places, but Alma had all the vigour that comes from generations of firm believers. It could have gone into anything and made a sensation. Well, that's how it was. There was no stopping her once she got started.

The home situation was indescribably bad. It was generally stated that Alma's mother had suffered a collapse and that her father was spending all his time praying, and there was some degree of truth in both reports. Very little sympathy for Alma came from the older residents of the community. Certain little perfunctory steps were taken to curb the girl's behaviour. The father got the car-key out of her pocket one night when she came in drunk and fell asleep on the sofa, but Alma had already had some duplicates of it made. He locked the garage one night. Alma climbed through the window and drove the car straight through the closed door.

'She's lost her mind,' said the mother. 'It's that hair-bleaching that's done it. It went right through her scalp and now it's affecting her brain.'

They sat up all that night waiting for her, but she didn't come home. She had run the course in that town, and the next thing they heard from Alma was a card from New Orleans. She had got all the way down there. 'Don't sit up,' she wrote. 'I'm gone for good. I'm never coming back.'

*

Six years later Alma was a character in the old French Quarter of New Orleans. She hung out mostly on 'Monkey-Wrench Corner' and picked up men around there. It was certainly not necessary to go into a good-time house to have a good time in the Quarter, and it hadn't taken her long to find that out. It might have seemed to some people that Alma was living a wasteful and profligate existence, but if the penalty for it was death, well, she was a long time dying. In fact she seemed to prosper on her new life. It apparently did not have a dissipating effect on her. She took pretty good care of herself so that it wouldn't, eating well and drinking just enough to be happy. Her face had a bright and innocent look in the mornings, and even when she was alone in her room it sometimes seemed as if she weren't alone — as if someone were with her, a disembodied someone, perhaps a remote ancestor of liberal tendencies who had been displeased by the channel his blood had taken till Alma kicked over the traces and jumped right back to the plumed-hat cavaliers.

Of course, her parents never came near her again, but once they dispatched as emissary a young married woman they trusted.

The woman called on Alma in her miserable little furnished room — or crib, as it actually was — on the shabbiest block of Bourbon Street in the Quarter.

'How do you live?' asked the woman.

'What?' said Alma, innocently.

'I mean how do you get along?'

'Oh,' said Alma, 'people give me things.'

'You mean you accept gifts from them?'

'Yes, on a give-and-take basis,' Alma told her.

The woman looked around her. The bed was unmade and looked as if it had been that way for weeks. The two-burner stove was loaded with unwashed pots in some of which grew a pale fungus. Tickets from pawnshops were stuck round the edge of the mirror along with many, many photographs of young men, some splitting their faces with enormous grins while others stared softly into space.

'These photographs,' said the woman, 'are these — are these your friends?'

'Yes,' said Alma, with a happy smile. 'Friends and acquaintances, strangers that pass in the night!'

'Well, I'm not going to mention this to your father!'

'Oh, go on and tell the old stick-in-the-mud,' said Alma. She lit a cigarette and blew the smoke at her caller.

The woman looked around once more and noticed that the doors of the big armoire hung open on white summer dresses that were covered with grass stains.

'You go on picnics?' she asked.

'Yes, but not church ones,' said Alma.

The woman tried to think of something more to ask but she was not gifted with an agile mind, and Alma's attitude was not encouraging.

'Well,' she said finally, 'I had better be going.'

'Hurry back,' said Alma, without getting up or looking in the woman's direction.

Shortly thereafter Alma discovered that she was becoming a mother.

She bore a child, a male one, and not knowing who was the father, she named it John after the lover that she had liked best, a man now dead. The son was perfect, very blond and glowing, a lusty infant.

Now from this point on the story takes a strange turn that may be highly disagreeable to some readers, if any still hoped it was going to avoid the fantastic.

This child of Alma's would have been hanged in Salem. If the Circle Girls had not cried out against Alma (which they certainly would have done), they would have gone into fifty screaming fits over Alma's boy.

He was thoroughly bewitched. At half-past six every morning he crawled out of the house and late in the evening he returned with fists full of gold and jewels that smelled of the sea.

Alma grew very rich indeed. She and the child went North. The child grew in a perfectly normal way to youth and to young manhood, and then he no longer crawled out and brought back riches. In fact that old habit seemed to have slipped his mind somehow, and no mention was ever made of it. Though he and his mother did not pay much attention to each other, there was a great and silent respect between them while each went about his business.

When Alma's time came to die, she lay on the bed and wished her son would come home, for lately the son had gone on a long sea-voyage for unexplained reasons. And while she was waiting, while she lay there dying, the bed began to rock like a ship on the ocean, and all at once not John the Second, but John the First appeared, like Neptune out of the ocean. He bore a cornucopia that was dripping with seaweed and his bare chest and legs had acquired a greenish patina such as a bronze statue comes to be covered with. Over the bed he emptied his horn of plenty which had been stuffed with treasures from wrecked Spanish galleons: rubies, emeralds, diamonds, rings, and necklaces of rare gold, and great loops of pearls with the slime of the sea clinging to them.

'Some people,' he said, 'don't even die empty-handed.'

And off he went, and Alma went off with him.

The fortune was left to The Home For Reckless Spenders. And in due time the son, the sailor, came home, and a monument was put up. It was a curious thing, this monument. It showed three figures of indeterminate gender astride a leaping dolphin. One bore a crucifix, one a cornucopia, and one a Grecian lyre. On the side of the plunging fish, the arrogant dolphin, was a name inscribed, the odd name of Bobo, which was the name of the small yellow bird that the devil and Goody Tutwiler had used as a go-between in their machinations.

THE FIELD OF BLUE CHILDREN

That final spring at the state university a restlessness came over Myra which she could not understand. It was not merely the restlessness of superabundant youth. There was something a little neurotic about it. Nothing that she did seemed quite satisfying or complete. Even when she returned from a late formal dance, where she had swung from partner to partner the whole evening through, she did not feel quite ready to tumble exhausted into bed. She felt as though there must be something still further to give the night its perfect fullness. Sometimes she had the almost panicky sensation of having lost or forgotten something very important. She would stand quite still for a moment with tightened forehead, trying to remember just what it was that had slipped from her fingers – been left behind in the rumble seat of Kirk's roommate's roadster or on the sofa in the dimly-lighted fraternity lounge between dances.

'What's the matter?' Kirk or somebody else would ask and she would laugh rather sharply.

'Nothing. I just feel like I'd forgotten something!'

The feeling persisted even when every article was accounted for. She still felt as though something were missing. When she had returned to the sorority house she went from room to room, exchanging anecdotes of the evening, laughing at them far more than their humour warranted. And when finally everyone else had gone to bed, she stayed up alone in her room and sometimes she cried bitterly without knowing why, crushing her pillow against her mouth so that no one could hear – or else she sat in pyjamas on the window seat and looked out across the small university town with all its buildings and trees and open fields a beautiful dusky blue in the spring night, the dome of the administration building like a snowy peak in the distance and the stars astonishingly large and close – she felt as though she would strangle with an emotion whose exact nature or meaning she could not understand.

When half-drunken groups of serenaders, also restless after late dances, paused beneath her house, she turned on the bed lamp and leaned above them, patting her hands together in a pantomime of delighted applause. When they left, she remained at the window, looking out with the light extinguished, and it was sad, unbearably sad, to hear their hoarse voices retreating down moonsplashed avenues of trees till they could not be heard any longer or else were drowned in the noise of a starting motor whose raucous gravel-kicking departure ebbed quickly to a soft, musical hum and was succeeded at length by the night's complete blue silence.

Still seated at the window, she waited with tight throat for the sobbing to commence. When it did, she felt better. When it did not, her vigil would sometimes continue till morning began and the restless aching had worn itself out.

That spring she took Kirk Abbott's fraternity pin. But this did not radically change her manner of living. She continued to accept dates with other men. She went out almost wherever she was asked with almost whoever asked her, and when Kirk protested she didn't try to explain the fever that made her behave in this way, she simply kissed him until he stopped talking and was in a mood to forgive her for almost anything that she might conceivably do.

From the beginning of adolescence, perhaps earlier, Myra had written a little verse. But this spring it became a regular practice. Whenever the rising well of unexplainable emotion became so full that its hurt was intolerable, she found that it helped her a little to scribble things down on paper. Single lines or couplets, sometimes whole stanzas, leapt into her mind with the instant completeness of slides flashed on the screen of a magic lantern. Their beauty startled her: sometimes it was like a moment of religious exaltation. She stood in a frozen attitude; her breath was released in a sigh. Each time she felt as though she were about to penetrate some new area of human thought. She had the sensation of standing upon the verge of a shadowy vastness which might momentarily flower into a marvellous crystal of light, like a ballroom that is dark one moment and is the next moment illuminated by the sunlike brilliance of a hundred glass chandeliers and reflecting mirrors and polished floors. At such times she would turn out the light in her bedroom and go quickly to the window. When she looked out across the purple-dark town and the snowy white dome above the quadrangle, or when she sat as in a spell, listening to the voices that floated down the quiet streets, singers of blues-songs or laughing couples in roadsters, the beauty of it no longer tormented her, she felt instead a mysterious quietness as though some disturbing question had been answered and life had accordingly become a much simpler and more pleasurable experience.

'*Words are a net to catch beauty!*'

She wrote this in the back of a notebook toward the close of a lecture on the taxing powers of Congress. It was late in April when she wrote this – and from then on it seemed that she understood what she wanted and the hurt bewilderment in her grew less acute.

In the Poetry Club to which Myra belonged there was a boy named Homer Stallcup who had been in love with her for a year or more. She could tell this by the way that he looked at her during the club sessions, which were the only occasions on which they met. Homer never looked directly at her, his eyes slid quickly across her face, but something about his expression, even about the tense pose of his body as he sat gripping his knees, made her feel his awareness of her. He avoided sitting next to her or even directly across from her – the chairs were usually arranged in a circle – and because of this she had at first thought that he must dislike her, but she had come gradually to understand that his shyness toward her had an exactly opposite meaning.

Homer was not a fraternity member. He waited on tables at a campus restaurant, fired furnaces and did chores for his room and board. Nobody in Myra's social *milieu* knew him or paid him any attention. He was rather short, stocky and dark. Myra thought him good-looking, but certainly not in any usual way. He had intense black eyes, a straight nose with flaring nostrils, full, mobile lips that sometimes jerked nervously at the corners. All of his movements were overcharged. When he rose from a chair he would nearly upset it. When he lighted a cigarette his face would twist into a terrible scowl and he would fling the burnt match away like a lighted firecracker.

He went round a great deal with a girl of his own intellectual type, a girl named Hertha something or other, who was rather widely known on the campus because of her odd behaviour. In classes she would be carried away by enthusiasm upon some subject, either literary or political, and she would talk so rapidly that nobody could understand what she was saying and she would splutter and gasp and make awkward gestures – as though she were trying to pluck some invisible object out of the air – till the room was in an uproar of amusement and the instructor had to turn his face to the blackboard to conceal his own laughter.

Hertha and this boy, Homer, made a queer picture together, she nearly a foot taller, often rushing along a foot or more in advance of him, clutching him by the coat sleeve as though afraid that he might escape from her, and every minute or so one or both of them bursting into violent laughter that could be heard for a block.

Homer wrote poetry of a difficult sort. It was uneven. Parts of it were reminiscent of Hart Crane, parts were almost as naïvely lucid as Sara Teasdale's. But there were lines and phrases which stabbed at you with their poignant imagery, their fresh observation. When he had given a reading at a symposium, Hertha would always leap out of her chair as though animated by an electric charge, her blinking, near-sighted eyes tensely sweeping the circle of superciliously smiling faces, first demanding, then begging that they concur in the extravagant praise which her moist lips babbled. Only Myra would say anything when Hertha had finished. The rest were too baffled or too indifferent or even too hostile. And Homer's face, darkly flushed, would be turned to his lap throughout the rest of the meeting. His fingers would fold down corners of the neat pages as though the poetry had been erased from them or had never been written on them, as though these pages were simply blank pieces of paper for his fingers to play with.

Myra always wanted to say something more, but her critical vocabulary was slight.

'I think that was lovely,' she would say. Or 'I liked that very much.' And Homer would not lift his eyes, his face would turn even darker, and she would bite her tongue as though in remorse for an unkind speech. She wanted to put her hands over his fingers, to make them stop crumpling the neat pages, to make them be still.

It was not till the last meeting of the year, in early June, that Myra had the courage to approach him. After that meeting she saw him standing by the water fountain at the end of the corridor. She rushed impulsively up to him and told him, all in one breath, that his was the best unpublished verse she'd ever heard, that he should submit it to some of the good literary magazines, that she thought the other members of the club were absolute fools for not understanding.

Homer stood with his fists clenched in his pockets. He did not look at her face the whole time she was speaking. When she had stopped, his excitement burst through. He tore a sheaf of manuscripts from his brief case and thrust them into her hands.

'Please read them,' he begged, 'and let me know what you think.'

They went downstairs together. On the bottom step he tripped or slid and she had to catch his arm to prevent him from falling. She was both touched and amused by this awkwardness and by his apparent delight in walking beside her. As they went out of the white stone building the late afternoon sun, yellow as lemon, met their faces in a beneficent flood. The air was filled with the ringing of five-thirty bells and the pliant voices of pigeons. A white feather from one of the stirring wings floated down and lighted upon Myra's hair. Homer lifted it off and thrust it in his hatband, and all the way home, after leaving him, Myra could feel that quick, light touch of his fingers. She wondered if he would keep the pigeon's feather; treasure it, possibly, for a long while afterward because it had once touched her person.

That night, when the sorority house was submerged in darkness, she took out the sheaf of poems and read them through without stopping. As she read she felt a rising excitement. She did not understand very much of what she was reading, but there was a cumulative effect, a growing intensity in the sequence. When she had finished she found herself trembling: trembling as when you step from warm water into chill air.

She dressed and went downstairs. She didn't know what she was planning to do. Her movements were without any conscious direction. And yet she had never moved with more certainty.

She opened the front door of the sorority house, ran down the brick-paved walk, turned to the left and continued swiftly through the moonlit streets till she had reached Homer's residence. It startled her to find herself there. There were cicadas burring in the large oaks – she had not heard them until this moment. And when she looked upward she saw a close group of stars above the western gable of the large frame house. The Seven Sisters. They were huddled together like virgin wanderers through a dark forest. She listened and there was not a voice anywhere, nothing except the chant of cicadas and the faint, faint rustling of her white skirt when she moved.

She went quickly around the side of the house to the door that she had seen Homer come out of in the mornings. She gave two short, distinct raps, then flattened herself against the brick wall. She was breathing rapidly. After waiting a while, she knocked again. Through the glass pane she could see down a flight of stairs into the basement. The door of a lamplit room was open. She saw first a moving shadow, then the boy himself, catching a heavy brown robe about his body and frowning up at the door as he mounted toward it.

As the door came open she gasped his name.

For a whole minute, it seemed, he said nothing. Then he caught her arm and pulled her inside the door.

'Myra, it's you.'

'Yes, it's me,' she laughed. 'I don't know what came over me. I've been reading your poetry, and I just felt like I had to see you at once and tell you . . .'

Her breath gave out. She leaned against the closed door. It was her eyes this time, and not his, that looked for concealment. She looked down at the bottom of his ugly brown bathrobe and she saw his bare feet beneath it, large and bony and white, and the sight of them frightened her. She remembered the intense, fleeting way of his eyes sliding over her face and body and the way he trembled that afternoon when she came up to him in the corridor, how those large feet had tripped on the bottom stair and she had been forced to catch him to keep him from falling.

'There was one thing in particular,' she went on with a struggle. 'There was something about a field of blue flowers . . .'

'Oh, yes,' he whispered. 'The blue children, you mean!'

'Yes, that was it!' Now she lifted her eyes, eagerly.

'Come down to my room, Myra.'

'I couldn't!'

'You couldn't?'

'No, of course not! If anyone caught me . . .'

'They wouldn't!'

'I'd be expelled!'

There was a slight pause.

'Wait a minute!'

He ran down three steps and turned.

'Wait for me just one minute, Myra!'

She felt her head nodding. She heard his running down the rest of the steps and into the basement room where he lived. Through the door she saw his shadow moving about the floor and the walls. He was dressing. Once he stepped into the portion of the bedroom that she could see through the half-open door and he stood in her sight naked from the waist up, and she was startled and strangely moved by that brief glimpse of his full, powerful chest and arms, strikingly etched with shadows thrown by the lamp. In that moment he acquired in her mind a physical reality which he had never had before. A very great physical reality greater than she had felt in Kirk Abbott or in any of the other young men that she had gone with on the campus.

A minute later he stepped out of the door and closed it and came quietly up the short flight of steps to where she was standing.

'I'm sorry I took so long.'

'It wasn't.'

He took her arm and they went out of the door and around to the front of the house. The oak tree in the front lawn appeared gigantic. Everything was peculiarly sharpened or magnified; even the crunch of gravel under their two pairs of white shoes. She expected to see startled, balloon-like heads thrust out of all the upstairs windows, to hear voices calling a shrill alarm, her name shouted from rooftops, the rushing of crowds in pursuit . . .

'Where are we going?' she asked as he led her south along the brick walk.

'I want to show you the field in the poem.'

It wasn't far. The walk soon ended and under their feet was the plushy coolness of earth. The moon flowed aqueously through the multitude of pointed oak leaves: the dirt road was also like moving water with its variations of light and shade. They came to a low wooden fence. The boy jumped over it. Then held out his arms. She stepped to the top rail and he lifted her down from it. On the other side his arms did not release her but held her closer.

'This is it,' he told her, 'the field of blue children.'

She looked beyond his dark shoulder. And it was true. The whole field was covered with dancing blue flowers. There was a wind scudding through them and they broke before it in pale blue waves, sending up a soft whispering sound like the infinitely diminished crying of small children at play.

She thought of the view from her window at night, those nights when she cried bitterly without knowing why, the dome of the administration building like a white peak and the restless waves of moonlit branches and the stillness and the singing voices, mournfully remote, blocks away, coming closer, the tender, foolish ballads, and the smell of white spirea at night, and the stars clear as lamps in the cloud-fretted sky, and she remembered the choking emotion that she didn't understand and the dread of all this coming to its sudden, final conclusion in a few months or weeks more. And she tightened her arms about the boy's shoulders. He was almost a stranger. She knew that she had not even caught a first glimpse of him until this night, and yet he was inexpressibly close to her now, closer than she had felt any person before.

He led her out over the field where the flowers rose in pale blue waves to her knees and she felt their soft petals against her bare flesh and she lay down among them and stretched her arms through them and pressed her lips against them and felt them all about her, accepting her and embracing her, and a kind of drunkenness possessed her. The boy knelt beside her and touched her cheek with his fingers and then her lips and her hair. They were both kneeling in the blue flowers, facing each other. He was smiling. The wind blew her loose hair into his face. He raised both hands and brushed it back over her forehead and as he did so his hands slipped down behind the back of her head and fastened there and drew her head toward him until her mouth was pressed against his, tighter and tighter, until her teeth pressed painfully against her upper lip and she tasted the salt of blood. She gasped and let her mouth fall open and then she lay back among the whispering blue flowers.

Afterward she had sense enough to see that it was impossible. She sent the poems back to the boy with a short note. It was a curiously stilted and formal prose, perhaps because she was dreadfully afraid of herself when she wrote it. She told him about the boy Kirk Abbott whom she was going to marry that summer and she explained to Homer how impossible it would have been for them to try and go on with the beautiful but unfortunate thing that had happened to them last night in the field.

She saw him only once after that. She saw him walking across the campus with his friend Hertha, the tall, weedy girl who wore thick-lensed glasses. Hertha was clinging to Homer's arm and shaking with outlandishly shrill laughter; laughter that could be heard for blocks and yet did not sound like real laughter.

*

Myra and Kirk were married in August of that year. Kirk got a job
with the telephone company in Poplar Falls and they lived in an
efficiency apartment and were reasonably happy together. Myra
seldom felt restless any more. She did not write verse. Her life
seemed to be perfectly full without it. She wondered sometimes if
Homer had kept on with his writing but she never saw any of it in
the literary magazines so she supposed it couldn't have amounted
to very much after all.

One late spring evening a few years after their marriage Kirk
Abbott came home tired from the office hungry for dinner and
found a scribbled note under the sugar bowl on the drop-leaf
table.

'Driven over to Carsville for just a few hours. Myra.'

It was after dark: a soft, moony night.

Myra drove south from the town till she came to an open field.
There she parked the car and climbed over the low wooden fence.
The field was exactly as she had remembered it. She walked
quickly out among the flowers; then suddenly fell to her knees
among them, sobbing. She cried for a long time, for nearly an
hour, and then rose to her feet and carefully brushed off her skirt
and stockings. Now she felt perfectly calm and in possession of
herself once more. She went back to the car. She knew that she
would never do such a ridiculous thing as this again, for now she
had left the last of her troublesome youth behind her.

THE MALEDICTION

When a panicky little man looks for a place to stay in an unknown
town, the countermagic of learning abruptly deserts him. The
demon spirits that haunted a primitive world are called back out
of exile. Slyly, triumphantly, then, they creep once more through
the secret pores of rocks and veins of wood that knowledge had
forced them out of. The lonely stranger, scared of his shadow and
shocked by the sound of his footsteps, marches through watchful
ranks of lesser deities with dark intentions. He does not look at
houses as much as they look at him. Streets have an attitude
toward him. Sign-posts, windows, doorways all have eyes and
mouths that observe him and whisper about him. The tension in
him coils up tighter and tighter. If someone smiles to offer a
sudden welcome, this simple act may set off a kind of explosion.
The skin of his body, as cramped as a new kid glove, may seem to
be split down the seams, releasing his spirit to kiss stone walls and
dance over distant roof-tops. The demons are once more dispersed, thrust back into limbo; the earth is quiet and docile and
mindless again, a dull-witted ox that moves in a circular furrow,
to plough up sections of time for man's convenience.

This was, in fact, the way that Lucio felt when he first
encountered his future companion, the cat. She was the first
living-creature in all of the strange northern city that seemed to
answer the asking look in his eyes. She looked back at him with
cordial recognition. Almost he could hear the cat pronouncing his
name. 'Oh, so it's *you, Lucio!*' she seemed to be saying, 'I've sat
here waiting for you a long, long time!'

Lucio smiled in return and went on up to the steps on which she
was seated. The cat did not move. Instead she purred very faintly.
It was a sound that was scarcely a sound. It was a barely
distinguishable vibration in the pale afternoon air. Her amber
eyes did not blink but they narrowed slightly – anticipating his
touch which followed at once. His fingers met the soft crown of
her head and moved down over the bony furred ridge of her back:

under his fingers he felt the faint, faint quiver of her body as she
purred. She raised her head slightly to gaze up at him. It was a
feminine gesture: the gesture of a woman who glances up at her
lover's face as he embraces her, a rapt, sightless glance, un-
deliberate as the act of breathing.

'Do you like cats?'

The voice was directly above him. It belonged to a large blonde
woman in a gingham dress.

Lucio flushed guiltily and the woman laughed.

'Her name is Nitchevo,' said the woman.

He repeated the name haltingly.

'Yes, it's peculiar,' she said. 'One of our roomers give her that
name Nitchevo. He was a Russian or something. Stayed here
before he took sick. He found that cat in an alley and brought her
home an' fed her an' took care of her an' let her sleep in his bed,
an' now we can't get rid of th' dog-gone thing. Twice already
today I thrown cold water on her and still she sits! – I guess she's
waitin' for him to come back home. But he won't, though. I was
havin' a conversation the other day with some boys he used to
work with down at the plant. It's too bad now. They tell me he's
right on the verge of kickin' the bucket out west where he went for
his lungs when he started to spit up blood. – Tough luck is what I
call it. – He wasn't a bad sort of a fellow as them Polacks go.'

Her voice trailed off and she turned away, smiling vaguely, as if
to go back inside.

'Do you keep boarders?' he asked.

'No,' said the woman. 'Everybody along here does but us. My
husband is not a very well man anymore. Got hurt in an accident
down at the plant and now he's not good for nothing except being
tooken care of. So me – ' she sighed, 'I got to work out at that
bakery down on James Street.'

She laughed and held up her palms, the sweating lines of which
were traced with a chalky whiteness.

'That's how I got all this flour. My next-door-neighbour, Mizz
Jacoby, tells me I smell like a fresh loaf of bread. Well – I don't
have time to keep boarders, all I can keep is roomers. I got rooms I
could show you – if you would be interested.'

She paused in good-humoured reflection – stroked her hips and
allowed her gaze to slide off on a gentle excursion among the
barren tree-tops.

'As a matter of fack,' she continued, 'I guess I could show you that room the Russian vacated. If you ain't superstitious about occupying the room that a man took sick in as bad as that. They say that it ain't contagious but I don't know.'

She turned and went into the house and Lucio followed.

She showed him the room that the Russian had lately moved out of. It had two windows, one that faced the brick wall of a laundry that smelled of naphtha, another that opened upon a narrow backyard where greenish-blue cabbage heads were scattered about like static fountains of sea-water among the casual clumps of unweeded grass.

As he looked out that back window and the woman stood behind him, breathing warmly upon the nape of his neck and smelling of flour, he saw Nitchevo, the cat, picking her way with slow grace among the giant cabbage-heads.

'Nitchevo,' remarked the woman.

'What does it mean?' he asked her.

'Oh, I don't know. I guess something crazy in Russian. — He told me but I forgotten.'

'I'll take the room if I can do like the Russian and keep the cat here with me.'

'Oh!' laughed the woman. 'You want to do like the *Russian*!'

'Yes,' said Lucio.

'Him an' me were pretty good friends,' she told him. 'He helped me out with things my husband ain't good for now that he's had that accident down at the plant.'

'Yes? — Well, how about it?'

'Well — ' she sat down on the bed. 'I never take nobody in without talking a little. There's some things I like to be sure of before I make final arrangements. — You understand that.'

'Oh, yes.'

'For instance, I don't like fairies.'

'What?'

'Fairies! — I had one once that used to go out on the street in a red silk scarf and bring men back to the room. — I don't like that.'

'I wouldn't do that.'

'Well, I just wanted to know. You looked kind of strange.'

'I'm foreign.'

'What kind of foreigner are you?'

'My folks were Sicilians.'

'What?'

'An island near Italy.'

'Oh. – I guess that's all right.'

She looked at him – winked and grinned.

'Musso!' she said. 'That's what I'll call you – *Musso!*'

Ponderously coquettish, she rose from the bed and poked him in the stomach with her thumb.

'Well – how about it?' he asked her.

'Okay. – Have you got a job yet?'

'Not yet.'

'Go down to the plant and ask for Oliver Woodson. Tell him Mizz Hutcheson sent yuh. – He'll give you a job all right with my recommendation.'

'Thank you – *thank* you!'

She grinned and chuckled and sighed and turned slowly away. 'My husband has got the war-news on the radio all of the time. – It gives me a pain in the place that I sit down on. – But a sick man's got to be humoured. – That's how it is.'

But Lucio wasn't listening. He had turned back to the window to look at the cat. She was still down there in the yard, patiently waiting between two large cabbage-heads to receive the verdict that settled her future existence. Oh, what a passion of longing there was in her look. But dignity, too.

Quickly he moved past the woman and down the front stairs.

'Where are you going?' she called.

'Out! In back! – For the cat!'

Lucio got a job at the plant through the man named Woodson. The work that he did was what he had always done, a thing that you did with your fingers without much thought. A chain clanked beneath you, you made some little adjustment, the chain moved on. But each time it moved beyond your place in the line it took a part of you with it. The energy in your fingers was drained out slowly. It was replaced by energy further back in your body. Then this was drained out also. When the day ended you were left feeling empty. What had gone out of you? Where had it gone to? *Why?* – You bought the evening papers the yelling boys poked toward you. Maybe here was a clue to all of these questions. Perhaps the latest edition would tell you what you lived for and why you laboured. But no! The papers avoided that subject. Instead they announced the total amount of tonnage now lost at sea. The number of planes brought down in aerial combat. Cities captured, towns bombarded. – The facts

were confusing, the paper fell out of your fingers, your head ached
dully . . .

Oh, my God, and when you got up in the morning, there was
the sun in the same position you saw it the day before – beginning
to rise from the graveyard back of the street, as though its nightly
custodians were the fleshless dead – seen through the town's
invariable smoke haze, it was a ruddy biscuit, round and red,
when it might just as well have been square or shaped like a worm
– anything might have been anything else and had as much
meaning to it . . .

The foreman seemed to dislike him, or maybe suspect him of
something. Often he stopped directly behind Lucio's back and
watched him working – stood there an unnecessarily long time
and before he moved off always grunted a little and in a way that
suggested any number of menacing possibilities.

Lucio thought to himself: I will not be able to keep this job very
long.

He wrote his brother a letter. – This brother named Silva was
serving a ten-year sentence in a Texas prison. He was Lucio's twin
but their natures were not alike. Yet they were close to each other.
Silva had been the rebel, a boy who loved music and whiskey,
whose life was nocturnal as the life of a cat, a sleek young man he
had been, with always the delicate scent of women about him. His
clothes flung carelessly about the flat, which they had shared in
the town further south, were faintly dusted with powder from
women's bodies. Small trinklets tumbled out of his pockets,
testimonials of intimacy with Gladys or Mabel or Ruth. When he
awoke he always wound up the victrola and when he wanted to
sleep, he switched the radio off. – Lucio rarely saw him either
awake or asleep. They very seldom discussed their lives with each
other but once Lucio found a revolver in his brother's coat-
pocket. He left the revolver on the bed which they used at opposite
hours – under it he placed a pencilled note. This is your death, said
the note. When he came home the revolver had disappeared. In its
place on the bed was a pair of workman's gloves that Lucio used
at the foundry. Pinned to it was a note in Silva's irregular hand.
Here is *yours*, said the note. – Shortly thereafter Silva had gone to
Texas and there was arrested and given a ten-year term on a hold-
up charge. Lucio started the letters which now had gone on for
eight years. Each time he wrote he informed his brother of some
purely fanciful advancement in his career. He told him that he had

become a foreman and a stockholder in the corporation. That he
belonged to a country-club and drove a Cadillac car – that
recently he had moved north to assume a much better position
with several times as much pay. These lies were further and
further elaborated: they began to comprise a sort of dream
existence. His face flushed while he wrote them – his hand shook
so that toward the end of the letter the writing would be illegible
almost. It was not that he wanted to arouse his unfortunate
brother's envy, it was not that at all. – But he had loved the
brother intensely and Silva had always been so contemptuous of
him in a kind sort of way. – Silva apparently believed the news in
the letters. How well you are doing! he wrote. You could see he
was startled and proud – so that Lucio thought with dread of the
time when the truth must be known, when his brother got out of
prison . . .

Lucio's feeling that he could not long hold the job became an
obsession with him: a certain knowledge that clung to his brain all
the time. In the evenings, with Nitchevo the cat, he could shut it
partly away. Nitchevo's presence was a denial of all the many
threatening elements of chance. You could see that Nitchevo did
not take stock in chance. She believed that everything progressed
according to a natural, predestined order and that there was
nothing to be apprehensive about. All of her movements were
slow and without agitation. They were accomplished with a
consummate grace. Her amber eyes regarded each object with
unblinking serenity. Even about her food she made no haste. Each
evening Lucio brought home a pint of milk for her supper and
breakfast: Nitchevo sat quietly waiting on her haunches while he
poured it into the cracked saucer borrowed from the landlady and
set it on the floor beside the bed. Then he lay down on the bed,
expectantly watching, while Nitchevo came slowly forward to the
pale blue saucer. She looked up at him once – slowly – with her
unblinking yellow eyes before she started to eat, and then she
gracefully lowered her small chin to the saucer's edge, the red
satin tip of tongue protruded and the room was filled with the
sweet, faint music of her gentle lapping. He watched her and as he
watched her his mind smoothed out. The tight knots of anxiety
loosened and were absorbed. The compressed and gaseous feeling
inside his body was forgotten and his heart beat more quietly. He
began to feel sleepy as he watched the cat – sleepy and entranced.
Her form grew in size and the rest of the room dwindled and

receded. It seemed to him, then, that they were of equal dimensions. He was a cat like Nitchevo – they lay side by side on the floor, lapping milk in the comfortable, secure warmth of a locked room beyond which no factories or foremen existed, nor large blonde landladies with hauntingly full-fleshed bosoms.

Nitchevo took a long time about drinking her milk. Often he was asleep before she had finished. He would awake later on and find her small warmth against him – he would sleepily raise his hand to caress her and he would feel the faint, faint vibration of the vertebral ridges along her back as she purred. She was getting fatter. Her sides filled out. – Of course there had been no spoken declaration of love between the two of them, but each understood that a contract existed between them to last their whole lives. Lucio talked to the cat in drowsy whispers – he never fabricated such stories as those that he wrote to his brother but merely denials of worries that plagued him most. He told her that he was not going to lose his job, that he would always be able to give her the saucer of milk night and morning and let her sleep on his bed; he told her that nothing disastrous was going to happen to them, that there was nothing to be afraid of between heaven and earth. Not even the sun, that rose newly-burnished each day from the heart of the cemetery, would break the enchantment which they had established between them.

One evening Lucio fell asleep with the light in his room still burning. The landlady, who was sleepless that night, saw it shining under the crack of his door and she came to the door and knocked and getting no response, she pushed it open. She found the strange man asleep on the bed with the cat curled against his bare chest. His face was sharp and prematurely aged and his eyes, when they were open, made it look older still, but now they were closed, and his body was thin and white and under-developed like that of a spindly boy. He did not look like very much of a man, she observed. But she wanted to test his manhood. The Russian had also been thin, cadaverous almost, and always coughing as though an army of vandals were tearing him down from inside. Nevertheless, there had been a great fire in his nature which magnified him as a lover, made him assume almost a great physical stature. So she remembered the Russian who occupied that room before and she came to the side of the bed and threw the cat down to the floor and placed her hand on the sleeping little man's shoulder. Lucio woke and found her seated beside him, smiling, still smelling of the bed's warmth and faintly of flour. Her face was double in his unfocused vision. Two large beaming moons that swam in the room's amber glow. Her hand on his shoulder burnt him, stung him painfully as the hide of a steaming horse had once stung his fingers when he touched it as a child. Her mouth was wet, the heat of her bosom engulfed him. The roses upon the wallpaper – how large they were! – And then they sank back into shadow . . .

When the landlady had gone he went back to sleep again, scarcely aware of what had happened between them – except that now he felt more completely rested and quiet and the bed, it seemed to have risen to a great height over the dark, huddled roofs and bristling stacks of the factory town – and to be floating loose among stars that were not as chill as they looked, but warm with a human warmth that was scented with flour . . .

The life in the house grew sweeter and familiar to him.

Sometimes when he entered the downstairs hall at fifteen after five on a wintry evening, he called out loudly and bravely. Heigho, Everybody, heigho! The blonde landlady moved out from the radio noise as though she was drugged, with a body stuffed full of honey-sweet popular songs – moons, roses, blue skies, rainbows after showers, cottages, sunsets, gardens, loves lasting forever! – She smiled with so much of it in her and touched her broad forehead and let her hand slide down her body, pressing herself here and there and enjoying the knowledge of so much sweet flesh on her and willing to share it . . . Yes, yes, moons, lovers, roses – followed him up the hallstairs and into his bedroom and spilled themselves over the bed in a great, wild heap of 'I love you!' – 'Remember me always' – and 'Meet me tonight by the moon-light!' – the radio filled her up like a ten-gallon jug which the dark little man un-stoppered upstairs before supper.

But the work-a-day life in the plant was more and more strained. Lucio went at his work with a feverish haste, his anxiety coiling up tight whenever the foreman stopped at his place in the line. The grunt which he uttered, somewhat louder each time, was like a knife thrust into the centre of Lucio's back: all his blood flowed out through the wound so that he scarcely had strength to remain on his feet. His hands went faster and faster until they lost their rhythm and the metal strips jammed and the machine cried out in a loud and furious voice, which ended abruptly the man's illusion as master.

'God damn!' said the foreman. 'Why dontcha watch whatcha doin'? I'm tired a the way yuh bung up things all a time with yuh jittery fingers!'

He wrote to his brother that night that he had received another considerable boost in salary: he enclosed three dollars for candy and cigarettes and said that he was planning to engage another great lawyer to re-open Silva's case and take it, if necessary, to the United States Supreme Court.

'In the meantime,' he ended, 'sit tight! – There is nothing to worry about – absolutely.'

This was the same type of statement he made every night to the cat.

But only a few days later there came a letter from the warden of the Texas prison, a man with the curious name of Mortimer J. Stallcup, returning the money and tersely announcing the convict brother, Silva, had recently been shot dead in an attempted jail-break.

Lucio showed this letter to his friend the cat. At first she seemed to observe it without much feeling. Then she became interested – she poked it with one white, tentative paw, mewed and set her teeth into a corner of the crisp paper. Lucio dropped it to the floor and she pushed it gently across the rug with her nose and her paws.

After a while he got up and poured out her milk which had grown rather warm in the steam-heated room. The radiators hissed. Her tongue lapped gently. – The roses on the wallpaper shimmered through tears that drained all the tension out of the little man's body.

Returning from the plant one evening that winter he had a rather curious adventure. There was a place a few blocks from the plant called the Bright Spot Cafe. Out of it on this particular evening stumbled a man who looked like a plain street beggar. He caught at Lucio's sleeve and after a long, steady glance with eyes as enflamed as the cemetery-horizon before daybreak, he made a remarkable statement:

'Don't be afraid of these stinking sons-of-bitches. They grow like weeds and like stink-weeds are cut down. They run away from their conscience and can't be still for a minute. – Watch for the sun! – It comes up out of their graveyard every morning!'

The speech rambled on for some time in prophetic vein – when at last he let go of Lucio's arm, to which he clung for support, he headed back to the swinging door he emerged from. Just before going inside he made a final statement which struck home profoundly.

'*Do you know who I am?*' he shouted. '*I'm God Almighty!*'

'*What?*' said Lucio.

The old man nodded and grinned – waved in farewell and passed back into the brightly-lighted cafe.

Lucio knew that the old man was probably drunk and a liar but like most people he sometimes had the ability to believe what he wanted to believe in despite of all logic. And so there were nights that harsh, northern winter when he comforted himself and the cat with the recollection of the old man's statement. God was perhaps, he remembered, a resident of this strangely devitiated city whose grey-brown houses were like the dried skins of locusts. God was, like Lucio, a lonely and bewildered man Who felt that something was wrong but could not correct it, a man Who sensed the blundering sleep-walk of time and hostilities of chance and wanted to hide Himself from them in places of brilliance and warmth.

Nitchevo the cat did not need to be told that God had taken up his residence in the factory town. She had already discovered his presence twice: first in the Russian, then in Lucio. It is doubtful that she really distinguished between them. They both represented the same quality of infinite mercy. They made her life safe and pleasant. From the alley they had brought her to the house. The house was warm, the rugs and the pillows were soft. She rested in perfect content, a content which was not, like Lucio's, merely nocturnal but stayed with her all through the days as well as the nights – which was never broken. (If He the Creator did not order all things well, He conferred one inestimable benefit in the animal kingdom when He deprived all but man of the disquieting faculty of examining the future.) Nitchevo, being a cat, existed in only one sliding moment of time: that moment was good. It did not occur to the cat that convicts might be attempting escapes from Texas prisons and being shot down (which accident terminated escape through dream) that wardens were writing terse letters announcing such facts, that foremen grunted contemptuously when they stood behind men whose fingers trembled with fear of doing things badly. That wheels cried out and cracked the whip as the master. That men were blind who thought they saw things plainly, that God had been driven to drink – Nitchevo

did not know that this curious accident of matter, the earth, was
whirling dangerously fast and some day, unexpectedly, it would
fly apart from its own excessive momentum and shatter itself into
little bits of disaster.

Nitchevo purred under Lucio's fingers in absolute contradic-
tion of all circumstances that threatened their common existence
– and that was perhaps why Lucio loved her so much.

It was now mid-January and every morning the wind with a
tireless impatience would grab at the smoke of the plant and
thrust it south-east of the town where it hung in a restless bank
above the graveyard: the sun rose through it at seven o'clock in
the morning, red as the eyeball of a drunken beggar, and stared
accusingly till it sank again on the opposite side, across the turgid
river: the river kept running away, polluted, ashamed, looking
neither to the right nor to the left, but steadily running and
running. The final week of the month the stockholders came in
town for a crucial meeting. Glittering black and rushing close to
the earth as beetles on desperate errands, the limousines sped
toward the plant: disgorged their corpulent contents at private
doorways and waited uneasily, like a nest of roaches, in cinder-
covered parkways back of the plant.

What was hatching inside the conference chambers no one who
actually worked at the plant could tell. It took some time for the
eggs to incubate: secret and black and laid in coagulate clusters,
they ripened slowly.

This was the problem: there was a slump at the plant. The
stockholders had to decide what action to take, whether to
cheapen the product and make it available thus to a wider market
or else cut down on production. The answer was obvious: they
would cut down on production, preserving the margin of profit,
and wait for the need of the people to make more demand. This
was promptly arranged. The wheels got their orders and stopped:
the workers were stopped by the wheels. One third of the plant
shut down and the men were laid off: the black roach-nest
dispersed from the cinder parkway: the problem was solved.

Lucio – yes – was among them.

There were sixty-eight of them given their notices that morning.
There was no protest, there was no demonstration, no angry
voices were lifted. It was almost as though these sixty-eight
factory workers had known from the beginning that this was in
store. Perhaps in the wombs of their mothers the veins that had

fed them had sung in their ears this song: Thou shalt lose thy job, thou shalt be turned away from the wheels and the bread taken from thee!

It was a glittering wasteland, the town that morning. All week the snow had fallen, lightless and thick. But now the sun shone upon it. Each separate crystal was radiant and alive. The roofs were exclamatory. The steep, narrow streets were ruthlessly brilliant as arrows.

Cold, cold, cold is the merciless blood of thy father!

In Lucio two things competed. One was the need to find his companion the cat. The other and equal need was that of his body to loosen its agonized tension, to fall, to let go, to be swept on like a river.

He managed to keep on walking as far as the Bright Spot Cafe.

There he was met by the man he had met once before, the beggarly stranger, the man who had called himself God.

Out of the lively, rotating glass door of this building the stranger emerged with an armful of empty beer-bottles the management had rejected because they were not purchased there.

'Like weeds,' he repeated glumly, 'like noxious weeds!'

He pointed south-east of the town with the arm not burdened with bottles.

'Watch for the sun. It comes from the cemetery.'

His spittle gleamed in the terrible glare of the morning.

'I clench my fist and this is the fist of God.'

Then he noticed the discharged worker before him.

'Where do you come from?' he asked.

'The plant,' said Lucio faintly.

The angry glow in the blood-shot eyes waxed brighter.

'The plant, *the plant*!' groaned the stranger.

His small black shoe, bound up with adhesive tape and wads of paper, spattered the snow as it stamped.

He shook his fist in the bristling stacks' direction.

'Cupidity and stupidity!' he shouted. 'That is the two-armed cross on which they have nailed me!'

An iron-loaded truck came by with sloshing thunder.

The old man's face convulsed with rage as it passed.

'Lies, lies, lies, lies!' he shouted. 'They've covered their bodies with lies and they won't stand washing! They want to be scabbed all over, they want no skin but the crust of their greediness on them! Okay, okay, let 'em have it! But let 'em have *more* and *more*! Maggots as well as lice! Yeah, pile th' friggin' dirt of their friggin' graveyard on 'em, shovel 'em under *deep* – till I can't *smell* 'em!'

The sound of this malediction was drowned in another truck's thunder, but Lucio heard the man's words. He stopped on the walk beside him. The stranger's vehemence was so great he had dropped his bottles. Together they crouched to the walk and picked them up with the grave and voiceless preoccupation of children gathering flowers. When they were finished and he, the stranger, had spat out the phlegm that choked him, he caught hold of Lucio's arm and peered at him wildly.

'Where are you going?' he asked.

'Home,' the little man told him, 'I'm going home.'

'Yes, go home,' said the stranger. 'Back to the bowels of earth. But not forever. The humble cannot be destroyed, they keep on going!'

'Going?' asked Lucio. '*Where?*'

'Where?' said the prophet, '*Where?*— I don't know *where*!' He began to sob – his sobbing shook him so that he dropped the bottles once more. And this time when Lucio crouched to assist in the gathering up, his strength went from him suddenly in a wave that swept far out and left him stranded, empty and flat and very nearly lifeless, upon the walk in the rapidly blackening snow outside the cafe.

'Drunk,' said the burly policeman.

The man who had called himself God protested but he could do nothing.

The wagon was called and Lucio thrust inside it.

'Nitchevo, Nitchevo,' was all he could say when they asked him where his home was. – So they bore him away.

For nearly an hour the man who called himself God remained on the corner outside of the Bright Spot Cafe. He appeared to be puzzled by something.

At last he shrugged and moved on down the street to the next beer-parlour.

What is your name? What did your mother die of? Do you have dreams at night?

No, no, no, no. No name, no mother, no dreams. Please leave me alone.'

He was a very bad patient. Refuses to co-operate, the doctors decided.

Finally after a week they turned him away.

He went directly back to the rooming-house. The door was unlocked. The hall was frosty and silent.

Where was the cat? Not there, he could tell without asking. If she had been there he would have been able to feel her breath in the stillness. There would have been something liquid and warm in the air like the womb of the mother remembered a long way off.

Mrs Hutcheson heard him and came from the rear of the house where the radio blared a ceaseless popular dream.

'I heard that you'd been laid off,' was all that she said.

It was easy to see that the Swanee and roses and moonlight had been turned off to meet a stricter occasion. Her amplitude was now hostile. It blocked the way.

He started to go upstairs but she blocked the staircase.

'The room has been taken,' she told him.

'Oh.'

'I can't afford to let my rooms be vacant.'

'No.'

'I got to be practical, don't I?'

'Yes.'

'Everyone's got to be practical. That's how it is.'

'I see. – Where is the cat?'

'The cat? – I turned her out Wednesday.'

Now for the last time vehemence stirred inside him. Energy. Anger. Protest.

'No, no, no!' he shouted.

'Be still!' said the woman. 'What do you think I am? The nerve of some people – expect me to play nursemaid to a sick alley-cat!'

'Sick?' said Lucio – he was suddenly quiet.

'Yes,' said the woman.

'What was the matter with her?'

'How should I know? – She cried all night and created an awful disturbance. – I turned her out.'

'Where did she go?'

The woman laughed harshly. 'Where did she go! How on earth should I know where that dirty cat went! She might have gone to the devil for all I know.'

Her great bulk turned and she climbed back up the stairs. The door of Lucio's former room stood open. The woman entered. A male voice spoke her name and the door was closed.

Lucio went back out of the enemy's house.

Dimly, remotely, and without any definite feeling, he knew that the game was up. Yes, he could see behind him the whole of his time on earth. Mad pilgrimage of the flesh. Its twisting and turnings, its seemingly empty excursions. He saw how the lines, delusively parallel-seeming, had now converged and had made all forward motion impossible from now on.

He was not conscious of fear nor self-pity nor even regret any more.

He walked to the corner and turned instinctively down.

Then there occurred once more and for the last time in his life a great and a merciful thing: an act of God.

At the entrance of an alley just beyond where he stood he saw abruptly the limping and oddly-misshapen figure of his lost companion. – The *cat*! Yes! Nitchevo!

He stood quite still and let his friend approach him. This she did, but with great difficulty. Their eyes were ropes that drew them slowly together in spite of the body's resistance. For she was hurt very badly, she could hardly move . . .

The consummation was gradual. Still it progressed. And all of the time the eyes of the cat stayed on him.

Her amber eyes regarded him with their usual dignified, unquestioning devotion, as though he had only returned from a few minutes' absence and not after days and days of hunger, calamity, cold.

Lucio reached down and gathered her into his arms. He observed now the cause of her limping. One of her legs had been crushed. It must have been for several days in that condition. It had festered and turned black and was very ill-smelling. Her body in his arms felt like a tiny bundle of bones and the sound that she made to greet him was less than a sound.

How had it happened, this injury? Nitchevo could not tell him. Neither could he tell her what had happened to him. He could not describe the foreman who watched and grunted, the calm superiority of doctors, nor the landlady, blonde and dirty, in whom desire could be satisfied as well by one man as another.

Silence and physical closeness spoke for them both.

He knew she could not go on living. She knew it, too. Her eyes were tired and dark: eclipsed in them now was that small, sturdy flame which means a desire to go on and which is the secret of life's heroic survival. No. The eyes were eclipsed. They were full to the amber brims with all of the secrets and sorrows the world can answer our ceaseless questioning with. Loneliness – yes. Hunger. Bewilderment. Pain. All of these things were in them. They wanted no more. They wanted now to be closed on what they had gathered and not have to hold any more.

He carried her down the steep, cobbled street toward the river. It was an easy direction. The whole town slanted that way.

The air had grown dark, no longer containing the terrible brilliance of sunlight reflected on snow. The wind took the smoke up quickly and sent it scudding across low roofs in a sheep-like surrender. There was cold in the air and a sooty gathering darkness. The wind whined a little as thin metal wires drawn taut.

High up on the bank, on the levee, a truck rumbled past. It was loaded with ingots of metal. Iron from the forge of the plant that was soaring away into darkness as the earth averted this side of its face from the stinging slap of the sun and gradually gave it the other.

Lucio spoke to the cat as the stream climbed about them.

'Soon,' he whispered. 'Soon, soon, very soon.'

Only a single instant she struggled against him: clawed his shoulder and arm in a moment of doubt. *My God, My God, why hast Thou forsaken me?* Then the ecstasy passed and her faith returned, they went away with the river. Away from the town, away and away from the town, as the smoke, the wind took from the chimneys—

Completely away.

THE ANGEL IN THE ALCOVE

Suspicion is the occupational disease of landladies and long association with them has left me with an obscure sense of guilt I will probably never be free of. The initial trauma in this category was inflicted by a landlady I had in the old French Quarter of New Orleans when I was barely twenty. She was the archetype of the suspicious landlady. She had a room of her own but preferred to sleep on a rattling cot in the downstairs hall so that none of her tenants could enter or leave the establishment during the night without her grudging permission. When finally I left there I fooled the old woman. I left by way of a balcony and a pair of sheets. I was miles out of town on the Old Spanish Trail to the West before the old woman found out I had gotten past her.

The downstairs hall of this rooming-house on Bourbon Street was totally lightless. You had to grope your way through it with cautious revulsion, trailing your fingers along the damp, cracked plaster until you arrived at the door or the foot of the stairs. You never reached either without the old woman's challenge. Her ghostly figure would spring bolt upright on the rattling iron cot. She would utter one syllable – *Who?* If she were not satisfied with the identification given, or suspected that you were taking your luggage out in a stealthy departure or bringing somebody in for carnal enjoyment, a match would be struck on the floor and held toward you for several moments. In its weirdly flickering light she would squint her eyes at you until her doubts were dismissed. Then she would flop back down in a huddle of sour blankets and if you waited to listen you would hear mutterings vicious and coarse as any that drunks in Quarter bar-rooms ever gave voice to.

She was a woman of paranoidal suspicion and her suspicion of me was unbounded. Often she came in my room with the morning paper and read aloud some item concerning an act of crime in the Quarter. After the reading she would inspect me closely for any guilty change of countenance, and I would nearly always gratify her suspicion with a deep flush and inability to return her look. I am sure she had chalked up dozens of crimes against me and was only waiting for some more concrete betrayal to call the police, a captain of whom, she had warned me, was her first cousin.

The landlady was a victim of dead beats, that much should be admitted in her defence. None of her tenants were regular payers. Some of them clung to their rooms for months and months with only promises of future payment. One of these was a widow named Mrs Wayne. Mrs Wayne was the most adroit sponger in the house. She even succeeded in finagling gratuities from the landlady. Her fortune was in her tongue. She was a wonderful raconteur of horribly morbid or salacious stories. Whenever she smelled food cooking her door would fly open and she would dart forth with a mottled blue and white saucepan held to her bosom coquettishly as a lace fan. Undoubtedly she was half starved and the odour of food set her off like a powerful drug, for there was an abnormal brilliance in her chatter. She tapped on the door from which the seductive smell came but entered before there could be any kind of response. Her tongue would be off before she was fairly inside and no amount of rudeness short of forcible ejection from the room would suffice to discourage her. There was something pitifully winning about the old lady. Even her bad-smelling breath became a component of her unwholesome appeal. To me it was the spectacle of so much heroic vitality in so wasted a vessel that warmed my heart toward the widow. I never did any cooking in my attic bedroom. I only met Mrs Wayne in the landlady's kitchen on those occasions when I had earned my supper by some small job on the premises. The landlady herself was not entirely immune to Mrs Wayne's charm and the stories unmistakably entranced her. As she put things on the stove she would always remark, If the bitch gets a sniff of this cookin' wild horses won't hold 'er!

In eight years' time such characters disappear, the earth swallows them up, the walls absorb them like moisture. Undoubtedly old Mrs Wayne and her battered utensil have made their protesting departure and I am not at all sure that with them the world has not lost the greatest pathological genius since Baudelaire or Poe. Her favourite subject was the deaths of relatives and friends which she had attended with an eye and ear from which no agonizing detail escaped annotation. Her memory served them up in the landlady's kitchen so graphically that I would find myself sick with horror and yet so fascinated that the risk of losing my appetite for a hard-earned supper would not prevail upon me to shut my ears. The landlady was equally spellbound. Gradually her gruff mumblings of disbelief and impatient gestures would give way to such morbid enjoyment that her jaws would slacken and dribble. A faraway mesmerized look would come into her usually pin-sharp eyes. All the while Mrs Wayne with the saucepan held to her bosom would be executing a slow and oblique approach to the great kitchen stove. So powerful was her enchantment that even when she was actually removing the lid from the stew-pot and ladling out some of its contents into her saucepan, although the landlady's look would follow her movements there would not appear to be any recognition. Not until the hapless protagonist of the story had endured his final conclusion – his eyeballs popped from their sockets and ghastly effluvia drenching his bed-clothes – did the charm loosen enough to permit the narrator's listeners any clear knowledge of what went on outside the scene that was painted. By that time Mrs Wayne had scraped her saucepan clean with wolfish relish and made her way so close to the door that if any unpleasantness attended the landlady's emergence from trance, the widow could be out of earshot before it achieved a momentum.

In this old house it was either deathly quiet or else the high plaster walls were ringing like fire-bells with angry voices, with quarrels over the use of the lavatory or accusations of theft or threats of eviction. I had no door to my room which was in the attic, only a ragged curtain that couldn't exclude the barrage of human wretchedness often exploding. The walls of my room were pink and green stippled plaster and there was an alcove window. This alcove window shone faintly in the night. There was a low bench beneath it. Now and again when the room was otherwise lightless a misty grey figure would appear to be seated on this bench in the alcove. It was the tender and melancholy figure of an angel or some dim, elderly madonna. The apparition occurred in the alcove most often on those winter nights in New Orleans when slow rain is falling from the sky not clouded heavily enough to altogether separate the town from the moon. New Orleans and the moon have always seemed to me to have an understanding between them, an intimacy of sisters grown old together, no longer needing more than a speechless look to communicate their feelings to each other. This lunar atmosphere of the city draws me back whenever the waves of energy which removed me to more

vital towns have spent themselves and a time of recession is called
for. Each time I have felt some rather profound psychic wound, a
loss or a failure, I have returned to this city. At such periods I
would seem to belong there and no place else in the country.

During this first period in New Orleans none of the small
encouragements in my life as a writer had yet come along and I
had already accepted the terms of anonymity and failure. I had
already learned to make a religion of endurance and a secret of my
desperation. The nights were comforting. When the naked light-
bulb had been turned off and everything visible gone except the
misty alcove set deeply and narrowly into the wall above
Bourbon, I would seem to slip into another state of being which
had no trying associations with the world. For a while the alcove
would remain empty, just a recess that light came faintly into: but
after my thoughts had made some dreamy excursion or other and
I turned again to look in that direction, the transparent figure
would noiselessly have entered and seated herself on the bench
below the window and begun that patient watching which put me
to sleep. The hands of the figure were folded among the colourless
draperies of her lap and her eyes were fixed upon me with a
gentle, unquestioning look which I came to remember as having
belonged to my grandmother during her sieges of illness when I
used to go to her room and sit by her bed and want to say
something or put my hand over hers but could not do either,
knowing that if I did I would burst into tears that would trouble
her more than her illness.

The appearance of this grey figure in the alcove never preceded
the time of falling asleep by more than a few moments. When I
saw her there I thought comfortably, Ah, now, I'm about to slip
away, it will all be gone in a moment and won't come back until
morning . . .

On one of those nights a more substantial visitor came to my
room. I was jolted out of my sleep by a warmth that was not my
own, and I awoke to find that someone had entered my room and
was crouching over the bed. I jumped up and nearly cried out, but
the arms of the visitor passionately restrained me. He whispered
his name which was that of a tubercular young artist who slept in
the room adjoining. I want to, I want to, he whispered. So I lay
back and let him do what he wanted until he was finished. Then
without any speech he got up and left my room. For a while
afterwards I heard him coughing and muttering to himself

through the wall between us. Turbulent feelings were on both sides of that wall. But at last I was drowsy again. I cocked an eye toward the alcove. Yes, she was there. I wondered if she had witnessed the strange goings-on and what her attitude was toward perversions of longing. But nothing gave any sign. The two weightless hands so loosely clasping each other among the colourless draperies of the lap, the cool and believing grey eyes in the faint pearly face, were immobile as statuary. I felt that she had permitted the act to occur and had neither blamed nor approved, and so I went off to sleep.

Not long after the episode in my room the artist was involved in a terrible scene with the landlady. His disease was entering the final stage, he coughed all the time but managed to go on working. He was a quick-sketch artist at the Court of the Two Parrots which was around the corner on Toulouse. He did not trust anybody or anything. He lived in a world completely hostile to him, unrelentingly hostile, and no other being could enter the walls about him for more than the frantic moments desire drove him to. He would not give in to the mortal fever which licked all the time at his nerves. He invented all sorts of trivial complaints and grudges to hide from himself the knowledge that he was dying. One of these subterfuges to which he resorted was a nightly preoccupation with bed-bugs. He claimed that his mattress was infested with them, and every morning he made an angry report to the landlady on the number that had bitten him during the night. These numbers grew and grew to appalling figures. The old woman wouldn't believe him. Finally one morning he did get her into the room to take a look at the bed-clothes.

I heard him breathing hoarsely while the old woman shuffled and rattled about the corner his bed was in.

Well, she finally grunted, I ain't found nothin'.

Christ, said the artist, you're blind!

Okay! You show me! What is there on this bed?

Look at that! said the artist.

What?

That spot of blood on the pillow.

Well?

That's where I smashed a bed-bug as big as my thumbnail!

Ho, ho, ho, said the landlady. That's where you spit up blood!

There was a pause in which his breathing grew hoarser. His speech when it burst out again was dreadfully altered.

How dare you, God damn you, say that!

Ho, ho, ho! I guess you claim you never spit up no blood?

No, no, never! he shouted.

Ho, ho, ho! You spit up blood all the time. I've seen your spit on the stairs and in the hall and on the floor of this bedroom. You leave a trail of it everywhere that you go, a bloody track like a chicken that runs with its head off. You hawk and you spit and you spread contamination. And that ain't all that you do by a long shot neither!

Now, yelled the artist — What kind of a dirty insinuation is *that*?

Ho, ho, ho! Insinuation of nothin' but what's known facts!

Get out! he shouted.

I'm in my own house and I'll say what I want where I please! I know all about you degenerates in the Quarter. I ain't let rooms ten years in the Quarter for nothin'. A bunch of rotten half-breeds and drunks an' degenerates, that's what I've had to cope with. But you're the worst of bunch, barring none! And it's not just here but at the Two Parrots, too. Your awful condition's become the main topic of talk at the place where you work. You spit all around your easel in the courtyard. It's got to be mopped with a strong disinfectant each night. The management is disgusted. They wish you would fold up your easel and get to hell out. They only don't ask you because you're a pitiful case. Why, one of the waitresses told me some customers left without paying their bill because you was hawking and spitting right next to their table. That's how it is, and the management's fed up with it!

You're making up lies!

It's God's own truth! I got it from the cashier!

I ought to hit you!

Go on!

I ought to knock your ugly old lying face in!

Go on, go on, just try it! I got a nephew that's a captain on the police force! Hit me an' you'll land smack in the House of Detention! A rubber hose on your back is what you'll git in there!

I ought to twist those dirty lies out of your neck!

Ho, ho, just try it! Even the effort would kill you!

You'll be punished, he gasped. One of these nights you'll get a knife stuck in you!

By you, I suppose? Ho, ho! You'll die on the street, you'll cough up your lungs in the gutter! You'll go to the morgue. Nobody will claim that skinny cadaver of yours. You'll go in a box and be dumped off a barge in the river. The sooner the better is how I look at it, too. A case like you is a public nuisance and danger. You've got no right to expose healthy people to you. You ought to go into the charity ward at Saint Vincent's. That is the place for a person in dying condition who ain't got the sense to know what is really wrong with him but goes about raising a stink about bugs putting blood on his pillow. Huh! Bugs! You're the bugs that puts blood all over this linen! It's you, not bugs, that makes such a filthy mess at the Court of Two Parrots it's got to be scoured with lye when you leave ev'ry night! It's you, not bugs, that drives the customers off without paying their checks. The management's not disgusted with bugs, but with you! And if you don't leave of your own sweet accord pretty quick you'll be given y'ur notice. And I'm not keepin' yuh neither. Not after y'ur threats an' the scene that you've made this mawnin'. I want you to gather all of y'ur old junk up, all of y'ur dirty old handkerchiefs an' y'ur bottles, and get 'em all out of here by twelve o'clock noon, or by God, an' by Jesus, anything that's left here is going straight down to the incinerator! I'll gather it up on the end of a ten-foot pole and dump it into the fire, cause nothing you touch is safe for human contact!

He ran from the room. I heard him running downstairs and out of the building. I went to the alcove window and watched him spinning wildly around in the street. He was crazed with fury. A waiter from the Chinese restaurant came out and caught at his arm, a drunk from a bar reasoned with him. He sobbed and lamented and wandered from door to door of the ancient buildings until the drunk had manœuvered him into a bar.

The landlady and a fat old Negress who worked on the place removed the young man's mattress from his bed and lugged it into the courtyard. They stuffed it into the iron pit of the incinerator and set it afire and stood at a respectful distance watching it burn. The landlady wasn't content with just the burning, she made a long speech at the top of her voice about it.

It's not bein' burned because of no bugs, she shouted. I'm burnin' this mattress because it's contaminated. A T.B. case has been on it, a filthy degenerate and a liar!

She went on and on until the mattress was fully consumed, and after.

Then the old Negress was sent upstairs to remove the young man's belongings. It had begun to rain and despite the landlady's objections the Negress put all of the things beneath the banana tree in the courtyard and covered them with a discarded sheet of linoleum weighted down with loose bricks.

At sundown the young man returned to the place. I heard him coughing and gasping in the rainy courtyard as he collected his things from under the fantastic green yellow umbrella of the banana tree. He seemed to be talking about all the wrongs he had suffered since he had come into the world, but at last the complaints were centred upon the loss of a handsome comb. Oh, my God, he muttered, She's stolen my comb, I had a beautiful comb that I got from my mother, a tortoise-shell comb with a silver and pearl handle on it. That's gone, it's been stolen, the comb that belonged to my mother!

At last it was found, or the young man gave up the search, for his talk died out. A wet silver hush fell over the house on Bourbon as daylight and rain both ended their business there, and in my room the luminous dial of a clock and the misty grey of the alcove were all that remained for me of the visible world.

The episode put an end to my stay at the house. For several nights after that the transparent grey angel failed to appear in the alcove and sleep had to come without any motherly sanction. So I decided to give up my residence there. I felt that the delicate old lady angel had tacitly warned me to leave, and that if I ever was visited by her again, it would be at another time in another place – which still haven't come.

THE RESEMBLANCE BETWEEN A VIOLIN
CASE AND A COFFIN

With her advantage of more than two years and the earlier maturity of girls, my sister moved before me into that country of mysterious differences where children grow up. And although we naturally continued to live in the same house, she seemed to have gone on a journey while she remained in sight. The difference came about more abruptly than you would think possible, and it was vast, it was like the two sides of the Sunflower River that ran through the town where we lived. On one side was a wilderness where giant cypresses seemed to engage in mute rites of reverence at the edge of the river, and the blurred palor of the Dobyne place that used to be a plantation, now vacant and seemingly ravaged by some impalpable violence fiercer than flames, and back of this dusky curtain, the immense cotton-fields that absorbed the whole visible distance in one sweeping gesture. But on the other side, avenues, commerce, pavements and homes of people: those two, separated by only a yellowish, languorous stream that you could throw a rock over. The rumbling wooden bridge that divided, or joined, those banks was hardly shorter than the interval in which my sister moved away from me. Her look was startled, mine was bewildered and hurt. Either there was no explanation or none was permitted between the one departing and the one left behind. The earliest beginning of it that I can remember was one day when my sister got up later than usual with an odd look, not as if she had been crying, although perhaps she had, but as though she had received some painful or frightening surprise, and I observed an equally odd difference in the manner toward her of my mother and grandmother. She was escorted to the kitchen table for breakfast as though she were in danger of toppling over on either side, and everything was handed to her as though she could not reach it. She was addressed in hushed and solicitous voices, almost the way that docile servants speak to an employer. I was baffled and a little disgusted. I received no attention at all, and the one or two glances given me by my sister had a peculiar look or resentment in them. It was as if I had struck her the night before and given her a bloody nose or a black eye, except that she wore no bruise, no visible injury, and there had been no altercation between us in recent days. I spoke to her several times, but for some reason she ignored my remarks, and when I became irritated and yelled at her, my grandmother suddenly reached over and twisted my ear, which was one of the few times that I can ever remember when she ever offered me more than the gentlest reproach. It was a Saturday morning, I remember, of a hot yellow day and it was the hour when my sister and I would ordinarily take to the streets on our wheels. But the custom was now disregarded. After breakfast my sister appeared somewhat strengthened but still alarmingly pale and as silent as ever. She was then escorted to the parlour and encouraged to sit down at the piano. She spoke in a low whimpering tone to my grandmother who adjusted the piano stool very carefully and placed a cushion on it and even turned the pages of sheet music for her as if she were incapable of finding the place for herself. She was working on a simple piece called *The Aeolian Harp*, and my grandmother sat beside her while she played, counting out the tempo in a barely audible voice, now and then reaching out to touch the wrists of my sister in order to remind her to keep them arched. Upstairs my mother began to sing to herself which was something she only did when my father had just left on a long trip with his samples and would not be likely to return for quite a while, and my grandfather, up since daybreak, was mumbling a sermon to himself in the study. All was peaceful except my sister's face. I did not know whether to go outside or stay in. I hung around the parlour for a little while, and finally I said to Grand, Why can't she practice later? As if I had made some really brutal remark, my sister jumped up in tears and fled to her upstairs bedroom. What was the matter with her? My grandmother said, Your sister is not well today. She said it gently and gravely, and then she started to follow my sister upstairs, and I was deserted. I was left alone in the very uninteresting parlour. The idea of riding alone on my wheel did not please me for often when I did that, I was set upon by the rougher boys of the town who called me Preacher and took a peculiar delight in asking me obscene questions that would embarrass me to the point of nausea . . .

In this way was instituted the time of estrangement that I could not understand. From that time on the division between us was ever more clearly established. It seemed that my mother and grandmother were approving and conspiring to increase it. They had never before bothered over the fact that I had depended so much on the companionship of my sister but now they were continually asking me why I did not make friends with other children. I was ashamed to tell them that other children frightened me nor was I willing to admit that my sister's wild imagination and inexhaustible spirits made all other substitute companions seem like the shadows of shades, for now that she had abandoned me, mysteriously and wilfully withdrawn her enchanting intimacy, I felt too resentful even to acknowledge secretly, to myself, how much had been lost through what she had taken away . . .

Sometimes I think she might have fled back into the more familiar country of childhood if she had been allowed to, but the grown-up ladies of the house, and even the coloured girl, Ozzie, were continually telling her that such and such a thing was not proper for her to do. It was not proper for my sister not to wear stockings or to crouch in the yard at a place where the earth was worn bare to bounce a rubber ball and scoop up starry-pointed bits of black metal called jacks. It was not even proper for me to come into her room without knocking. All of these proprieties struck me as mean and silly and perverse, and the wound of them turned me inward.

My sister had been magically suited to the wild country of childhood but it remained to be seen how she would adapt herself to the uniform and yet more complex world that grown sisters enter. I suspect that I have defined that world incorrectly with the word uniform; later, yes, it becomes uniform, it straightens out into an all too regular pattern. But between childhood and adulthood there is a broken terrain which is possibly even wilder than childhood was. The wilderness is interior. The vines and the brambles seem to have been left behind but actually they are thicker and more confusing, although they are not so noticeable from the outside. Those few years of dangerous passage are an ascent into unknown hills. They take the breath sometimes and bewilder the vision. My mother and maternal grandmother came of a calmer blood than my sister and I. They were unable to suspect the hazards that we were faced with, having in us the turbulent blood of our father. Irreconcilables fought for supremacy in us; peace could never be made: at best a smouldering sort of armistice might be reached after many battles.

Childhood had held those clashes in abeyance. They were somehow timed to explode at adolescence, silently, shaking the earth where we were standing. My sister now felt those tremors under her feet. It seemed to me that a shadow had fallen on her. Or it had fallen on me, with her light at a distance? Yes, it was as if someone had carried a lamp into another room that I could not enter. I watched her from a distance and under a shadow. And looking back on it now, I see that those two or three years when the fatal dice were still in the tilted box, were the years of her beauty. The long copperish curls which had swung below her shoulders, bobbing almost constantly with excitement, were unexpectedly removed one day, an afternoon of a day soon after the one when she had fled from the piano in reasonless tears. Mother took her downtown. I was not allowed to go with them but was told once more to find someone else to play with. And my sister returned without her long copper curls. It was like a formal acknowledgment of the sorrowful differences and division which had haunted the house for some time. I noted as she came in the front door that she had now begun to imitate the walk of grown ladies, the graceful and quick and decorous steps of my mother, and that she kept her arms at her sides instead of flung out as if brushing curtains aside as she sprang forward in the abruptly lost days. But there was much more than that. When she entered the parlour, at the fading hour of the afternoon, it was as momentous as if brass horns had sounded, she wore such beauty. Mother came after her looking flushed with excitement and my grandmother descended the stairs with unusual lightness. They spoke in hushed voices. Astonishing, said my mother. She's like Isabel. This was the name of a sister of my father's who was a famed beauty in Knoxville. She was probably the one woman in the world of whom my mother was intimidated, and our occasional summer journeys to Knoxville from the Delta of Mississippi were like priestly tributes to a seat of holiness, for though my mother would certainly never make verbal acknowledgment of my aunt's surperiority in matters of taste and definitions of quality, it was nevertheless apparent that she approached Knoxville and my father's younger sister in something very close to fear and trembling. Isabel had a flame, there was no doubt about it, a lambency which, once felt, would not fade from the eyes. It had an awful quality, as though it shone outward while it burned inward. And not long after the time of these recollections she was to die, quite abruptly and irrelevantly, as the result of the removal of an infected wisdom tooth, with her legend entrusted to various bewildered eyes and hearts and memories she had stamped, including mine, which have sometimes confused her with very dissimiliar ladies. She is like Isabel, said my mother in a hushed voice. My grandmother did not admit that this was so. She also admired Isabel but thought her too interfering and was unable to separate her altogether from the excessively close blood-connection with my father, whom I should say, in passage, was a devilish man, possibly not understood but certainly hard to live with . . .

What I saw was not Isabel in my sister but a grown stranger whose beauty sharpened my sense of being alone. I saw that it was all over, put away in a box like a doll no longer cared for, the magical intimacy of our childhood together, the soap-bubble afternoons and the games with paper dolls cut out of dress catalogues and the breathless races here and there on our wheels. For the first time, yes, I saw her beauty. I consciously avowed it to myself, although it seems to me that I turned away from it, averted my look from the pride with which she strolled into the parlour and stood by the mantel mirror to be admired. And it was then, about that time, that I began to find life unsatisfactory as an explanation of itself and was forced to adopt the method of the artist of not explaining but putting the blocks together in some other way that seems more significant to him. Which is a rather fancy way of saying I started writing . . .

My sister also had a separate occupation which was her study of music, at first conducted under my grandmother's instruction but now entrusted to a professional teacher whose name was Miss Aehle, an almost typical spinster, who lived in a small frame house with a porch covered by moonvines and a fence covered by honeysuckle. Her name was pronounced *Ail*-ly. She supported herself and a paralysed father by giving lessons in violin and piano, neither of which she played very well herself but for which she had great gifts as a teacher. If not great gifts, at least great enthusiasm. She was a true romanticist. She talked so excitedly that she got ahead of herself and looked bewildered and cried out, What was I saying? She was one of the innocents of the world, appreciated only by her pupils and a few persons a generation older than herself. Her pupils nearly always came to adore her, she gave them a feeling that playing little pieces on the piano or scratching out little tunes on a fiddle made up for everything that was ostensibly wrong in the world made by God but disarrayed by the devil. She was religious and ecstatic. She never admitted that anyone of her pupils, even the ones that were unmistakably tone-deaf, were deficient in musical talent. And the few that could perform tolerably well she was certain had genius. She had two real star pupils, my sister, on the piano, and a boy named Richard Miles who studied the violin. Her enthusiasm for these two was unbounded. It is true that my sister had a nice touch and that Richard Miles had a pure tone on the fiddle, but Miss Aehle dreamed of them in terms of playing duets to great ovations in the world's capital cities.

Richard Miles, I think of him now as a boy, for he was about seventeen, but at that time he seemed a complete adult to me, even immeasurably older than my sister who was fourteen. I resented him fiercely even though I began, almost immediately after learning of his existence, to dream about him as I had formerly dreamed of storybook heroes. His name began to inhabit the rectory. It was almost constantly on the lips of my sister, this strange young lady who had come to live with us. It had a curious lightness, that name, in the way that she spoke it. It did not seem to fall from her lips but to be released from them. The moment spoken, it rose into the air and shimmered and floated and took on gorgeous colours the way that soap bubbles did that we used to blow from the sunny back steps in the summer. Those bubbles lifted and floated and they eventually broke but never until other bubbles had floated beside them. Golden they were, and the name of Richard had a golden sound, too. The second name, being Miles, gave a suggestion of distance, so Richard was something both radiant and far away.

My sister's obsession with Richard may have been even more intense than mine. Since mine was copied from hers, it was probably hers that was greater in the beginning. But while mine was of a shy and sorrowful kind, involved with my sense of abandonment, hers at first seemed to be joyous. She had fallen in love. As always, I followed suit. But while love made her brilliant, at first, it made me laggard and dull. It filled me with sad confusion. It tied my tongue or made it stammer and it flashed so unbearably in my eyes that I had to turn them away. These are the intensities that one cannot live with, that he has to outgrow if he wants to survive. But who can help grieving for them? If the blood vessels could hold them, how much better to keep those early loves with us? But if we did, the veins would break and the passion explode into darkness long before the necessary time for it.

I remember one afternoon in fall when my sister and I were walking along a street when Richard Miles appeared suddenly before us from somewhere with a startling cry. I see him bounding, probably down the steps of Miss Aehle's white cottage, emerging unexpectedly from the vines. Probably Miss Aehle's because he bore his violin case, and I remember thinking how closely it resembled a little coffin, a coffin made for a small child or a doll. About people you knew in your childhood it is rarely possible to remember their appearance except as ugly or beautiful or light or dark. Richard was light and he was probably more beautiful than any boy I have seen since. I do not remember if he was light in the sense of being blond or if the lightness came from a quality in him deeper than hair or skin. Yes, probably both, for he was one of those people who move in light, provided by practically everything about them. This detail I do remember. He wore a white shirt, and through its cloth could be seen the fair skin of his shoulders. And for the first time, prematurely, I was aware of skin as an attraction. A thing that might be desirable to touch. This awareness entered my mind, my senses, like the sudden streak of flame that follows a comet. And my undoing, already started by Richard's mere coming toward us, was now completed. When he turned to me and held his enormous hand out, I did a thing so grotesque that I could never afterwards be near him without a blistering sense of shame. Instead of taking the hand I ducked away from him. I made a mumbling sound that could have had very little resemblance to speech, and then brushed past their two figures, his and my beaming sister's, and fled into a drugstore just beyond.

That same fall the pupils of Miss Aehle performed in a concert. This concert was held in the parish house of my grandfather's church. And for weeks preceding it the pupils made preparation for the occasion which seemed as important as Christmas. My sister and Richard Miles were to play a duet, she on the piano, of course, and he on the violin. They practised separately and they practised together. Separately my sister played the piece very well, but for some reason, more portentous than it seemed at the time, she had great difficulty in playing to Richard's accompaniment. Suddenly her fingers would turn to thumbs, her wrists would flatten out and become cramped, her whole figure would hunch rigidly toward the piano and her beauty and grace would vanish. It was strange, but Miss Aehle was certain that it would be overcome with repeated practice. And Richard was patient, he was incredibly patient, he seemed to be far more concerned for my sister's sake than his own. Extra hours of practice were necessary. Sometimes when they had left Miss Aehle's, at the arrival of other pupils, they would continue at our house. The afternoons were consequently unsafe. I never knew when the front door might open on Richard's dreadful beauty and his greeting which I could not respond to, could not endure, must fly grotesquely away from. But the house was so arranged that although I hid in my bedroom at these hours of practice, I was still able to watch them at the piano. My bedroom looked out upon the staircase which descended into the parlour where they practised. The piano was directly within my line of vision. It was in the parlour's lightest corner, with lace-curtained windows on either side of it, the sunlight only fretted by patterns of lace and ferns.

During the final week before the concert – or was it recital they called it? – Richard Miles came over almost invariably at four in the afternoon, which was the last hour of really good sunlight in late October. And always a little before that time I would lower the green blind in my bedroom and with a fantastic stealth, as if a sound would betray a disgusting action, I would open the door two inches, an aperture just enough to enclose the piano corner as by the lateral boundaries of a stage. When I heard them enter the front door, or even before, when I saw their shadows thrown against the oval glass and curtain the door surrounded or heard their voices as they climbed to the porch, I would flatten myself on my belly on the cold floor and remain in that position as long as they stayed, no matter how my knees or elbows ached, and I was so fearful of betraying this watch that I kept over them while they practised that I hardly dared to breathe.

The transference of my interest to Richard now seemed complete. I would barely notice my sister at the piano, groan at her repeated blunders only in sympathy for him. When I recall what a little puritan I was in those days, there must have been a shocking ambivalence in my thoughts and sensations as I gazed down upon him through the crack of the door. How on earth did I explain to myself, at that time, the fascination of his physical being without, at the same time, confessing to myself that I was a

little monster of sensuality? Or was that actually before I had
begun to associate the sensual with the impure, an error that
tortured me during and after pubescence, or did I, and this seems
most likely, now, say to myself, Yes, Tom, you're a monster! But
that's how it is and there's nothing to be done about it. And so
continued to feast my eyes on his beauty. This much is certain.
Whatever resistance there may have been from the 'legion of
decency' in my soul was exhausted in the first skirmish, not
exterminated but thoroughly trounced, and its subsequent
complaints were in the form of unseen blushes. Not that there was
really anything to be ashamed of in adoring the beauty of Richard.
It was surely made for that purpose, and boys of my age are made
to be stirred by such ideals of grace. The sheer white cloth in
which I had orginally seen his upper body was always worn by it,
and now, in those afternoons, because of the position of the piano
between two windows that cast their beams at cross angles, the
white material became diaphanous with light, the torso shone
through it, faintly pink and silver, the nipples on the chest and the
armpits a little darker, and the diaphragm visibly pulsing as he
breathed. It is possible that I have seen more graceful bodies, but I
am not sure that I have, and his remains, I believe, a subconscious
standard. And looking back upon him now, and upon the devout
little mystic of carnality that I was as I crouched on a chill
bedroom floor, I think of Camilla Rucellai, that highstrung mystic
of Florence who is supposed to have seen Pico della Mirandola
entering the streets of that city on a milk-white horse in a storm of
sunlight and flowers, and to have fainted at the spectacle of him,
and murmured, as she revived, *He will pass in the time of lilies!*
meaning that he would die early, since nothing so fair could
decline by common degrees in a faded season. The light was
certainly there in all its fulness, and even a kind of flowers, at least
shadows of them, for there were flowers of lace in the window
curtains and actual branches of fern which the light projected
across him; no storm of flowers but the shadows of flowers which
are perhaps more fitting.

The way he lifted and handled his violin! First he would roll up
the sleeves of his white shirt and remove his necktie and loosen his
collar as though he were making preparations for love. Then there
was a metallic snap as he released the lock on the case of the violin.
Then the upper lid was pushed back and the sunlight fell on the
dazzling interior of the case. It was plush-lined and the plush was

emerald. The violin itself was somewhat darker than blood and even more lustrous. To Richard I think it must have seemed more precious. His hands and his arms as he lifted it from the case, they said the word love more sweetly than a speech could say it, and, oh, what precocious fantasies their grace and tenderness would excite in me. I was a wounded soldier, the youngest of the regiment and he, Richard, was my young officer, jeopardizing his life to lift me from the field where I had fallen and carry me back to safety in the same cradle of arms that supported his violin now. The dreams, perhaps, went further, but I have already dwelt sufficiently upon the sudden triumph of unchastity back of my burning eyes; that needs no more annotation . . .

I now feel some anxiety that this story will seem to be losing itself like a path that has climbed a hill and then lost itself in an overgrowth of brambles. For I have now told you all but one of the things that stand out very clearly, and yet I have not approached any sort of conclusion. There is, of course, a conclusion. However indefinite, there always is some point which serves that need of remembrances and stories.

The remaining very clear thing is the evening of the recital in mid-November, but before an account of that, I should tell more of my sister in this troubled state of hers. It might be possible to wilfully thrust myself into her mind, her emotions, but I question the widom of it: for at that time I was an almost hostile onlooker where she was concerned. Hurt feelings and jealous feelings were too thickly involved in my view of her at that time. As though she were being punished for a betrayal of our childhood companion-ship, I felt a gratification tinged with contempt at her difficulties in the duet with Richard. One evening I overheard a telephone call which mother received from Miss Aehle. Miss Aehle was first perplexed and now genuinely alarmed and totally mystified by the sudden decline of my sister's vaunted aptitude for the piano. She had been singing her praises for months. Now it appeared that my sister was about to disgrace her publicly, for she was not only unable, suddenly, to learn new pieces but was forgetting the old ones. It had been planned, originally, for her to play several solo numbers at the recital before and leading up to the duet with Richard. The solos now had to be cancelled from the programme, and Miss Aehle was even fearful that my sister would not be able to perform in the duet. She wondered if my mother could think of some reason why my sister had undergone this very inopportune and painful decline? Was she sleeping badly, how was her appetite, was she very moody? Mother came away from the telephone in a very cross humour with the teacher. She repeated all the complaints and apprehensions and questions to my grandmother who said nothing but pursed her lips and shook her head while she sewed like one of those venerable women who understand and govern the fates of mortals, but she had nothing to offer in the way of practical solutions except to say that perhaps it was a mistake for brilliant children to be pushed into things like this so early . . .

Richard stayed patient with her most of the time, and there were occasional periods of revival, when she would attack the piano with an explosion of confidence and the melodies would surge beneath her fingers like birds out of cages. Such a resurgence would never last till the end of a piece. There would be a stumble, and then another collapse. Once Richard himself was unstrung. He pushed his violin high into the air like a broom sweeping cobwebs off the ceiling. He strode around the parlour brandishing it like that and uttering groans that were both sincere and comic; when he returned to the piano, where she crouched in dismay, he took hold of her shoulders and gave them a shake. She burst into tears and would have fled upstairs but he caught hold of her by the newel post of the staircase. He would not let go of her. He detained her with murmurs I couldn't quite hear, and drew her gently back to the piano corner. And then he sat down on the piano stool with his great hands gripping each side of her narrow waist while she sobbed with her face averted and her fingers knotting together. And while I watched them from my cave of darkness, my body learned, at least three years too early, the fierceness and fire of the will of life to transcend the single body, and so to continue to follow light's curve and time's . . .

The evening of the recital my sister complained at supper that her hands were stiff, and she kept rubbing them together and even held them over the spout of the teapot to warm them with the steam. She looked very pretty, I remember, when she was dressed. Her colour was higher than I had ever seen it, but there were tiny beads of sweat at her temples and she ordered me angrily out of her room when I appeared in the doorway before she was ready to pass the family's inspection. She wore silver slippers and a very grownup-looking dress that was the greenish sea-colour of her eyes. It had the low waist that was fashionable at that time and there were silver beads on it in loops and fringes. Her bedroom was steaming from the adjoining bath. She opened the window. Grandmother slammed it down, declaring that she would catch cold. Oh, leave me alone, she answered. The muscles of her throat were curiously prominent as she stared in the glass. Stop powdering, said my grandmother, you're caking your face with powder. Well, it's my face, she retorted. And then came near to flying into a tantrum at some small critical comment offered by Mother. I have no talent, she said, I have no talent for music! Why do I have to do it, why do you make me, why was I forced into this? Even my grandmother finally gave up and retired from the room. But when came time to leave for the parish house, my sister came downstairs looking fairly collected and said not another word as we made our departure. Once in the automobile she whispered something about her hair being mussed. She kept her stiff hands knotted in her lap. We drove first to Miss Aehle's and found her in a state of hysteria because Richard had fallen off a bicycle that afternoon and skinned his fingers. She was sure it would hinder his playing. But when we arrived at the parish house, Richard was already there as calm as a duckpond, playing delicately with the mute on the strings and no apparent disability. We left them, teacher and performers, in the cloakroom and went to take our seats in the auditorium which was beginning to fill, and I remember noticing a half-erased inscription on a blackboard which had something to do with a Sunday School lesson.

No, it did not go off well. They played without sheet music, and my sister made all the mistakes she had made in practicing and several new ones. She could not seem to remember the composition beyond the first few pages; it was a fairly long one, and those pages she repeated twice, possibly even three times. But Richard was heroic. He seemed to anticipate every wrong note that she struck and to bring down his bow on the strings with an extra strength to cover and rectify it. When she began to lose control altogether, I saw him edging up closer to her position, so that his radiant figure shielded her partly from view and I saw him, at a crucial moment, when it seemed that the duet might collapse altogether, raise his bow high in the air, at the same time catching his breath in a sort of 'Hah!' a sound I heard much later from bullfighters daring a charge, and lower it to the strings in a masterful sweep that took the lead from my sister and plunged them into the passage that she had forgotten in her panic . . . For a bar or two, I think, she stopped playing, sat there motionless, stunned. And then, finally, when he turned his back to the audience, and murmured something to her, she started again. She started playing again, but Richard played so brilliantly and so richly that the piano was barely noticeable underneath him. And so they got through it, and when it was finished they received an ovation. My sister started to rush for the cloakroom. But Richard seized her wrist and held her back. Then something odd happened. Instead of bowing she suddenly turned and pressed her forehead against him, pressed it against the lapel of his blue serge suit. He blushed and bowed and touched her waist with his fingers, gently, his eyes glancing down . . .

We drove home in silence, almost. There was a conspiracy to ignore that anything unfortunate had happened. My sister said nothing. She sat with her hands knotted in her lap exactly as she had been before the recital, and when I looked at her I noticed that her shoulders were too narrow and her mouth a little too wide for real beauty, and that her recent habit of hunching made her seem a little bit like an old lady being imitated by a child.

At that point Richard Miles faded out of our lives for my sister refused to continue to study music, and not long afterwards my father received an advancement, an office job as a minor executive in a northern shoe company, and we moved from the South. No, I am not putting all of these things in their exact chronological order, I may as well confess it, but if I did I would violate my honour as a teller of stories . . .

As for Richard, the truth is exactly congruous to the poem. A year or so later we learned, in that northern city to which we had moved, that he had died of pneumonia. And then I remembered the case of his violin, and how it resembled so much a little black coffin made for a child or a doll . . .

SUGGESTIONS FOR FURTHER READING

Williams's stories have been collected and are available in an edition with an introduction by Gore Vidal (New York, 1985). Most critical evaluations of his work have concentrated on his drama but it is worth consulting the various biographies, including Ronald Hayman, *Tennessee Williams: Everyone Else is an Audience* (New Haven, 1993), Benjamin Nelson, *Tennessee Williams: His Life and Work* (London, 1961), Donald Spoto, *The Kindness of Strangers: The Life of Tennessee Williams* (Boston, 1985), Nancy Tischler, *Tennessee Williams: Rebellious Puritan* (New York, 1961), Dakin Williams and Sheperd Mead, *Tennessee Williams: An Intimate Biography* (New York, 1983), and Edwina Dakin Williams, *Remember Me to Tom* (New York, 1963). Williams's own *Memoirs* appeared in New York in 1975, while Donald Windham's *Tennessee Williams' Letters to Donald Windham 1940–1965* (New York, 1976) throws interesting light on all aspects of the early Williams.

AMERICAN LITERATURE
IN EVERYMAN

A SELECTION

Selected Poems
HENRY LONGFELLOW
A new selection spanning the whole
of Longfellow's literary career **£7.99**

Typee
HERMAN MELVILLE
Melville's stirring debut, drawing
directly on his own adventures in the
South Seas **£4.99**

Billy Budd and Other Stories
HERMAN MELVILLE
The compelling parable of innocence destroyed by a fallen world
£4.99

The Last of the Mohicans
JAMES FENIMORE COOPER
The classic tale of old America, full
of romantic adventure **£5.99**

The Scarlet Letter
NATHANIEL HAWTHORNE
The compelling tale of an
independent woman's struggle
against a crushing moral code **£3.99**

The Red Badge of Courage
STEPHEN CRANE
A vivid portrayal of a young
soldier's experience of the
American Civil War **£2.99**

Essays and Poems
RALPH WALDO EMERSON
An indispensable edition celebrating
one of the most influential
American writers **£5.99**

The Federalist
HAMILTON, MADISON AND JAY
Classics of political science, these
essays helped to found the
American Constitution **£6.99**

Leaves of Grass and Selected Prose
WALT WHITMAN
The best of Whitman in one volume
£6.99

£5.99

SHORT STORY COLLECTIONS
IN EVERYMAN

A SELECTION

The Secret Self 1:
Short Stories by Women
'A superb collection' *Guardian* **£4.99**

Selected Short Stories
and Poems
THOMAS HARDY
The best of Hardy's Wessex in a
unique selection **£4.99**

The Best of
Sherlock Holmes
ARTHUR CONAN DOYLE
All the favourite adventures in one
volume **£4.99**

Great Tales of Detection
Nineteen Stories
Chosen by Dorothy L. Sayers **£3.99**

Short Stories
KATHERINE MANSFIELD
A selection displaying the remarkable range of Mansfield's writing
£3.99

Selected Stories
RUDYARD KIPLING
Includes stories chosen to reveal the
'other' Kipling **£4.50**

The Strange Case of
Dr Jekyll and Mr Hyde
and Other Stories
R. L. STEVENSON
An exciting selection of gripping
tales from a master of suspense **£3.99**

The Day of Silence and
Other Stories
GEORGE GISSING
Gissing's finest stories, available for
the first time in one volume **£4.99**

Selected Tales
HENRY JAMES
Stories portraying the tensions
between private life and the outside
world **£5.99**

£4.99

DRAMA
IN EVERYMAN

A SELECTION

Everyman and Medieval Miracle Plays

EDITED BY A. C. CAWLEY
A selection of the most popular medieval plays **£3.99**

Complete Plays and Poems

CHRISTOPHER MARLOWE
The complete works of this fascinating Elizabethan in one volume **£5.99**

Complete Poems and Plays

ROCHESTER
The most sexually explicit – and strikingly modern – writing of the seventeenth century **£6.99**

Restoration Plays

Five comedies and two tragedies representing the best of the Restoration stage **£7.99**

Female Playwrights of the Restoration: Five Comedies

Rediscovered literary treasures in a unique selection **£5.99**

Poems and Plays

OLIVER GOLDSMITH
The most complete edition of Goldsmith available **£4.99**

Plays, Poems and Prose

J. M. SYNGE
The most complete edition of Synge available **£6.99**

Plays, Prose Writings and Poems

OSCAR WILDE
The full force of Wilde's wit in one volume **£4.99**

A Doll's House/The Lady from the Sea/The Wild Duck

HENRIK IBSEN
A popular selection of Ibsen's major plays **£4.99**

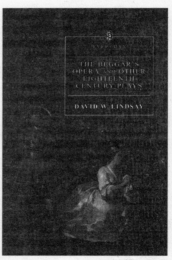

£6.99

AVAILABILITY

All books are available from your local bookshop or direct from
Littlehampton Book Services Cash Sales, 14 Eldon Way, Lineside Estate, Littlehampton, West Sussex BN17 7HE. PRICES ARE SUBJECT TO CHANGE.

To order any of the books, please enclose a cheque (in £ sterling) made payable to Littlehampton Book Services, or phone your order through with credit card details (Access, Visa or Mastercard) on 0903 721596 (24 hour answering service) stating card number and expiry date. Please add £1.25 for package and postage to the total value of your order.

In the USA, for further information and a complete catalogue call 1-800-526-2778.

CLASSIC FICTION
IN EVERYMAN

A SELECTION

Frankenstein
MARY SHELLEY
A masterpiece of Gothic terror in its
original 1818 version **£3.99**

Dracula
BRAM STOKER
One of the best known horror stories
in the world **£3.99**

The Diary of A Nobody
GEORGE AND WEEDON
GROSSMITH
A hilarious account of suburban life
in Edwardian London **£4.99**

Some Experiences
and Further Experiences
of an Irish R. M.
SOMERVILLE AND ROSS
Gems of comic exuberance and
improvisation **£4.50**

Three Men in a Boat
JEROME K. JEROME
English humour at its best **£2.99**

Twenty Thousand Leagues
under the Sea
JULES VERNE
Scientific fact combines with
fantasy in this prophetic tale of
underwater adventure **£4.99**

The Best of Father Brown
G. K. CHESTERTON
An irresistible selection of crime
stories – unique to Everyman **£4.99**

The Collected Raffles
E. W. HORNUNG
Dashing exploits from the most glam-
orous figure in crime fiction **£4.99**

£5.99

AVAILABILITY

All books are available from your local bookshop or direct from
**Littlehampton Book Services Cash Sales, 14 Eldon Way, Lineside Estate,
Littlehampton, West Sussex BN17 7HE.** PRICES ARE SUBJECT TO CHANGE.

To order any of the books, please enclose a cheque (in £ sterling) made payable to
Littlehampton Book Services, or phone your order through with credit card details (Access,
Visa or Mastercard) on 0903 721596 (24 hour answering service) stating card number and
expiry date. Please add £1.25 for package and postage to the total value of your order.

In the USA, for further information and a complete catalogue call 1-800-526-2778.